PLAYLIST

Don't Fade – Vance Joy
Green Eyes – JOSEPH
Someone Like You – Danielle Ponder
Quietly Yours – Birdy
Non Avere Paura –Tommaso Paradiso
Lose Your Head – London Grammar
Let Me Love You Like A Woman – Lana Del Rey
The Chain – Fleetwood Mac
Bigger Than The Whole Sky – Taylor Swift
Disfruto – Carla Morrison
Run Away to Mars – Talk
Nobody Gets Me – Sza
Todo Pasa – Carla Morrison
Horizon (feat. Leon Bridges) – Diplo, Leon Bridges
L-L-Love – Astaire
Daylight – Daivd Kushner
How Do I Say Goodbye – Dean Lewis
Holding Me Down – Danielle Ponder
I remember Everything (feat. Kacey Musgraves) –Zach Bryan, Kacey
Musgraves

Something Real —Post Malone
Right Where You Left Me – Taylor Swift

RIGHT WHERE YOU LEFT ME

VANESSA STOCK

To the reader,
Thank you for giving me a chance.

CONTENT WARNING

In this book, I talk about subjects that can be sensitive to others. The following is a list of topics mentioned in the book.

- Cheating Trope
- Suicide
- Death
- Mental Health
- Substance abuse

Reminder: You are worthy. You are needed. You are loved.

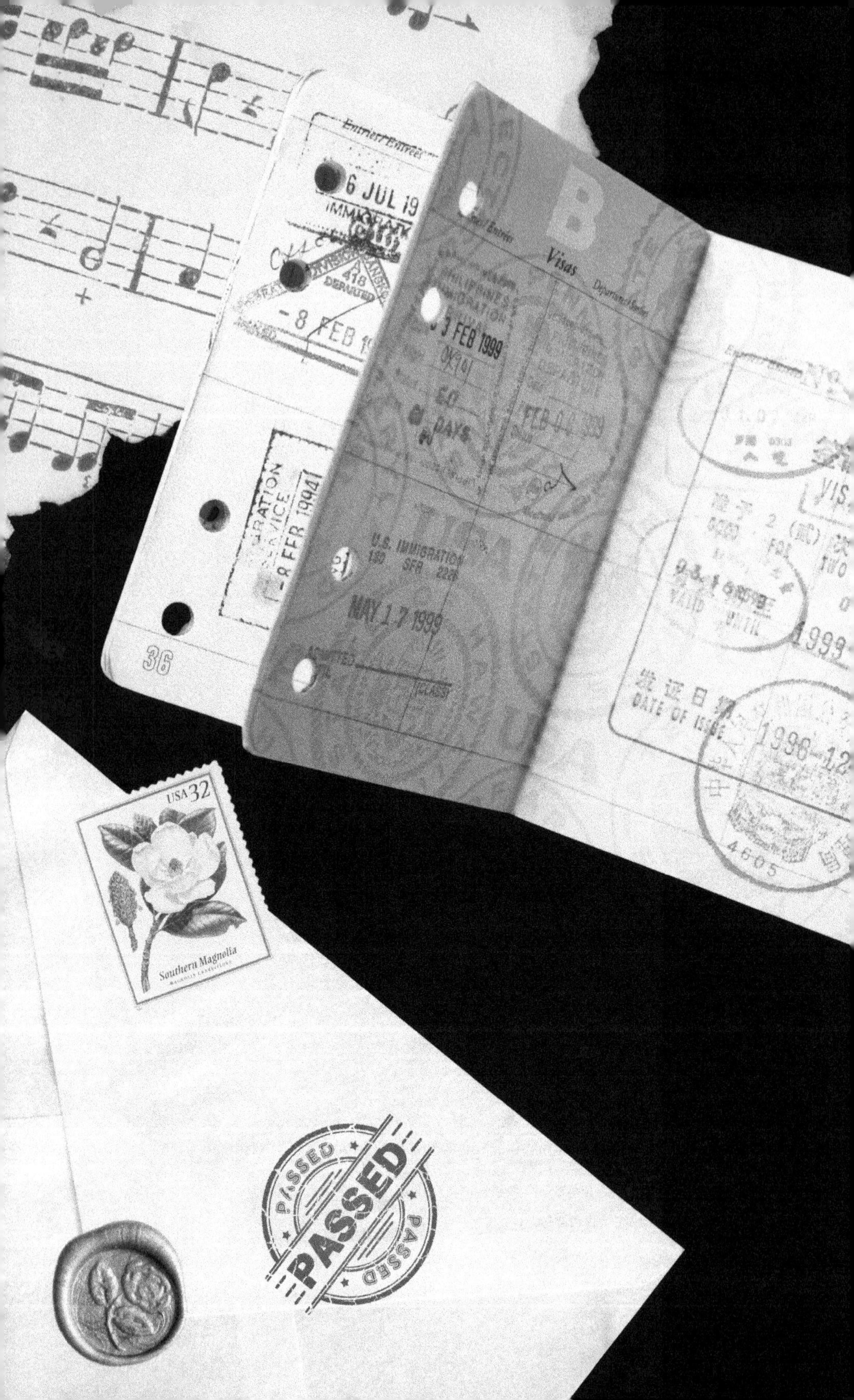

Entries/Entrées
6 JUL 19
IMMIGRANT
418
DEPARTED
- 8 FEB 19
B
Visas
Départ/Sortie
PHILIPPINES
IMMIGRATION
3 FEB 1999
OK101
60 DAYS
FEB 04 1999
GRATION
SERVICE
-8 FEB 1994?
U.S. IMMIGRATION
180   SFR   22a
MAY 1 7 1999
ADMITTED
CLASS
36
VISA
TWO
VALID UNTIL
1999
DATE OF ISSUE
1998-12
4605
USA 32
Southern Magnolia
MAGNOLIA GRANDIFLORA
PASSED
PASSED
PASSED
PASSED

PROLOGUE

Six Years Old

Zelda

I lay in the back of the car because Mommy told me we needed to. She said we're camping, but we didn't have a tent. I shook, but she kept her arms around me for warmth. We had run away again. I thought this would be different this time, but I guess I was wrong.

"Mommy?" I snuggled against her chest. "Is this a new home?" I wanted a room to sleep in. I thought our apartment was good, but Mommy said it wasn't.

"Baby." She kissed my forehead. "I thought it would be fun for the night to sleep here. Don't worry, I will find a space tomorrow."

She would; I knew she would.

"Derrick is mean to you, Mommy." I cuffed her hands with mine. That's when I felt her cry against my back. The past couple of nights, he yelled at her. He would scream so loud that I could hear her crying.

I didn't like hearing her cry.

"Baby, he was a bad man. We had to get away from him." She whispered, "But don't you worry, I will make things right."

She always said that. That she would fix it. That it was her fault.

"I think you need to find Prince Charming." I laughed.

She pushed her fingers through my hair as she held me tight. "What I need is for my daughter to become the most amazing girl in the world. You don't ever let a man take hold of who you are. You hear me?"

"Okay, Mommy." I shrugged.

"Listen to me, Zelda. One day, a man will make you feel like you're floating in the sky. He will make you laugh. Make you smile. He is the missing piece in that heart of yours. Don't ever ignore that feeling."

Mom fell asleep against me while I looked up through the foggy window, hoping that I would feel what she said one day.

PART I

"don't want to live—I want to love first, and live incidentally…"-Zelda Fitzgerald

Entrée/ Entrée
6 JUL 19
IMMIGRATION
418
DEMATU
- 8 FEB 1
Visas
Départ/ Sortie
PHILIPPINES
IMMIGRATION
3 FEB 1999
60
DAYS
FEB 4 1999
RATION
SERVICE
RFR 1994
U.S. IMMIGRATION
150   SFR   2226
MAY 1 7 1999
ADMITTED
CLASS
36
B
VISA
TWO
VALID
UNTIL
1999
DATE OF ISSUE
1996-12
4605
USA 32
Southern Magnolia
PASSED
PASSED

Zelda

Mom's only rule in a relationship was never to settle, or you'd be a shadow. This from the woman who never held down a proper relationship.

Mom could have had her own book of one-line advice. There was a catch, though. They always led to a mess. One that she said on the day I graduated from university was still tattooed on my brain: you need someone to drive you mental in order to feel the fire. Deep down, I told myself I could never grasp that blaze because it terrified me. Having seen my mom's heart shatter multiple times left a nasty taste in my mouth for love. There would be no prince to be my true love. Growing up with my mom, I saw firsthand how men tried to destroy a beautiful soul.

Yet I was playing house, being this man's girlfriend, and pretending to be the person I should be. Despite that, I was in a relationship, and it was picture-perfect. James checked off the ideal list for a significant other. There'd be no plunging off the path and falling for fairy tales for me. *Because romance stories aren't real.* I thought.

James was forcing our headboard into our doorway. I had a box in my arms as I climbed up the steps of our new apartment. He'd suckered his friend Billy into helping us move by promising him a night of Dungeons and Dragons at our space if he helped. Billy's new girlfriend disapproved of the game, and he was looking for a free night to play. So Billy growled and moaned, but he would not surrender.

"This"—Billy paused, taking a deep breath—"is fucking heavy!" His voice echoed through the hallway as I made it up to the landing. He was James's friend from childhood, and initially, they were supposed to move in together, but things changed when James decided to take a chance and asked me to move in, which took us to another stage of our relationship. I wasn't ready to admit that being at this stage scared me the most. The word "our" felt more of a drag than an excitement.

Our bedroom. Our furniture. Our future.

Our.

Our.

That word frightened me. It felt foreign. It shouldn't feel that way, but the wave of emotions attacked me like I was in danger every time it was mentioned.

"Zelda found it! It was on the side of the road. She thought it could fit on the roof of my Mini!" James rested his hands on his knees, gasping for air. The two guys did not work out. They were decently fit, but they were more of the nerdy type. Awkward artists with a dash of seventies inspiration.

James and I had been dating for four years, and in the previous couple of months, he decided we should enter the "next stage" of our relationship. I liked my independence and the eight-hundred-square-foot Brooklyn apartment I'd managed to get a deal for. Probably because it was not in the safest part of the neighborhood, yet I felt the most secure there.

Being raised above the strip joint your mother worked at had its benefits. One was being friends with a bouncer who taught me how to do a sucker punch. Thanks to Joe, the bouncer, I can flip a guy and crack his nose. It had been one of the first show-and-tells I did in school, and I almost got suspended.

James came from the ideal family, though. That was part of the reason it was unsettling for me to move in with James. His parents were in love, and his brother and sister had their lives together—blah,

blah, blah. My mom had loved and protected me, but she was not James's mother, Mrs. Marissa Cummings. She baked pies and sold them at the PTA meetings. She would flash her beautiful clothes, dazzling charm, and headstrong attitude to anyone.

My mom took care of me in the ways she knew how. She always managed to have food in the fridge and never skimped on clothes for me. She never missed a night of helping me finish my homework. We ordered Chinese food on Christmas, watched planes take off at midnight, and attended a nightmare film fest every Halloween season —all while she tried her best to make ends meet. I loved her. Yet I was embarrassed about that life.

"There are at least seven more boxes in the moving van." I scrunched my nose as the men looked at each other in frustration. I placed the box on our kitchen counter and watched James scratching his head as he took a deep breath.

"Why did we choose this place again?" he asked in defeat.

"Because it has the original flooring from the forties, and there is a huge art-deco-influenced design," I said matter-of-factly. He rolled his eyes. I studied interior design but managed to work at a magazine talking about it. I never got a chance to make a stamp in the world. But this place was my dream come true.

When James asked me to take the next step, he wanted my opinion on choosing our future place together. I remember seeing the crown molding on the ceiling when we walked into this place, and I knew it had me. The arched hallway, the herringbone floors, and the stunning details of the brass light fixtures were even more reasons for us to sign right away. We knew it might break the budget, but we had managed to get a good deal—because there was a death in it.

Not a murder but a natural death—a brain aneurysm. All deaths suck, but at least I would not see some creepy ghost haunting us from a murder. I have seen my fair share of ghost shows to know that would not be a pleasant place to stay.

When James told his parents about the death, they insisted on doing a blessing in the home, but we declined the offer. My mom had insisted I sage the place to remove previous sadness. That was a no too.

"I guess you're right." James rolled his eyes as he walked over and planted a kiss on my lips. He was tall and lanky. His hazel eyes illuminated as the hues of the sunshine bounced from the mirror and to his iris. His hair was sandy and messy, and a bead of sweat chased down his neck. His white shirt tightened, clinging to his natural definition.

James was a dream boat, an artist. He went against his parents' wishes by creating his own art shop. Inspired by Banksy, James was creating a graffiti statement that was starting to become the next big thing. I was so proud of him. We met in our final year of college. I stumbled upon him painting the concrete steps with his thesis mural. I tripped on his paint gear and twisted my ankle as I rushed to my final exams. That was when I fell for him—literally. James panicked and lifted me into his arms, then rushed to the university paramedic program, not the doctor's office on campus. It was embarrassing, but he was trying to be heroic. He was the "taking care" kind.

"I'm going to get the next box." Billy scratched his head as he walked out of the apartment, mumbling something. I wrapped my arms around James and kissed his unshaven cheek to convince my heart this would be a good thing. Anxiety was overtaking me, but I had to let it go.

"You okay, Zel?" He ran his hands through my hair as I leaned away from his face, watching him. He knew I closed off when I felt overwhelmed, but I needed to live more. I could not allow myself to fall down that path again. I became isolated when I felt something wasn't right. To shut the world off when I could be happy.

"Of course." My lips stretched to a cheeky smile, beaming as I tried to soak in our embrace.

"I don't get why you're always this emotional. Just calm down and let things flow." James pulled away, seemingly annoyed with the way I was acting.

"I'm sorry." I watched him walk away to talk to Billy about something I had no interest in. Taking a deep breath, I continued to be the girl he wanted, but not the girl I was in my heart.

∿

THE AIR-CONDITIONING WAS out of commission, so the heat was unbearable. The windows were open on that hot July night, and I had switched into a tank top and jean shorts while unpacking my clothes into the dresser. James had gone to bring back the rental truck while I started to get things in order when there was a knock on the door.

Tiptoeing to the entrance, I peeked into the peephole and saw Tony. He was the manager of the complex and an eighty-five-year-old Italian man with the sweetest heart. He reminded me of Carl from *Up* with his thick black-rimmed glasses, silver-gray hair, and stocky frame. He had dark olive-weathered skin and the brightest green eyes I'd ever seen.

I swung the door open. "Hello, Tony!" He grinned as he held a bunch of papers in his hands.

"*Buona sera*, Zelda." He nodded. "How is the move going?"

"It's going really well; the place is coming along." I glanced back into the apartment, not noticing its disarray. It looked like a tornado had ransacked the apartment because nothing had a home yet.

He peered in too. "Yeah, it is." Tony narrowed his eyes as he shrugged. "Heck, I didn't expect to find anyone to take this space. Especially after what happened…" He did the sign of the cross with his other hand. "What a beautiful soul she was. Sweet woman."

We stared at each other awkwardly as a couple of seconds passed. "So…" I rocked on my feet. "What can I help you with?"

"Oh!" He tapped his head with one hand while the other still had a bunch of papers. "Can you do me a favor? I haven't had the chance to empty the mailbox, and I need to deal with the air-conditioning situation with the repairman. Do you mind clearing it out? I need to send it to the family tomorrow."

"Yes, that's not a problem," I responded. Tony did everything by himself here with little help. It was the least I could do. "I'll go down now."

"Perfect, I greatly appreciate it, and welcome to the family." He patted my arm as he walked away. I watched him trail along the hallway as I rested against the doorframe.

I don't know whether I was intrigued to find out about the previous owner, but I wanted to know who she was. I couldn't be the only one who liked doing that. So I reached for the keys in the dining room and headed down the main stairs.

Jiggling the keys and scanning the faded carvings of each box number, I found mine. I traced the indent of the number two sign. It was a mausoleum of the woman's life. A part of me had this weird feeling of excitement, while the other part considered this an invasion of her space.

Once unlocked, I unpacked a bunch of mail. At least a month's worth was stuffed inside this small little metal box. I placed them on the small shelf and reviewed them. "Daisy Anderson," I uttered her name as I flipped through the envelopes. There were bills, catalogs, insurance, and other stuff. But there was also a letter at the bottom of the pile.

It was a lavender envelope addressed to her. I rubbed the top of the stamp. "Scotland," I whispered. "Who were you seeing, Daisy?" I asked her as if she was next to me. I flipped it over to see a name printed in the middle, Edmund Hughes. Something about letters always intrigued me. Every time I went to a museum, I always end up in the exhibit of correspondents. It was like seeing another life through words. Now that I was holding a letter in my hands, I wanted to know who this person was. Why was there a letter? It could be something silly, but it drew me in.

As I climbed the stairs, my eyes couldn't break away from this piece of Daisy's life, but I noticed Tony walking back down the hall toward me, so I stuffed the letter into my back pocket.

"Is that from her box?" he asked as his eyes widened at the pile of mail in my hand.

"Yes, I figured I'd get it to you while you're still here to make it easy for you."

"Thank you, Zelda," he said as he reached for the mail, not knowing I kept something from him in my back pocket. I watched him walk down the stairs as I realized I was breaking the law. I took a last glimpse over the banister before I headed inside the apartment.

Closing the door behind me, I rested against it and wondered if this was the worst thing I could have done. I held the envelope, clutching it tight, and took a deep breath.

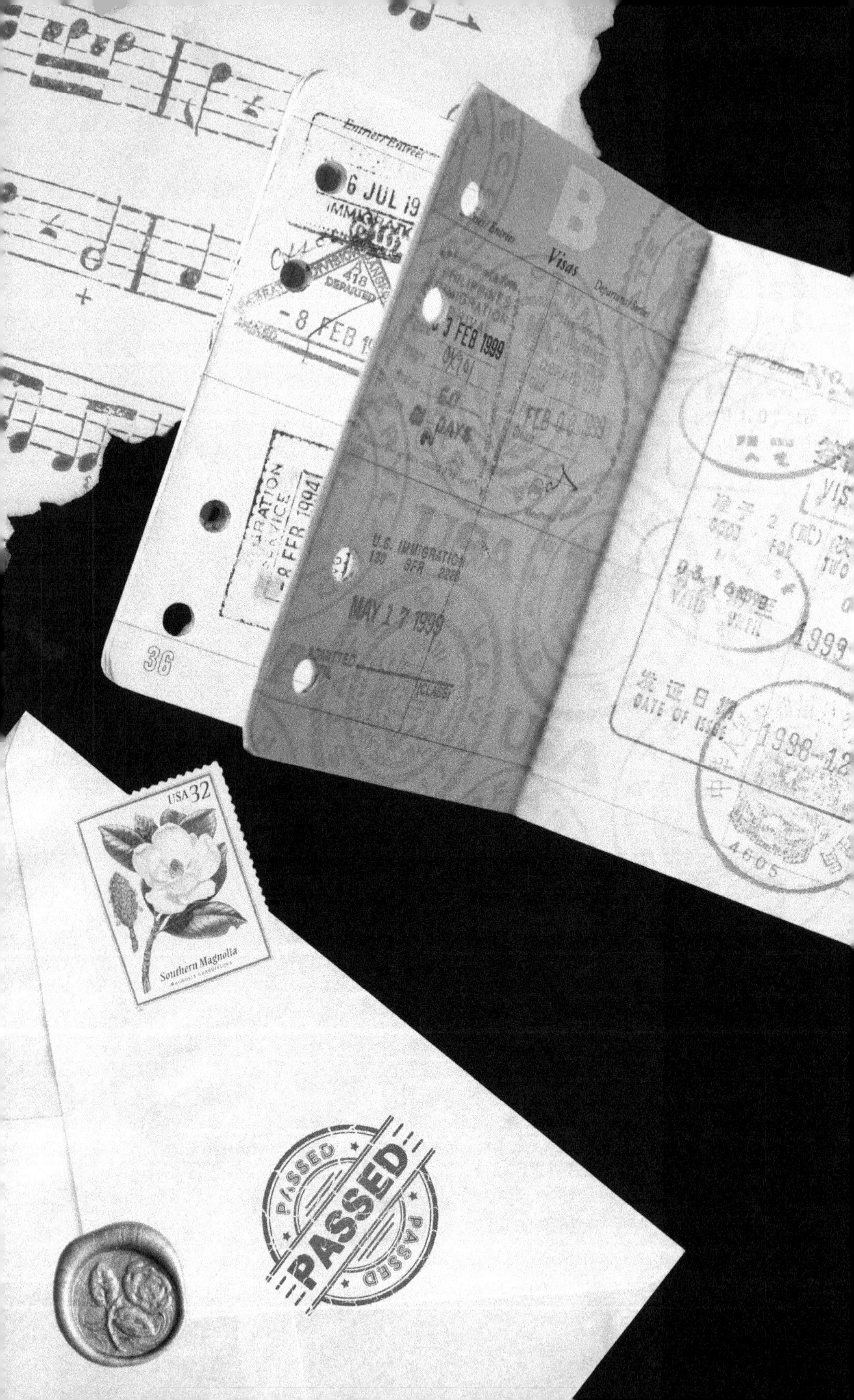
Entree/Entree
6 JUL 19
IMMIGRATION
418
DEPARTED
- 8 FEB 19
GRATION SERVICE
FEB 1994
36
Visas
Departure/Arrivee
B
PHILIPPINES
IMMIGRATION
3 FEB 1999
60
DAYS
FEB
U.S. IMMIGRATION
MAY 1 7 1999
ADMITTED
DATE OF ISSUE
1998-12
4605
USA 32
Southern Magnolia
PASSED
PASSED
PASSED
PASSED

Zelda

onday rolled around after an exhausting weekend of moving. I stormed into the office with the letter burning a hole in my purse. I knew I needed to get advice from someone emotionally stable. I filled Clara in on the fiasco of a weekend as she sat there completely dumbfounded.

"What do you mean, you kept the letter?" We were both senior writers at the women's magazine called *BLAZE*. Clara and I had been friends since childhood. She was the sister I never had, my truest soulmate. We had both lucked out by landing positions here after graduating from college.

At the magazine, I oversaw the interior design advice online while Clara reviewed books and films. Being able to get endless amount of advance copies and movie tickets were a sweet deal for her. I would always be her plus-one for any event she had to do. My job didn't get the same perks, but we did happen to share an office. So when Clara saw me looking frazzled as I scrambled my way down the aisle holding her favorite hot chocolate from Starbucks, she knew something was up.

"What are you going to do?" She examined the letter like it was evidence of a crime. Technically, it was because it fell under theft.

"Should I give it back?" I felt guilty. There was nothing I would hide from her. She was my courage and strength in times when I needed a push. She was my common sense when I could not process my thoughts. "I wanted to know what Edmund said, but another part of me thought, what if he doesn't know she's dead?"

"We can look him up," Clara offered.

"There isn't fun in that, though." I paused, grinding my teeth. "There has to be a reason they sent letters. What if they were pen pals?"

"As adults?"

"Maybe." I shrugged.

"I don't know." She pinched the bridge of her perfect nose. "Maybe Daisy is rolling in her grave, telling you not to touch her shit," Clara answered.

I bit my bottom lip and scratched my forehead in worry, but really, I shouldn't. Nothing was wrong because the only person who knew I had it was Clara. Tony didn't even see the letter, and Daisy can't say anything about it because she's six feet underground.

Do it, Zelda.

I pulled it out of her hand and tugged it roughly, which ripped the side of the envelope.

"Now you have done it!"

"It was the easiest way to get it open!" I squealed as I tore the rest of the envelope. I glanced at the glimpse of white paper. Clara was typically noisy, and she moved closer to me as I slowly slipped out the contents.

Dear Daisy,

I am terrible at writing. I write song lyrics but not letters. You didn't leave many details, but I wanted to send you something. Our time together was brilliant. I can't explain it. You made the darkness go away for a little bit. I know we left on open terms, and I want nothing more than for you to be happy, but one day, if you ever decide to come

back, I would love to spend time with you in Edinburgh.
And maybe go to the Highlands like we kept saying we
would.

I hope to hear from you.
Love,
Edmund.

"That's it? No sex? No details?" Clara frowned. It was a brief letter, but the word *love* had caught my eye. What if he loved her and never knew what happened?

"Maybe he was worried about someone reading it," I suggested.

"Like you?" She flashed a smirk.

"Touché." I pointed at her. "But what if he doesn't know she passed? What if he thought she was totally ghosting him? The poor guy needs to know."

"He could check on social media. We do not live in medieval times where you cannot search. I can find anyone without a name."

I rubbed my neck. "But he mentioned he had no information. What if she was private? I tried to find her details last night, and there were none. There is not even an obituary. How do we know she is dead?" I reached for my hot chocolate and took a sip. My thoughts were pouring in. Part of my heart said it was a complicated situation, and the other part wanted to tell him. I was curious—and that was never a good sign. I never liked the idea of the unknown. It probably stemmed from the lack of details of not knowing who my father was, or how my mom tended to keep hush about everything before I existed. So let's just say curiosity always got the best of me.

"The dead body your new landlord found was probably the give-away," Clara said.

I exhaled as I crashed my face into my hand. "Something is telling me to do it."

"Zelda, I've known you for twenty-three years of your twenty-eight years of life. I know how you act," she responded. "This"—she dragged her finger up and down at me —"is you scoping for excitement."

"Stop reminding me how old I am."

"We are talking about you having a quarter-life crisis." Clara turned toward me fully.

"A what?" I shook my head.

"Everything is all going well for you. You have a house, a boyfriend, and a retirement fund."

"You need that," I said, pointing at her.

"Everything is perfect, and you don't like it. This is your imperfection. You get unsettled or bored when everything is complete. You like the idea of freedom, which you hate to admit." She crossed her arms and narrowed her gaze. "James tends to control every situation in your life. He doesn't allow you to have a voice. This is why you want to respond. I don't want you to get hurt."

"I won't." She was right even though it was hard to admit to myself. I looked at the letter and traced Edmund's writing.

"Look at me." Clara touched my hand, and I focused on her hazel eyes." Be truthful, Zel."

I held her hand in mine. "What would you do?"

She leaned back in her chair and exhaled. "I would want to know about Edmund." She turned back to her computer. I watched her for a couple of seconds as I processed her answer. Maybe I was looking for something to create a thrill when all I felt was shadows.

LOUD MUSIC HIT me as I swung open the door. James was painting our walls, so I took off my shoes. Everything was taped off and prepped. "My Sweet Lord" blared from the speakers. James was in his paint-covered faded jeans and a ruined Metallica shirt. His hair was messy, and I watched him absorbed in his own world. When he finally looked my way, his eyes were darker, almost black from the low lighting of the sconces.

"Hey, babe." James lowered the paintbrush into the can before he picked me up in his arms. The smell of paint, sweat, and his cologne surrounded me as I wrapped my arms around his neck.

"James, you are dirty!" I cried out as he kissed the nape of my neck.

"You like it," he teased, running his hand along my cheek as he kissed me, a simple kiss that fit perfect and right.

Pulling away, I gazed at him. "You have no proof," I teased back, and he placed me down as I gave him a peck.

"It's coming along," I said while I scanned the room. There were not as many boxes as the previous day. James had worked a lot these past few nights.

I thought of telling him about the letter. It was not that I didn't want to tell him about it—it was more that I already knew what he would say. That this was chaotic or absurd. It was not my place to tell the person to move on. Yet here I was, thinking of the possible outcome that this could lead to. I wondered whether it would blow up in my face or if this man would appreciate that I gave the time and effort to let him know. It was all the more reason I wanted to do it.

"Yeah, but you have to finish up your boxes in the bedroom. I hate that I have to remind you again, Zelda. You know it messes with my thought process." His voice was stern, as if I annoyed him. "Tonight, I need to run to the studio and teach a class." He kissed my cheek again. "I'm going to shower and head out."

I brushed his comment aside and changed the subject. "No dinner?"

"Sorry, babe." He rubbed his chin. "Riley can't do tonight, and it's my space plus the lack of employees…" He started to close the can of paint by pounding it with a hammer. I knew he was trying to hire more artists, but he was strict about others joining. When he hired Riley, she burst into the studio like an atomic bomb, crying the second she walked in because her girlfriend had broken up with her, and she needed to rage. James gave her the paint, and she went to town. She ended up selling that art and making a large profit the next weekend. Riley had been the golden child ever since.

"That's fine. I have work to finish anyway," I lied. I'd wanted to spend time with him. That had been the purpose of living together. We'd barely seen each other prior to moving in. I was overthinking things, but it was hard.

James showered and packed his things for the studio while I finished dinner and got ready for bed. Before he left, he kissed me good night and told me he would be back tomorrow. His classes would run late, and instead of heading home, he slept at the studio a lot. It was how he made sure he finished his projects. Sometimes, I felt weird about him doing it, but I trusted him. I asked him once about it, but he got annoyed thinking I was being a clingy girlfriend.

I watched a cheesy reality show and was about to do the boxes when my thoughts became clouded by the letter. I walked into the hallway and headed to the fire escape at the window to catch a breath and look up at the stars.

"Daisy, if you can hear me..." I paused and shook my head in disbelief at looking for wisdom from a dead girl. "You got any words to say to Edmund?" I pressed my hands to my face and closed my eyes as a cool breeze hummed around my warm body. "This is ridiculous," I snapped.

I pulled the notebook I had rested on my windowsill and started to write.

Entrée/ Entrée
Visas
Départ/ Partos
B
6 JUL 19
- 8 FEB 19
3 FEB 1999
60
DAYS
U.S. IMMIGRATION
130   SFR   224
MAY 1 7 1999
RATION
FER 1994
36
USA 32
Southern Magnolia
VISA
VALID UNTIL
1999
DATE OF ISSUE
1998-12
4605
PASSED
PASSED

3

Two weeks later

Edmund

When it rains, it pours. Especially in Edinburgh.

"You know it isn't your break yet, right?" Tom strolled into the back alley as I sucked on a cigarette and blew out a puff of smoke as I scratched my beard. I felt aggravated, irritable, and exhausted. Being a bartender at a tourist trap at McCandless Pub was the bane of my existence, but it paid the bills.

I was a thirty-year-old bartender living miles away from my family because I chose not to be what they wanted me to be. I was raised in York with a prominent family who considered me the black sheep. I couldn't stay out of jail. My father had wanted me to be like my brothers—in the military, clean-cut, married, and with children. But I'd said fuck that and took off on my motorcycle with a backpack and maybe three hundred pounds to my name. Moving to Edinburgh was my best friend Andrew's idea.

I moved in with Andrew, and he hooked me up with a job through a friend for the time being. He was the smarter one of us. He had gone to university and done all the wonderful things parents wanted. And here I was—doing nothing with my life.

Andrew insisted that I do piano for Tom's band at the pub. He'd thought I could do some good with it and keep my mind at ease, or at least off drugs. That was the thing he'd wanted me to remember—get the fuck off drugs.

Playing music was a passion of mine, but I hadn't thought anything could help me. I was in a cloud of misery.

"Listen"—I pointed at Tom—"I took your shift twice this week." I took another drag. "If I want to have a break, no one will stop me."

Tom shook his head and bummed a smoke off me. "Aye." He sat across from me on a storage box. The narrow alley was seven feet wide with extremely tall buildings and tourists walking up and down the stairs as they found their way through the city. Urine, smoke, and garbage was the aroma we had to endure. The pub's history was long and deadly. Founded in the seventeen hundreds, it had managed to stay in the same family for generations, despite many deaths and hauntings being attached to this building. I hated to admit that I kind of like the fact it was eerie.

"How's the girl?" I asked him as he took a sip of his water.

"She's well." Tom's fling for the week was Abby, the bar's latest hire. She attended the local university and wanted to become something I don't remember. Tom seemed to be short on brain cells the minute he talked about her. He was a golden retriever with a heart of gold. For a person to write love songs, he sure sucked at keeping a relationship. In the past two months, he claimed to have fallen for three girls. This was probably going to be number four.

After I had moved in with Andrew, he'd insisted on meeting new friends. We came to this pub one night, and lo and behold, Tom came out of nowhere and became the third wheel in our friendship. That was about two years ago, yet it feels like we'd known him for decades.

"Isn't she out of your league?" I teased and licked my bottom lip.

"Way out of this league." He patted his chest. "But something I did attracted her to me." He let out a deep laugh as we both put out our smokes. He had wild blond hair and fair skin. Women always crushed on him.

I leaned against the stone wall and felt an unexpected warmth take over the narrow alley.

"Whatever happened with that American girl?" Tom questioned.

Daisy. She left about four months back. She had a wild spirit. She'd had this fire in her eyes, the kind that startled you. I couldn't imagine being with her for my whole life, but it had been a delightful time. We'd had our fair share of moments together when we enjoyed exploring each other's bodies. It had been a just-fucking kind of relationship. She had gotten me into some drugs I was not too happy about, which was more of a reason to keep a distance. I regretted sending her that letter.

"I haven't heard from her," I said. I sent her a letter wishing to stay in contact if she ever decided to return because to be honest, the sex was mind-blowing. It helped with the lonely nights to think of her.

Andrew hated that I took over the apartment when Daisy was around. And by taking over, I mean I fucked her everywhere. He made me wipe down all the surfaces with bleach when she left.

"Too bad she was crazy," Tom replied, leaning against the pub's door.

"Yeah."

Lily swung the door open and said, "Guys! Get in! We are fucking busy with tourists!"

I was tired of dealing with annoying tourists obsessed with my accent.

It was close to one in the morning when I finally called it a night. I closed the pub and watched the last drunks stumble out. Because of my fearlessness, the owner had given me the task of closing. My curly, long hair was uncontrollable, and my stern demeanor unnerved people —I looked like a Viking ready to attack with an ax.

I placed my hoodie on and lit a smoke as I watched Lily and Abby walk to their bus stop before I headed in the opposite direction. The bar was in the Grassmarket, which was only a ten-minute walk from the flat on the Royal Mile. It didn't take long to get there as I climbed up the curved street, yet the crazies came out at night.

Throwing in my earbuds, I shoved my hands in my jacket pocket and made the trek home, watching people stumble upon the cobblestones. A beggar asked for money, so I gave him the money I had in my pocket before crossing the street to my apartment.

We were on the top floor, and I still didn't know how Andrew afforded this place. It was costly. Andrew was from money too, and he had managed to keep his inheritance, while I hadn't. He wanted to become a doctor while living in the city. To be truthful, his parents wanted him to be a doctor too. We'd grown up together. His parents banned him from seeing me because they heard it through the grapevine that I was into drugs, liquor, and gangs.

Guess what, Margret, I moved in with your son!

I unlocked our building door and headed up the stairs to the third floor. It was a big unit for the top floor—two bedrooms, a kitchen, and a living space that opened toward the front of the building. The big windows had the perfect view of the castle, while the other side looked toward the North Sea in the distance. Flipping the lights on, I glanced at the note on the counter: Edmund—Gone to Fiona's. See you in the morning.

"Could have texted me," I muttered as I threw the keys on the table. Heading to the fridge, I pulled out a bottle of water and drank it as I shuffled through the mail left for me.

"Rubbish, rubbish." I flipped through the letters to my name. I stopped on a pale pink letter. I placed the water down and scanned it. I didn't recognize the person's name, nor the address, yet it was from the United States.

"It's 223 Kingsdown Street," I said when I clued in.

Daisy, I thought.

Dear Edmund,

This is awkward. I'm not Daisy; I don't even know who she is. The reason I'm responding to this is to tell you she has passed away. She had a brain aneurysm.

You are also probably wondering why I wrote you a letter. I

moved into this space and found this in her mailbox untouched. After her death, no one claimed any of her belongings, and I couldn't reach out to her family because I had no details. She seemed like she was in hiding. Weird.

If you already knew, then ignore this, and I'm sorry for reading your letter.

I'm sorry for your loss. I didn't want you to wonder what-if. I don't know why I care so much, but maybe my heart (or her ghost) pushed me to do it. I sound like a nut job.

I figured that maybe you would want to know what became of Daisy.

I'm here if you want to write back. I promise I won't be weird and send you more. This is a one-time thing.

Goodbye,

Zelda

I pressed my hand against my mouth. A wave of regret drenched my heart for Daisy. I was sad for her; she was such a beautiful soul with the potential for a good life. She was plucked from this world and was just a memory. I reached for the whiskey we stored in the cabinet and grabbed a glass.

The heavy peat of scotch ran down my throat as it rippled through my blood. Taking the bottle with me, I headed to my room. I felt an ache in my body that I loathed. It was misery, outrage, and frustration. Deep down, I felt rage taking me over. Everything seemed to fade to black.

My eyes flicked as I felt sunshine stream through my window. "Edmund!" I felt a kick at my foot as I moaned. The pain in my head was unbearable. I pulled my pillow to cover my face. "Fucker! You drank my single malt scotch! That was a fucking two-hundred-quid bottle!"

I moaned again. "Leave me be," I snapped back. "Fuck off."

"Eddie! What the hell happened to you? This room is a mess, and you're wasted. What did we say about drinking?" Andrew was about to get my fist.

"Leave me alone. Go screw Fiona or something."

"No!"

I snapped up from my bed as I glanced around my bedroom. It was a mess. My notepad was scattered with words and lyrics, but I didn't remember any of it. Andrew looked at the bed and read the letter from Zelda.

"She died?"

I nodded as I cradled my head in my hands and applied pressure to help with the pain.

"You've went barbaric last night. Look at these. You were able to write?" He reached for my notebook. I didn't remember what I had put down on the paper. I had been consumed by liquor, anger, and maybe some weed? The room smelled of it, which Andrew hated.

Andrew's eyes widened. "This is it! This is the song!" He handed it to me as I reached for the notebook. I looked at the words, and the title name overtook me in a way I didn't expect it.

"Zelda." I was at a loss of words.

4

ZELDA

It has been a month since I sent the letter with no response. Every day at ten in the morning, the intern would walk down the aisles of desks with the mail. I'd peek up from behind my screen, expecting to hear my name be called and watching each person receive their items. I tried to keep my mind at ease, hoping not to search or become a closet detective into finding out who this Edmund was. I also didn't want the letter to end up in James's hand, who would think I was an idiot for doing this. This was why I made sure I kept this secret letter at my work.

I never expected a letter to be so daunting. Walking to the post office to deliver it weeks back, I was excited to think I could get a response. But when the weeks passed, my anticipation was dreading the outcome. Part of me was struggling with the idea of the unknown. Yes, he had a right not to respond back, but I felt this itch pleading for something. I'd never felt so incomplete. I should be happy with what I have, not involving myself in someone else's life.

This sounded farfetched, I thought.

Here I was informing a person about a woman's death, and I was intrigued. It felt like being in a room with random people and making eye contact with someone you don't know. It's a weird sensation. One that leaves you haunted by the what-ifs. It's what I felt when I read the letter.

I wondered what their connection and their involvement was. A part of me wanted to know what Edmund looked like. Was he attractive? Did he have a dark and edgy demeanor, or was he a simple man? Did Daisy love him? Maybe it was because I'd read enough romance books to contribute to this addiction. I wanted something to keep me on a positive side of life because James has insisted on trying to change everything about me these past weeks. Moving in with him felt like I couldn't do anything without him approving, hence why this letter couldn't end up at my apartment.

In my heart, I craved a distraction. Something tangible. James was gone every night, working on his art to be the next big thing while I was living day-after-day with nothing to look forward too.

I typed furiously at my desk with my headphones in. I was finishing another decor article for the week when Clara came back from her meeting. She sat down next to me as I looked up from my screen.

"What happened?" I swiveled toward her. Clara had seen better days. She had her head in her hands, releasing deep breaths. I paused my music.

"I was given a book, and I hate it so much. Marissa is begging me to finish it and review it by Friday. I'm in dire need of drinks tonight." She leaned her head to the side, watching me. It was Thursday, and realistically, she should get her shit together. Getting that done by tomorrow would be brutal. Couldn't she leave the book unfinished?

"That's rough. Want some help? I can recon some videos online to tell us about it."

"It's okay, Zel. You will die of boredom." Clara rolled her eyes as she pulled the book out, inspecting the cover. "There isn't even any sex in this book."

"That's boring," I teased.

"This lonely woman needs some loving too!" She pouted. Clara reached for her coffee as she took a sip, and I took off my headphones fully. "Have you heard back from that guy?" She winked. Clara had mentioned Edmund every week because she was also intrigued by the entire situation.

I let out a defeated breath. I shook my head. *He's not going to write back to you. Stop thinking about it! He isn't yours,* my thoughts taunted me.

"Earth to Zelda! You here?" Clara waved at me.

"Sorry." I shook away the thoughts as I tried to come to terms. "I don't know why I have a fascination with him." When an idea or something is in my head, it's like an addiction. I need to know. In the past month, I tried to occupy myself hoping to forget everything about this letter, but somehow it was the center of my own thoughts.

"Maybe because you've always been this way. It's like a new hobby for you," she indicated. Clara had known me since kindergarten. We had hung out with each other every chance we got. Her mom and dad were not well off, but they would do anything to make their family happy. They would take me in on days my mom was working late and never judged her life choices.

"It isn't that," I lied. It was that. As much as I thought I wanted everything perfect and straightforward, I wished for the adventure—a curve in a road, the unknown that came along the corner. It screamed of my mom's personality. She was a firecracker, and as much as I fought to be more stable or grounded, I was ending up like her.

"You can't lie," she teased, but before I could respond, my name was called out.

"Zelda St. Claire! Mail!" One of the interns called.

Before she could get to my desk, I ran toward her and I grabbed the letter from her hands. My co-workers shot me a look of confusion. The intern handed me a letter.

It was his response. Edmund Hughes.

"Thanks!" I said as I rushed back to my best friend.

"Is that what I think it is?" Clara moved closer to me; her full curls bounced in the air. She watched me giggle in delight. "He wrote back?"

"He wrote back!" My eyes widened in disbelief. I couldn't comprehend it. My hands were clammy with the sudden anxiety taking over me.

"For fuck's sake, open it!" Clara snapped.

"Okay! Okay!" I took a deep breath and glanced down at the back.

For a second, it felt like I was touching his hand for the first time like an imprint had been left. I knew it was my mind playing tricks. It was stupid to think that way, but I felt his presence around me.

Dear Zelda,

What a cool name. I've never met a Zelda before. How did you get that name? I quite like it. Thank you for telling me about Daisy. I was devastated to learn that she had died. It took me a while to come to terms with writing you back. It isn't your fault. You didn't know her, and I'm glad you opened the letter. I won't tell anyone.

I guess I'm trying to say I hadn't expected it. Daisy was a free spirit who didn't want anything holding her down. We only had a few weeks together because she was on a trip. Maybe this was her way of connecting me to you. She was a bit of a nut to be honest. So I wouldn't be surprised if this was her in the afterlife.

Tell me about yourself.

I'm from London, but I left a couple of years back. Now, I live in Edinburgh in a flat with my friend. I am trying to figure out what I want to do. I sound like a problem case. Let's face it; it's hard to write down who I am. I don't know how to write a stupid profile. I'm currently on a break at work, wondering what to say to you. My friend thinks this is foolish, but I'm giving it a go. What made you decide to write to me? I'm intrigued.

Sometimes things happen that can't be explained. Maybe this is one. It must have been odd to write to me.

If it's okay, I'd like to write to you more. If that's weird, then don't bother to respond. Look forward to hearing from you. If not—have a good life.

Edmund

"He's intrigued." Clara wiggled her eyebrows.

I paused for a moment. My heart was in my throat as I lifted my eyes from the letter to Clara. *Calm down, Zelda.*

"I...I..." I shook my head at a loss for words. "What do I do?" I asked her.

"That's your call, Zel. Think about it, okay?" Clara touched my knee as if I was holding some kind of artifact. I had a piece of information I didn't know what to do with. Edmund wanted to talk to me. He wanted to have a conversation. I reached out and he had responded. That was what a letter was. He didn't need to write back, and neither did I. Maybe it was best not to answer.

JAMES HAD A SHOW TONIGHT, and I wanted to support him. It was small, but it was something he was looking forward to. After work, I changed into something more fitting, my red silk dress and black heels.

I placed on my headphones to occupy my mind as I got on the train to head to his studio because to be truthful, all I was thinking about was Edmund. I didn't even know him, but something inside me ignited in a way I had never felt.

After reading his letter, I told myself to wait twenty-four hours to think about my next move, not to to dive in until I was for sure ready. I convinced myself this was not harmful. Nothing would come out of it. So why did I feel guilty? Why did I feel like something was off?

I stepped onto the street where the studio was and made my way toward the art show when something inside me stopped me dead in my tracks. I reached for the letter in my purse and glanced down at it for a second. There was a bench outside of the art studio, and I had time before going in. I took a deep breath and pulled out the notepad I carried around with me and began to write. I felt like someone else took over my body and needed to speak. So I did it.

After finishing the letter, I went over to the convenience store and got an envelope and a stamp for the letter. I was late for the showing, but I couldn't wait. I needed to send it as soon as I could, so that is what I did. When I placed the letter in the slot of the mailbox, I took a deep breath and headed back to the studio for the event.

The studio was filled with people I didn't recognize other than Riley who kept dodging me. James was mid-conversation with clients. A ton of art pieces hung on the wall, and I did not like a single one. I always lied to James, which was bad, but I didn't want to hurt him. James could be cocky at times and thought he was the greatest thing since sliced bread. Being raised by people who had given him a silver spoon growing up had contributed to that attitude. I tried to be a supportive girlfriend, even if I despised his arrogance.

Rebecca and Louis Cummings strolled toward me as I tried to comprehend what the hell a painting was when Rebecca intruded into my space. "Zelda, you look nice. Have you been attending Eloise's club?" Rebecca jabbed at me every time about my mother's previous profession.

"You mean my mom's successful yoga studio that she won awards for? Yes, it's fantastic. Maybe you should try it out sometime. I heard she is doing pole dancing soon," I snapped. Rebecca's eyes narrowed with disapproval.

James's parents were the people I dreaded the most. Rebecca and Louis Cumming were never accepting of me, and they liked to remind me that my mom was a stripper every time. I'm convinced since Louis cheats on her, she is out for blood for anyone who is a tad sexier than her.

James insisted that I was being ridiculous and overly dramatic when I brought up how his parents treated me. I pleaded with him multiple times about the way they always put me down, but he brushed it off like I was the one causing problems.

"Hello!" Ignoring Rebecca, I flashed a fake smile as I shook Louis's hand. "It's so nice to see you again!"

"It has felt like forever, right, Louis?" Rebecca hit Louis's chest. Even he was annoyed by his wife. "How's the apartment?"

"It's coming along. We love it."

"I'm glad. That thing was horrendous, but we told James that our money should be going toward something else, not that place..." She continued talking, but I took a moment to process what she had said.

"I'm sorry? Your money?" I gave a confused look.

"Oh honey." She reached for my hand, with her polished manicure and her Hermes bag hanging off her arm. "You thought you and James could afford that place? We bought it for him."

"But I'm paying part of it. I don't understand." I felt a sudden heat overtake me. "Excuse me." I didn't let her finish as I headed toward James who was once again consumed by clients.

"And here is my lovely girlfriend, Zelda." He reached for my hand. I felt irritable in front of everyone. I tried to calm my frustration, but I wanted to discuss where my money was going. We had made a plan that I would split the rent with him. It was impossible that his parents were paying for it because I'd seen the documents—unless he'd forged them for me.

"I need to speak to you," I whispered as James smiled to the others.

"About what, babe?" He looked at me with worried eyes.

"Your parents told me that they bought the apartment." I'd never seen his face go so rigid as the color drained to white. He took a deep breath and held my arm.

"Excuse us for a minute," he said to the people around us as he pulled me roughly toward the back room.

He closed the door of his office, but I didn't let him talk. "How could you? Why didn't you tell me?"

"Because I knew this is how you would respond. We couldn't afford the apartment. Not with the studio and how much you get paid." He gestured at me like I was incompetent.

"What does that have to do with anything? We could have found a cheaper place. Where is my money going?" I snapped. Before signing, I told him I would have covered the first and last month's payment, including the deposit. He appreciated me doing that and said he would organize all the paperwork for it. James was tight on cash because of the studio. So I figured I would make it work for us. Now, I found out his parents bought it outright. "The documents you gave me were fake. How could you? I had to take an advance out."

"Listen, your money was needed for the studio. I was going to tell you, but I felt like everything was stable and good. I'm sorry I lied to you. I felt terrible." He reached for my hand, but I pulled away. "I need to go. This is ridiculous." I was livid as I walked toward the door, but he reached for me.

"Please, all I wanted to do was give you the best, and I couldn't."

"James, I would've lived in a cardboard box with you." I bit back tears. "I lived in a car for months as a kid. Life doesn't need to be flashy like your parents."

"I didn't want that life!" He pressed his hand on the bridge of his nose. "Let's drop it tonight. We can start over tomorrow. I will give you back all your money. I promise."

"Whatever, I'll see you at home." I swung the office door open and beelined for the entrance but bumped into Riley.

"Hey," I said quickly, but she only flashed me a small smile and walked away. I looked over my shoulder, wondering what her problem was, but I was done with today. All I wanted to do was hide from my thoughts.

Entrer Entrée
6 JUL 19
-8 FEB 19
Visas
Départ Visa
B
PHILIPPINE
IMMIGRATION
3 FEB 1999
60
DAYS
FEB
IMMIGRATION
SERVICE
R FEB 1994
36
U.S. IMMIGRATION
100   SFR   226
MAY 1 7 1999
VISA
TWO
1999
DATE OF ISSUE
1998-12
4605
USA 32
Southern Magnolia
PASSED
PASSED

5

One Week Later

Edmund

"Concentrate, Eddie! He's going to knock you out!" My trainer Callum rested on the ropes. My mind was somewhere else at that exact moment. My opponent took cheap shots without me defending myself. I'd checked out before I arrived in this ring.

"Stop! It's over!" Callum screamed for the other boxer to back off. "What the hell, Eddie? Did you drink last night?"

My hands rested on my waist as I took a deep breath, feeling the sharp pain on my side thanks to the punch by my opponent. I'd been waiting for what feels like forever since I mailed that letter. I needed to hear from Zelda. I played more piano, which surprised Andrew. Every night, I was on the piano at the pub performing while people gave tips. Something had brought me back to music.

"I'm having a hard time!" I snapped in one breath as I climbed down the ring, pulling off my gloves. I'd been trying my best to get myself away from the thoughts of Zelda. I had no idea who she was or what to expect from her. Fuck. It could be fake. Yet there I was, mesmerized by some unknown woman.

"With the way you're boxing, you will probably die the first round." Callum shook his head and handed me my water bottle.

"Next time, I'll be in the right mindset," I responded as I took a gulp of water and sat down on the bench. I glanced at my phone, then stared at the messages that came in.

I wish I could just text her, I thought. If she responded, I was going to give her my email to make things faster. Walking home from Waverley station, I had my headphones on, listening to music when Tom called.

"What the hell do you want? I am not taking your shift," I snapped.

"It's not that." He sounded desperate.

"What do you want then?"

"The piano guy in our band quit. We need a replacement, please. I beg of you. Just until we find someone else."

I stopped in my tracks and took a deep breath as I licked my bottom lip and watched the traffic light finally change. "Fuck," I said, letting out a deep breath. "Aye, but only until you find someone else."

"Yes! Thank you!" He was thrilled. "Tonight at the pub. We start at nine."

He hung up before I could respond.

I swung the door open of our apartment when the echo of music came from Andrew's room. The sound of moaning and screaming made me roll my eyes. I should walk out, but on the counter was a letter for me to read. I reached it, suddenly excited, knowing it was what I had been waiting for.

Dear Edmund,

Hi again. I know this could be weird—I thought about not responding back. It took forever to get your letter, and I knew deep down I didn't want to wait any longer.

I need to let you know that I have a boyfriend. I like the idea of writing to you as a friend. Someone to talk too. It's kind of like free therapy, somewhere to vent to. If you don't want this, I get it.

But if you do, here is my email: zzelstclaire11@hmail.com.
Talk to you soon,
Zelda

SHE HAS A BOYFRIEND.

As my fingers touched the paper, I could swear I saw her finger-prints. I rubbed over it as I thought about what I was going to do. This wasn't something I could do knowing there is someone else. I rubbed my face and shoved the paper in my jacket pocket, then threw it on the chair. I needed to think about tonight's performance and not worry about Zelda for a moment, even if there was an urge to send her an email.

~

WALKING ONTO THE STAGE, I felt eyes on me. Tom gave me the list of songs he wanted to do with the sheets of music ready to go. I watched the crowd swarm us as the excitement took over. I never thought playing in a band was something I wanted, but I absorbed the crowd like it was a drug, feeling the vibration through my bones every time I played a key. The world dissolved in front of me, and I sat there in my space haunted by the music.

The crowd cheered as I lifted my face from the piano, and Tom turned around and flashed me a cocky grin. It seemed pointless to be excited about something I knew I would fuck up, but for once, I felt like I could control myself and make this my future.

When we took a break, I went outside to the alley and sat there to smoke, twitching from the adrenaline I collected onstage. It made me do something I hadn't expected.

To: zelstclaire11@hmail.com
From: eddie_h2020@hmail.co.uk
Subject: To our first email

Hi.

I got your letter today. I was not going to respond because of the boyfriend thing, but a part of me liked the idea of having free therapy. Why did everything suddenly make sense with you in my mind when I barely know you? Maybe having someone who knows nothing of me with no judgment is nice to have.

I just played for the first time in a band, and the first person I wanted to tell was you. How ridiculous is that? I promise not to stalk you with this email, even if I want to see what you look like.

Edmund

I headed toward the stage to set up for the second round of music when I looked down at my phone to see an email message alert.

To: eddie_h2020@hmail.co.uk
From: zelstclaire11@hmail.com
Subject: I'm glad.

Hey Edmund,

I got your email at work, and I'm not going to lie to you—I got extremely excited. I didn't think you would want to chat, but I too felt something connecting me to you.

Wow, you're in a band? What kind of music? I'd love to hear you play.

I found out some not-so-great stuff about the boyfriend, and I feel kind of overwhelmed by it all. It's been a rough week, so you sending that made me feel so happy.

Let's play twenty questions. You can go first.
Zel.

To: zelstclaire11@hmail.com
From: eddie_h2020@hmail.co.uk
Subject: 21 questions? lol

Zel,

Can I call you that? I like it. Yeah, not in a band. My friend Tommy has a band, and his guy who plays the piano decided he didn't want to continue with them. So Tommy reached out to me. I didn't want to do it, but something told me to do it. I'd love for you to hear me play one day.

What's happening with the boyfriend? You okay?

What is your favorite flower?

Edmund

THE NIGHT CONTINUED AS I played with the band. I knew it was a different high for me. I felt the sweat drip down as my fingers graced the keys of the piano. I closed my eyes as I heard the music come alive. The fire took over when I hadn't thought I could feel that way. I lost myself in the sounds.

The band came up together as we bowed with a full cheer from the crowds all. I hadn't thought it was possible, but I felt excitement in ways I hadn't expected. But one thing was more desirable. Talking to Zelda.

To: eddie_h2020@hmail.co.uk

From: zelstclaire11@hmail.com

Subject: A little hello from afar

Edmund,

You can call me whatever you want lol. I'm joking! I go by Zel. I forgot to tell you about my name. My mom loved the story of Zelda Fitzgerald. But most people think I was named after a video game character. It's a normal thing for me.

Well, I'm happy about the band. Do you have a name? Is it a legit band or a drinking band that plays the songs from the eighties? Wait!

Second question: I never asked how old are you?

My favorite flower are forget-me-nots. My mom would get a bunch to fill our house. I know it's a weed. I thought that even the worst kinds of weeds could still look beautiful. I loved them. Every chance I get, I save them and create a bookmark with them.

Why did you leave London? (Technically, I should let you do three, but I couldn't wait).

Your friend,

Zel.

To: zelstclaire11@hmail.com

From: eddie_h2020@hmail.co.uk

Subject: Morning but too early for you.

Zel,

I was utterly exhausted and had some drinks last night, which is why I didn't respond sooner. My best friend Andrew insisted on having a good ole time with our buddies, so I didn't get home until three in the morning.

I love that about your name. Her story was quite tragic. But I promise I won't reference the video game.

I'm a sixty-two-year-old divorced man with three baby mommas. I'm kidding. Just turned thirty. Trying to navigate life when I have no idea on how to do that.

PS not cool with taking two questions. But I will grant you another answer.

My family comes from wealth. I left because I wasn't what they wanted me to be. They had a perfect home with perfect children, and I was the one who ruined the image. I have two brothers, both married with outstanding careers, and they live in the countryside. It wasn't for me. I haven't spoken to them in two years.

I sound like a problem case, apologies for that. I just never fit the idea of what my parents wanted for me. I was the middle kid. Older brother was the golden child, and the last was the baby.

Question four: What is your family like?

Edmund

To: eddie_h2020@hmail.co.uk
    From: zelstclaire11@hmail.com
    Subject: You awakened the beast

Edmund,

I'm five hours behind. I heard the notification, and I had to respond. Listen! I'm asleep—respect my beauty sleep lol.

I'm down to be a fourth momma. I will strive to be the best one yet.

I'm sorry about your family. Why do they make you feel that way? You shouldn't compromise your life to fit into others'. Your brothers sound boring, and they must live unhappily. Kidding—they have a different character than you.

My family is different. My mom had me out of wedlock at the age of seventeen. She wanted to go to school for dance, but I killed that. She and I managed to do the best we could with whatever we got. I lived through rough times when we slept in my mom's car. Or she would sacrifice meals for herself to make sure I was okay. She even became a stripper to earn more money for us. James doesn't like me mentioning my life story. His family is repulsed by the thought of poor people. As if there isn't such a thing. I tried the best I could not to go down that path. I felt so ashamed.

Mom is now an owner of a yoga shop. She practices some kind of energy stuff that I can't for the life of me figure out, but she's happy. We try to see each other at least once a week.

Question 6: Why did you send a letter to Daisy? Did you love her?

Yours,
Zelda.

To: zelstclaire11@hmail.com
    From: eddie_h2020@hmail.co.uk
    Subject: Blaze of glory with this one.

Zel,

Never let others make you feel ashamed of your upbringing because if they try to, they are fucking assholes. Besides, it sounds like your mom is amazing. You're better than them. James shouldn't make you feel that way. His parents sound a lot like mine. It's why we aren't on speaking terms. Your mom did the best she could to make things happen for you. I bet she's so proud of you, even if she practices magic.

Going for the jugular with the questions, aren't you, Zellie?

To be honest, I liked her but could never love her. Daisy never liked the idea of a relationship. It was daunting to her, having to be stuck with one person. But she could be a tad wild. Andrew didn't like her at all. She would get me into party drugs, which would end in me being in a bender. I couldn't love a woman like that. Maybe for a minute I could love her, but that's it. She was on a bad path and a temptation.

What happened with James?

Your pal,

Edmund

To: eddie_h2020@hmail.co.uk

From: zelstclaire11@hmail.com

Subject: Eddie — not cool

Eddie

I will never in my life answer to Zellie.

Sorry for the delay. I had to attend an interior design expo for work. I handle the design articles at the magazine I work at. It's a decent job and I get to work along side my best friend, Clara.

Side note, I wasn't even going to respond to your terrible choice of a nickname for me! I need one for you. Eddie is predictable. Edmund. It sounds rich. Gosh, what next? Are you going to tell me there is a third in there?

Regarding James, he has been keeping the money I've been paying for the rent. His parents bought the apartment, and he lied just so he could keep my money for his art studio. We haven't really talked much since the fight last week. He's been sleeping at the studio while I've been here. It's been hard. I feel like it's all or nothing with him. If he had told me he needed money for the studio, I would have helped. But he hasn't apologized. I struggle to see how this is a good thing with him. I had an idea that everything would eventually get better, and I wouldn't end up alone.

I'm feeling rough right now.

Zel

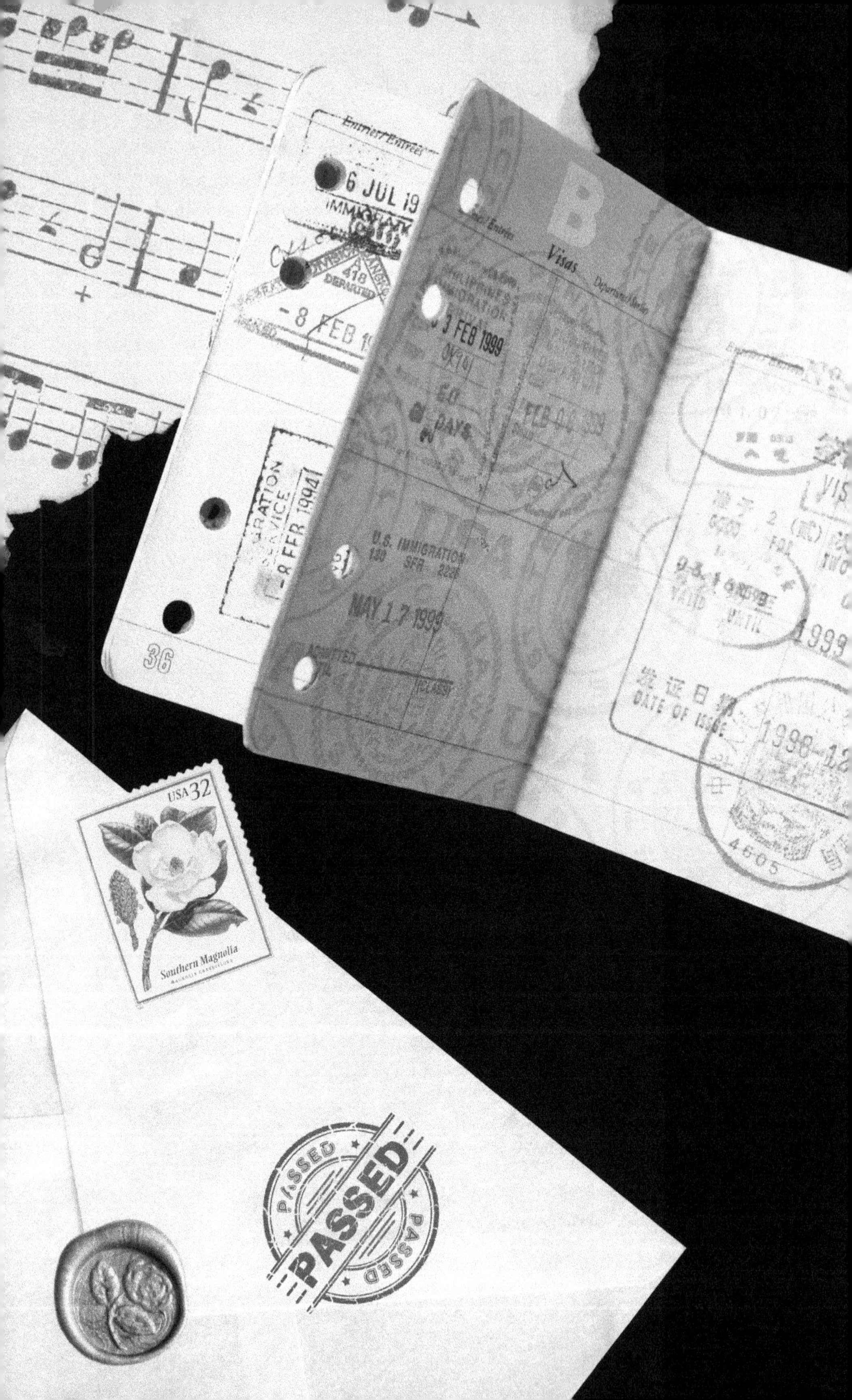
Entrée/Entrée
6 JUL 19
IMMIGRATION
418
DEPARTED
8 FEB 19
Visas
Départ/Partir
B
PHILIPPINES
IMMIGRATION
3 FEB 1999
OK14I
60 DAYS
RATION SERVICE
8 FEB 1994
36
U.S. IMMIGRATION
180   SFR   2220
MAY 17 1999
ADMITTED
74   CLASS
DATE OF ISSUE
1998-12
4605
USA 32
Southern Magnolia
MAGNOLIA GRANDIFLORA
PASSED
PASSED
PASSED
PASSED

Zelda

Within the past five days, I had sent numerous emails to a stranger, which brought me more happiness than what existed in my life. It was a bold statement, but something had ignited in me in a way I couldn't explain.

You're right; I need to stand up to James. He always makes me feel incapable of doing anything. It's as if I need approval before being judged. It's strange to think that way or even confess it. A part of me always feels like I'm missing something. I may be terrified to end up like my mom. I hate admitting that. I sound so childish, but I just want to feel like I'm worthy.

Throughout our conversations, we openly shared personal experiences that were typically kept secret.

I never talk about this, not even to Andrew. My demons appeared when we lost our friend, Rupert. When I was sixteen, Rupert died from suicide. I could've saved him, but I was too busy being some hotshot.

He called me that day, and I pressed ignore because I cared about fucking a girl more than his mental health. He struggled a lot. I promised him that I would always answer him.

Not that day.

Andrew showed up at my house with tears in his eyes, and I knew. We rushed to the hospital, but it was too late. I was so angry with myself because I failed him. That night, I had my first run-in with the police.

Edmund confided in me about his fears, doubts, and inner struggles that hindered him from pursuing his dreams.

I want to feel happiness once and not let darkness take over me.

Likewise, I had revealed my checklist of tasks I must accomplish.

My mom thinks I'm nuts, but I've always been a person who needs structure. If I don't, I fall off, and everything becomes chaos. Maybe it's because I am not too fond of the unknown. Not knowing what will happen next terrifies me the most.

I told him it felt uncompleted regardless of whether I did them all. It was like something was missing.

Maybe, Zelda, you can teach me how to stay on track, and I can help you live a little bit on the wild side.

Edmund described his world, and he sent me photos of his prized possession, his motorcycle. I shared a picture of my library, which he was impressed with, minus the romance collection. I told him he should invest in at least one and maybe get some new techniques.

We talked a lot about his music, including his lyrics. He sent me a sample of his voice, and God help me, I felt every word ignite my bones. A chill shivered down my body as his voice rasped with each lyric. His husky laughter at the end and his accent taking life—I was surprised by how utterly turned on I was. I closed my eyes, swaying as I listened to his voice repeatedly.

"I hold you tight, hoping you know I will take your darkness away."

I lay in my bed at night, alone. Watching my ceiling as I had my headphones in, I listened to his words over and over again. I was on thin ice, and I knew I had to put a stop to it. I was feelings something that was foreign and alluring.

"You have a boyfriend, Zelda!" I repeated. I had to draw a line in our friendship. I was starting to have a crush on Edmund and had to control myself.

~

CLARA NOTICED the change in my expression. I couldn't lie to her. She was the only saving grace I had. "Zel, what are you doing? Maybe you're realizing that James isn't the right one?" she whispered, and I watched her worried eyes. We went for dinner after work because I wanted to get her opinion.

"I love James, and I won't do anything to ruin our relationship. I don't know why I feel this way," I confessed.

"Because you're alone. James distanced himself from you. He doesn't give you what you want. You're his doormat, always giving and never taking. Maybe it's time to end it," she said.

She was right, but I was afraid.

I was terrified of being alone and watching my world crumble over a man I'd never met. I didn't even know what he looked like. How could someone have feelings from emails? "Maybe I should work on making me and James better." I nodded confidently. "We've been together for four years. I can't give that up. We have everything together."

"What would you say if I already know what he looks like?"

I sat frozen in my seat. "Pardon? How?" I was dumbfounded by what she said. "What do you mean? How?"

"I have my ways," She winked. "Would you like to see what Edmund looks like?" she asked.

Clara sipped her wine as I processed what I wanted to do. *Should I look and see, or should I not,* I thought. If I did do this, it would change everything. Writing to him was a place for me to escape; however, my feelings were becoming entangled with lust. What if I found him attractive? What if he's everything I've ever dreamed of? Or could he be nothing like I picture? I couldn't risk it.

"No." As I sipped my wine, I firmly declared, "No, I don't want to."

Clara nodded, reaching for my hand and squeezing. "Whatever you want to do, I support you."

I sat in my chair as guilt overtook me. I needed to stop whatever this was between Edmund and me. Or at least come to terms with the fact that we could only stay friends and nothing more.

I CONVINCED Edmund that we shouldn't ever take any steps toward meeting each other in person. Not that I didn't want to see him; it drove me insane not to look him up. Hearing him sing had been one thing, but seeing the person behind the emails would change everything.

My real world cracked every chance it got because of the tension between James and me. Since that night at the studio, I had been walking around on eggshells and barely speaking to him because it resulted in constant fights. He'd never apologized. James brushed it off and made it out like I was being childish by making it a big deal. Maybe I was. I told him that I was tired of always fighting, but James insisted I was the one causing all the problems.

Yesterday, he became unhinged about something that occurred at the studio. I tried to speak to him, but it only fueled his anger. James yelled at me, blaming our fight for his lack of concentration. I distracted him from his work, he told me. But what hurt the most was when he said something I didn't expect he would say to me.

"You like to ruin everything good, Zelda. You are such a fucking mess. I don't want to deal with you." James slammed his hands on the counter before storming out of the room.

I cried that night in bed while he lay there, not even consoling me.

I vented to Edmund that James was purposely trying to stay away from me. James had only texted me, stating I needed to cool down and figure my shit out. When I showed the text message to Edmund, he sent me a message saying James was a tosser, which I had to look up. There was a mutual agreement on that.

To: zelstclaire11@hmail.com
From: eddie_h2020@hmail.co.uk
Subject: Get yourself together, friend.

Good morning,

I know you've had a rough week since the fight with James. I secretly want to punch the idiot because of what he said to you. I couldn't stop thinking about it. You should tell James he needs to get a grip. But that isn't my place. I'm here to talk more if you want to.

Here's something to distract you: I thought about you when I passed by the Central Library heading to Greyfriars. Usually, on my days off, I sit in the cemetery and write. While I sat there and watched people taking photos of graves, I wondered how often you'd go to the library if you were here. Would you spend most of your time there? I've only been there once since I moved to the city. It's a pretty building, though. Most of the time, I sit under a tree, minding my business and conversing with the dead.

They are quiet, at least.

E.

Ps. I've attached a photo of the area.

WHEN THE EMAIL dinged onto my screen at work, I bit my bottom lip. I'd been trying my best to keep strong, but it was too damn hard. I was trying to keep with my daily routine, and Edmund was part of it. He was there, and James wasn't.

After the fight with James, he found peace at his studio again. He didn't even call or text me, as if I didn't exist to him, even if I tried to reach out. I felt like I was nothing to him.

"What are you doing?" Clara asked as I minimized the email.

"I…" I hesitated while glancing at her, but it was written all over my face. "He's been making me happy," I confessed.

"I can see." Clara nodded at the screen. "What did I tell you about this 'situation'?" She air quoted.

"He has been respectful and kind. I told him we need to keep it friendly," I assured her.

"You like him." She pointed at me accusatorily. "I can tell."

"Not in that way. We're just friends, Clara."

"You don't need any more friends," she hissed. "What does he say?"

"We talk about ourselves and our lives." I shrugged. "Basic stuff." I couldn't lie to my best friend; she knew my ins and outs.

Clara reached for my hand. "Don't be stupid. I know what this is."

"What do you mean?" I shot her a confused look as I watched her expression go stern.

She took a deep breath and reached for the bridge of her nose. "I love you, but as much as you fight it, you settled with James. I said it before, you need to choose."

I couldn't put words to it because I didn't know what to say. "No...I—"

The sudden buzz of my phone caught me off guard. James's face was on the screen as I held my breath. I looked at Clara, and she slowly shook her head.

"He hasn't come home in days," I said as I looked back at the screen.

"Don't give him the time of day." Clara rolled her eyes as she reached for my phone. "Let me chat," she snapped.

"No! Don't!" It was too late.

"What do you want?" Clara snapped into the phone.

I watched her react with a narrowed stare at me.

"You know you're in the wrong, right?"

She exhaled a deep breath, shaking her head, and handed me the phone. "James wants to talk." She sighed and shook her head.

I took a deep breath and reached for my phone. "Hi," I said.

"Babe, please listen to me. Meet me on the roof tonight, okay?"

"Why?"

"Don't ask, please."

I glanced back at Clara as she flashed me a saddened face that surprised me.

"Okay, I'll be there tonight."

To: eddie_h2020@hmail.co.uk
    From: zelstclaire11@hmail.com
    Subject: Hello from New York.

Edmund,

That photo was beautiful. I wish I had a place to flee. Mine is currently the emergency fire escape outside my window. I sit there with my notepad, writing away. It is the only time when I do not have to please or do anything for anyone else. I wrote my first letter there as I watched the stars.

I want to go to Scotland. I looked up at that cemetery; it's pretty

Gothic. I love it! Did you know there were body snatchers? Wait, you would know there were. I sound like a tourist already.

Here is my twentieth question (wait, I lost count of how many were asked).

If you're ready, can we do this through text?

Zelda

xx

~

THIS WAS a wicked game I was playing; pressing send, I knew it was going to open something further than expected. My emotions were unsettling, and I crossed another barrier without stopping. I was making a mess.

As I walked down the street heading home from a long workday, I got a phone call from the one person who would help me in the right direction.

I heard my mom yell, "Baby girl!" and I took my earbud out.

"Mom! Stop yelling." She sounded breathless. "What are you doing?"

"I'm doing this crazy home spin class! It's glorious!" I heard a commotion followed by someone screaming in the background.

"Can you pause it for a minute?"

"Hold on, let me pause it for a minute."

Rolling my eyes, I said, "Thank you."

"Lord, that was fun."

"I'm glad you liked it." Since her new life endeavors, she'd decided to get into the groove of self-love. At least once a day, she sent me an article on life improvements and love. I wouldn't be surprised if she went to Bali one day to eat, pray, and love her way around the world.

"Let's chat, baby. What's going on? I could feel your mood. It's throwing me off."

"How?"

"I'm an empath, you know that!"

Rolling my eyes again, I said, "Right, so you know about the dead woman?"

"Is she there? Do you want to do a séance?"

"No, Mom, it's not like that. I kept one of her letters."

"Oh, that's not good. Especially with the dead."

"Mom, just listen to me! I wrote back to a letter from a guy she had a fling with. His name is Edmund, and we've been chatting for six weeks or so."

"Okay."

"Okay?" I asked.

"Well, what do you want me to say?"

I was dumbfounded. "Advice?"

"You're in a relationship with James. You're chatting with another man. You're bored."

"It's not like that."

"What is it then? Why did you write to a man who you didn't know?"

"I-I don't know." It was the truth. I didn't understand why I had done it.

"Listen, I love you, and I want what is best for you. Let this flow. I've always known that James wasn't ever your forever guy."

"Mom! I love him!"

"Honey, you can love one person but also love another. That's a natural thing, but he isn't your forever. He pulls you down in ways you shouldn't allow anyone to do. You have a fire, even if you pretend you want structure. Zelda, I support you in this."

I fought back the tears in my eyes. Deep down, I knew she was telling the truth. I wanted to have that lifestyle I'd seen growing up. I was ashamed to admit that I wanted that perfect love story, even if I made fun of it.

"Mom, I think I need to stop talking to him."

"Why? There is a reason he responded back. There is a reason you got that apartment. Maybe Edmund is someone you need to check out before letting it go." I stopped in front of my apartment and looked up, wishing that something would end this Groundhog Day lifestyle. "Give yourself another month and see."

"Okay, I love you."

"I love you more than you will ever know."

I smiled, then hung up with her. James and I had come so far and built this all to make a life. I needed to stop creating a messy situation and focus on us. I headed up our stairs to get to the rooftop and each step left me with a smile. It was the right thing for me.

When I opened the roof's security door, I realized James wasn't there. I checked my phone, and the text message I received made me hurt.

JAMES

I'm sorry I can't make it tonight. I'll make it up to you. Can we reschedule? Got invited to a big party! Love you.

Entrée/ Entrée
6 JUL 19
IMMIGRAT
8 FEB 1
Visas
B
PHILIPPINE
IMMIGRATION
3 FEB 1999
DAYS
FEB 06 1999
RATION
FER 1994
U.S. IMMIGRATION
SFR
MAY 1 7 1999
ADMITTED
36
VISA
1999
DATE OF ISSUE
1996-12
4605
USA 32
Southern Magnolia
PASSED
PASSED

7

———

Edmund

"Thank you, my gorgeous audiences!" Tom roared into the microphone as I leaned away from the keyboard and watched the crowd pour their excitement into cheering. My body was drenched in sweat from the stage lights, and my heart beat against my chest from the pure adrenaline. It was a high I'd never felt before.

I'd been going hard on this band thing since Tom decided not to look for a replacement. It had been a calling pulling me in ways I'd never felt before. It was something tangible I could call my own and be proud of.

My attitude had improved over the past weeks as a result of talking to Zelda. Andrew insisted I was less asshole lately, which was all the more reason to thank her. Talking to Zelda had helped me push myself to do something more in my life. I wasn't proud of what I'd been falling into, and I knew I was going to end up being how I was before, an uncontrollable storm determined to ruin everything in its path.

At our first band meeting, Tom had insisted on one rule for the rest of the guys, and it was not to piss me off. I'd let out a snicker. One of the guys had even said I needed to get laid, and I'd thought, *That may help*.

Malcom came on stage and took the microphone from Tom. "Don't you love these guys?" he asked the crowd. It was the same lineup every night. I played five nights a week while bartending before the show. It was the busiest pub on the Grassmarket. Crowds huddled around the entrance way listening to our songs. A part of me hoped Zelda would walk in and listen to me.

I could picture her, in my mind, and I felt like I would be able to pick her out of the crowd. After getting to know her more, I wanted to video chat with her. I had never felt this addicted to a person before. She was a new drug I wanted to sample, but I had to remind myself that we were only friends.

She had a boyfriend.

She was complicated.

I fucking loved complicated.

I was bonded to my phone all the time. It was the only way I could read whatever she wrote to me. I was glad she had accepted my email suggestion because I couldn't fucking wait any longer for her letters. It was even better that she'd asked to swap phone information. But I wanted to see her. The thought of videoing her was always on my mind, but I couldn't.

I stood from the keyboard, and a couple of women waited at the edge for me to talk, but I didn't give them the opportunity.

"You know…" Tom patted my shoulder. "Your imaginary girlfriend won't mind if you have sex with a groupie."

"Fuck off!" I nudged him as I reached for the beer Grace handed to me. She was the new hire who finally made it to a month. She was short with strawberry-blond hair and evergreen eyes. Her skin was ivory, and she had a wicked body. She continually wore the shortest dresses knowing I'd take a glance. She was friendly and flirty, yet I felt like I was attached to someone. But Zelda was taken, and I was allowed to have fun.

"Thank you." I nodded at her as she pushed a loose curl away from her face and flashed me a small smile. She turned away, showcasing her curvy ass in her tight black dress.

"Now that is something nice to look at," Tom commented, and all I wanted him to do was go away.

"I'm heading outside for a smoke. Give me five before we pack up," I called out as I walked to the back.

I swung the door open, sat on the fold-up chair, and lit my smoke, then I placed my beer on the makeshift table. And that was when Grace walked out.

"You're working," I teased her.

"I can't come out and say hello?" She leaned against the wall with her arms behind her back, making her breasts unavoidable. I took a deep breath, rubbed my chin, and took a drag. "You played well tonight," she continued.

"Thank you," I replied. "It's busy tonight."

"Yeah." She cocked her head to the side, and she pushed off the wall. She walked over to me as I took a deep breath. "I want to do something, but only if you want to." She straddled me and wrapped her arms around my neck. My dick pulsed in my jeans as my chest tightened at the inhale of her perfume. Grace's lips were so close to mine that I could feel her hot breath brush against my skin. I gripped her hips tight, and I devoured her mouth. I tasted her, and my aggression wanted to take hold of her. She was a distraction or maybe a substitute for the woman I really wanted.

I moved my hands up to her breasts and explored her forbidden territory. Grace moaned as she started to rock her hips. I wanted nothing more than to shove her against the wall, put my dick in her wet pussy, and make her scream as loud as she could. I trailed my lips down to the nape of her neck and her head fell back.

"Fuck me," she cried. "I want you so bad." She reached for my hand and placed it under her skirt so I could feel how wet she was for me.

A vibration interrupted us.

"Ignore it," she demanded as she unbuckled my pants. I was in dire need of sex. So I ignored the call, but I started to think of Zelda and fucking her.

I lifted Grace, wrapped her legs around my waist, and pushed her against the wall. She let out a moan as I devoured her mouth once more. My dick was out, ready to fuck her in the alley. But as I pushed her underwear to the side, the phone distracted me.

"Fuck!" I groaned as Grace dropped to her feet. She moved away before I could do anything.

"Maybe later?" she responded as she patted her dress and fixed her hair. Her lips looked raw as I watched her chest heave for me. I fixed myself up, zipping up my jeans.

"Come over tonight?" I asked.

"Sure. It's probably better on a bed than an alley." She winked as she reached for the door handle and disappeared.

I ran my hands through my hair to calm my arousal. Fucking blue balls suck. I took a swig of my beer before acknowledging my ringing phone. When I pulled my phone out, I was surprised by the name across the screen: Zelda.

I froze. We didn't call each other. Ever.

She had called me twice.

I didn't know what to do. Was there a reason for the call? I thought about it, then pressed her name to call her back.

It rang once.

Twice.

"I'm so sorry to bug you!" Her voice was sweet and perfect. I was dumbfounded by hearing her voice. It was like a melody playing in my mind. I swallowed hard and leaned against the wall. "I didn't know what to do. I'm having a bad day, and I was with my friend Clara, and we went to happy hour, and the first person I thought of was you—"

"Hey," I said. I didn't know what to say to her. I was about to have sex in an alley, and suddenly, Grace was nowhere in my mind.

"Your voice. I love it. It's so deep. So British," Zelda's voice squeaked.

I could feel my lips turn into a smile. "I love your voice too."

There was silence for a second.

"I love your voice. Did I say that already?" She giggled.

"Yeah, you did, Zelda." I paused, listening to her laugh. It was intoxicating.

"Repeat my name."

I licked my bottom lip. "Zelda."

"I get chills from your voice," she admitted. "I can't stop thinking about you. It's like every moment I get, I think of you. What you're doing…who you are. I don't know how, but you've done something to me." Her confession was a turn-on.

"Zelda, I want to talk to you so fucking bad. I do…" I paused. "But I have to finish work. Can I call you when I'm done? Please?"

"I'll wait for you."

"Please answer when I get home. You can tell me all about your day, babe," I said.

"You called me babe."

"I won't call you that."

"No, I like it." I could picture her smiling.

"Are you home at least?" I asked.

"No, I'm with Clara at her apartment. We're going to watch a movie. But she's going to pass out shortly. She can't handle liquor." She snorted.

"Did you snort?" I teased.

"Yeah! Get used to it."

For a second, we both were quiet. *Get used to it*, as if Zelda wanted more. "I will talk to you soon."

"Have a good night at work, and don't think of me too much."

"I will." *I think about you all the time*, I thought.

We both hung up, and I felt like the air in that alley evaporated as my chest tightened at the foreign feeling. I didn't know how to handle it. My hands were clammy, but my heart was pounding. I didn't care about helping the band pack up; I just wanted to talk to her.

Entrées/Entrees
6 JUL 19
IMMIGRANT
418
-8 FEB 19
Entrées/Entrees
Visas
Départ/Home
B
PHILIPPINE
IMMIGRATION
3 FEB 1999
OK TO
60
DAYS
FEB-0 1999
U.S. IMMIGRATION
190   SFR   228
MAY 1 7 1999
ADMITTED
CLASS
ARATION
RVICE
FER 1994
36
入電
VISA
GOOD 2 (INC)
FOR TWO
VALID UNTIL
1999
DATE OF ISSUE
1996-12
4605
USA 32
Southern Magnolia
MAGNOLIA GRANDIFLORA
PASSED
PASSED
PASSED
PASSED

8

Edmund

om begged me to do one more song before the pub closed, but I told him I had plans. He wanted me to play the one I had written. He insisted that I sing the song, but I wasn't ready to release it into the world.

I was the backup singer, not the center stage type. Tom knew that was the only way that I agree to be in the band. But I had had to remind him constantly as his drunkenness persisted that I go for it.

The band thought I was on Adderall because I packed the van with the instruments with such focus that nothing stopped me. Grace was trying to make an advance, but she wasn't on my radar anymore. All I wanted was to get home and call the only woman in my mind.

I couldn't stop thinking about her voice. It was the perfect melody that I wanted to hear. I wanted to devour her voice when she was mad and when she was aroused.

When Malcom locked the pub doors, I wasn't waiting for anyone. Grace came over as I grabbed my stuff, packed my keyboard, and placed it into the lockers. "So…tonight?" She winked.

"About that…" I passed by her and reached for my bag. "Some

other time." I kissed her cheek, grabbed my jacket, and headed out with a quick wave before she could respond.

Nothing mattered at that moment other than calling Zelda. I'd never walked to the apartment so fast. I rushed up the stairs to our flat like I was on a mission. Once inside, I kicked off my boots and threw my gear down. The lights were off, and I heard Andrew calling from his bedroom. I said hi before heading to my room to pace like a fucking loser.

Sitting on the edge of the bed, I glanced at my phone. I called her as Zelda answered on the first ring.

"You called back." She was cheerful.

"I promised I would."

"I don't believe in promises," she said.

"Why?"

"Because most people break them. It's wasteful. Most people don't know what it means to hold on to a promise."

"Who broke your heart?"

She paused as I lay down on my bed.

"I watched it happen with my mom when others used her. I've seen it when I'm with James."

James. I forgot about him. I didn't want anything to do with him.

"What did he do?"

"Your voice is super sexy."

"Don't change the subject but thank you."

"What is there to say? He's an asshole. After canceling the other day and what he did last night, I can't handle it. All he cares about is his career. James showed up at one in the morning completely wasted and told me about some woman who was all over him. It isn't right. It isn't us—not me."

"He hasn't apologized?"

"No, he hasn't. We barely talk. I don't know; he's off, I guess."

"Change the subject?" I felt a weird tension.

"How was your night? I want to see you play," she said with a soft voice.

"I thought of you when I was playing the piano," I said as I grabbed my headphones and put them on.

"Did you? What did you think about?" she asked.

"I thought about what it'd be like if you were in the pub."

"I wish I could."

"Come visit me. Come be with me for a couple of weeks," I begged. "I want to see you."

Zelda didn't respond. Maybe it was too forward.

"Never mind, I don't want you to—"

"What if I did? What if I came to visit you, Edmund? I can't stop thinking about you, and I want nothing more than to be with you—in certain ways." She giggled.

My fucking dick twitched at her words. "What kind of ways?"

"I want to kiss you," she whispered.

I scratched my chin. "Do you think of me in the nude?"

"I don't even know what you look like," she squeaked.

"We can solve that Zel, video chat?" I asked, wanting nothing more than to see her. I wanted to see her smile and her eyes. I wanted to watch her laugh or blush. I wanted to hear her say my name over and over again. I wanted her.

"Tempting, but if I do, it becomes real," she said.

"What we share and what we write isn't real?"

"It's over for me once I see you. It's all I want to do. I want to see you. I want to know you. I want to be able to touch you. I've had dreams of you."

"Were they hot?" I half-joked.

"Edmund, not all of them involves that type of dream."

"Oh?" I perked up at the thought of "not all the time."

"I'm not going down that path."

"Fine, but I think it's time, Zelda."

She was silent. "I'm not pretty, okay?"

"I highly doubt it."

I reached for my phone and clicked on the screen to video.

"I'm not ready! I'm in my sweats. I look like shit."

"Answer the fucking phone, Zelda. I want to see you."

"No!"

"Answer the phone!"

Her lips were full and rosy against her ivory skin. Her loose hair fell on her face, and her eyes were big and emerald green. She hid under a blanket to avoid being in the camera frame. And she was the only woman in the world who would fucking ruin me.

"You're unbelievably beautiful." My lips parted, and I felt overwhelmed.

"Are your eyes brown?" she asked as she bit her bottom lip. Those lips. I desired to touch them so badly. Tasting Zelda was now the first thing on my bucket list.

"Yeah, I wasn't given bright eyes like my siblings. I look like the adopted one with my dark features. It's from my mum's side." I leaned against my headboard.

"I like your eyes."

I brought my knee closer to rest my hand on it. "Do you think I look like a Viking?"

"You look like guys I've had crushes on but never talked to me."

"I would talk to you."

She rolled her eyes as she fell back on her pillow. Her hair draped around her head as she watched me. "You definitely look like a Viking. I love your curls."

"This hair doesn't tame."

"Don't cut it. You will lose your attractiveness," she teased.

"Ouch! I was going to get it cut tomorrow," I lied.

"A dimple!" She made an O with her lips as I rubbed my cheek.

"You saw nothing."

"Edmund?" Her smile was gone before I knew it.

"Zelda?"

"What are we doing? I'm not the type who does this. I can't be."

"I won't push unless you want me to."

She paused. "I don't know why I feel something for you. I don't want to do things I will regret."

"I get that."

Guilt was written all over her face, and she looked down. "I don't want to lose you."

"Zel…" I paused. "You can never lose me, darling."

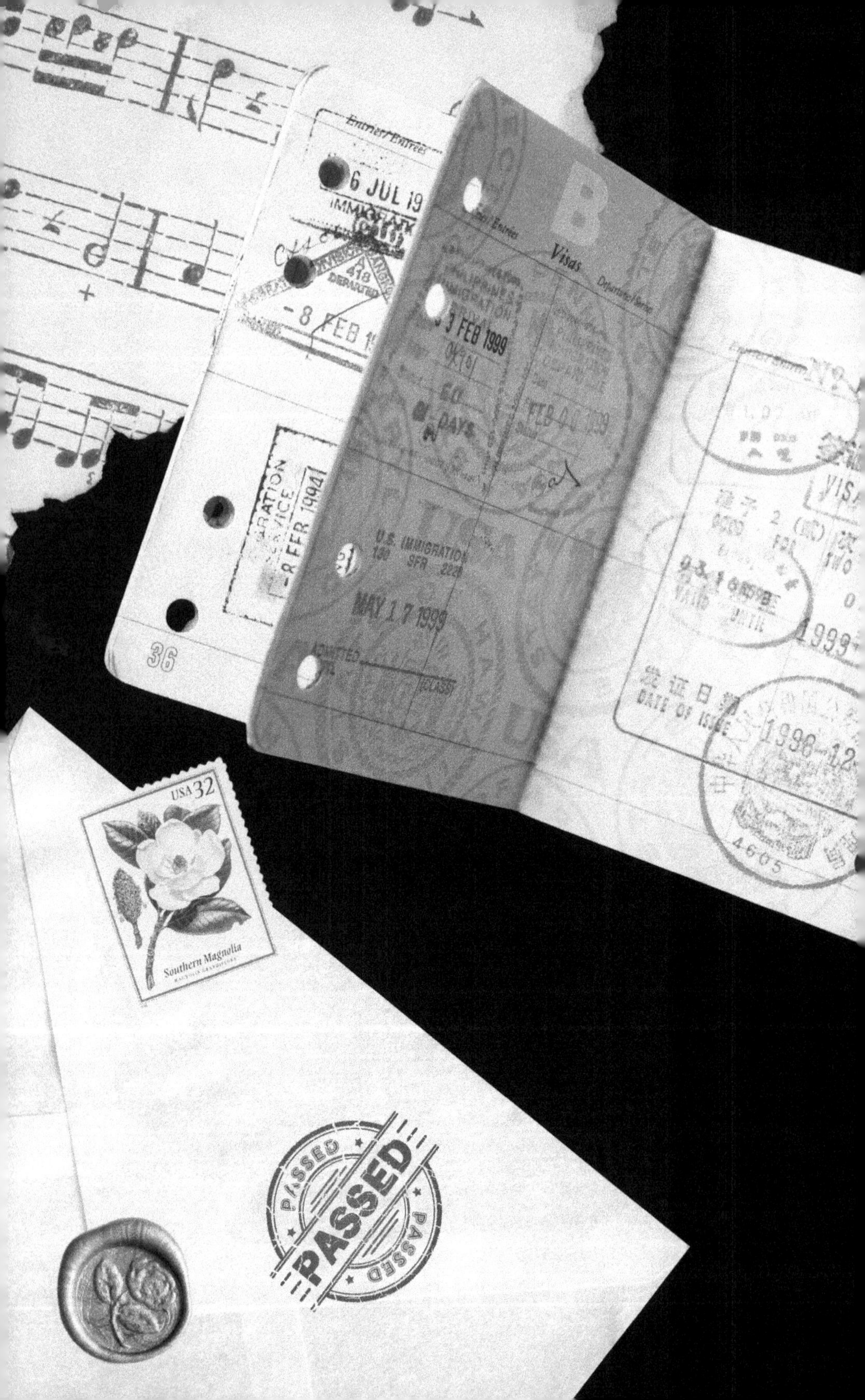
Entrées/Entrees
6 JUL 19
IMMIGRATION
418
DEPARTURE
8 FEB 1
Visas
Départ/Sortie
B
3 FEB 1999
DAYS
U.S. IMMIGRATION
SFR
MAY 1 7 1999
ADMITTED
CLASS
36
USA 32
Southern Magnolia
MAGNOLIA GRANDIFLORA
VISA
DATE OF ISSUE
1996-12
4605
PASSED
PASSED
PASSED

9

———

Zelda

The night I saw Edmund altered everything I thought was right. Awakened by spirits I'd never felt, my eyes watched the raindrops hit the window as tears overtook my vision. My heart was being pulled in a direction I could never recover from.

I didn't tell Clara I had seen him yet; I was waiting for the right moment to open up. When I headed to my office the following day, I walked in to see Clara holding a bouquet of my favorite flowers in her hand.

"Is it our friend-aversary?" I joked, heading to my seat.

"No." She gave a little smile before handing them to me. There was a note in a green envelope. I pulled out the little card and read the words.

I couldn't forget you even if I wanted to try.

E.

I bit my bottom lip while my heart burst in ways I couldn't explain.

Not a single time had James ever purchased my favorite flowers. It sounded childish, but the little effort by Edmund took hold of me.

"They're from Edmund, aren't they?" Clara crossed her arms.

I looked up at her, still holding the card close to my heart. I couldn't lie to her.

"I've seen him," I confessed.

If her eyes could explode, they would've. "What do you mean, you saw him?"

"We video chatted. And his voice! God! His voice! I loved it!"

Clara pressed her hands to her forehead. "Are you fucking kidding me? So? What is it? Are you two going to make it happen?"

"We are friends."

"Friends don't buy flowers for each other."

"I buy you flowers all the time." I said, rolling my eyes.

"I meant a man. The man you've been secretly writing too. This means something."

"He is respectful. He isn't pushing me."

Clara pressed on the bridge of her nose. "Zel, I love you, but this is a hot mess waiting to explode. You need to end it."

I narrow my glance. "Why? I'm only talking to him."

"End it with James."

She was right. I needed to end it. There had to be a plan in order for me to end it with James. It made sense. I was petrified in doing so because I was risking it all for Edmund. I had to focus on what I wanted.

"I will do so, but tonight, I need to support James." I knew she wouldn't understand, but I had to play the part. I had to attend an event for James, which was different from what I wanted to do.

James had been invited to a gala for the arts, and I was supposed to go with him. After finally sleeping at home last night, he begged me to attend it as if we were the picture-perfect couple he wanted us to be. He would stroll in and talk about art, and I felt a sudden numbness. Was it regret? Betrayal? Or was it realizing that I was better than this. I deserved better.

~

"My parents are excited to see you tonight," James said while fixing his tie. He stood in front of the mirror, but his eyes watched me. I did my final touches, placing my lipstick on in the bathroom. I glanced down to the counter and see that Edmund has messaged me, but I tried to stay focused. I swiped quickly and turned to James and flashed him a smile.

We'd been coasting for a couple of days. James had been home and tried to make things right with us. But I was battling fear and confusion every moment I had.

Nothing was worth saving at this moment.

"It has been a while," I replied as I closed the lipstick. "I can't wait to see them." They hated me, which was why I'd never felt like I was good enough for their son.

"Good because tonight is going to be a wonderful night." James headed toward me, looking clean and ready. His hair was slicked back, and his day-old stubble was gone. He was the perfect clean-cut man his parents adored. I couldn't handle this. This was slowly making me feel like I couldn't breathe.

"God…" James watched me from the bathroom doorway. His eyes darkened as he crossed his arm against his chest. His head rested on the frame as he gave me a cocky smirk.

"What?" I grinned at him. "Why are you looking at me like that?"

"I can't help but stare at the most beautiful person in the world."

I watched him walk toward me as I leaned against the vanity. He stood in front as he cradled my head in the palm of his hands. "I love you, Zelda. I want nothing more than to make you happy. These past few weeks have been crazy, and I've ignored you, but I want to make things right. I know you did some stuff that wasn't okay—but let's get past it, all right?"

I swallowed hard, and my eyes widened under his stare. He pressed a kiss on my lips deeply. The feeling of our love held on, and I wanted to make things right with him. I had to. Even before that letter, James was my everything. We were building a life together.

He pulled away with his cocky smile I adored. "The car is waiting for us. Tonight's going to be a fun time." James left the bathroom, and I stood silently for a few minutes. I glanced at the screen and ignored Edmund.

~

WALKING into a room filled with rich people enjoying expensive champagne and food that cost an average year's wage wasn't me. I sat at the table, watching James in his element as he talked about his latest art project, and I felt utterly alone. My soul screamed, demanding freedom, but I was too much of a coward.

"Sweetie," James whispered into my ear as I turned my head toward him.

"Are you having fun?" I asked.

"Yeah, this is incredible. I've made some great connections tonight."

"I'm proud of you," I said as I flashed him a pleased look.

"Can you come with me?"

"Okay." He reached for my hand and pulled me through the crowds. We walked through the gala as music and chatter surrounded us.

He whisked us up the grand staircase to escaped the chaos below. We laughed as we hurried through the halls of the historic building; James pulled me into a room. He then closed the door. My eyes adjusted quickly to the darkness, and I saw walls of books and a balcony.

"What are we doing here?" I asked as James walked toward me with a devilish grin.

"I came here as a kid when my dad worked here. It was a place I used to escape."

"It's beautiful," I said, still looking around.

"Come with me." He pulled me into him and kissed me gently. "There is another view that is better than this one." He opened the French doors to the balcony, and I saw the perfect view of the city lights. I held the railing and gazed at the night sky.

"I love this. Downstairs was fun, but this is my ideal night," I confessed. James wrapped his arms around my waist and kissed the nape of my neck. "I miss this," I admitted.

"I miss us," he said. "Can we start over?"

I turned to him and wrapped my arms around his neck. I watched him as he parted his lips. "You are the only thing that matters to me. I want nothing more in this world than to spend my life with you."

My eyes widened at his last statement because I knew where it was going. James bent down on one knee.

"I know things have been different, and I know I haven't been myself, but I want us. I want a life with you, Zelda. I want this with you. Please be my wife. Be my everything."

"James…is…" I was too stunned to talk as he flashed me the ring in his hand, waiting for an answer. A heavy weight overtook me as my chest tightened. James watched my every move as I stood there, at a loss for words.

"Yes."

James stood and placed the ring on my finger. It was not what I should be doing.

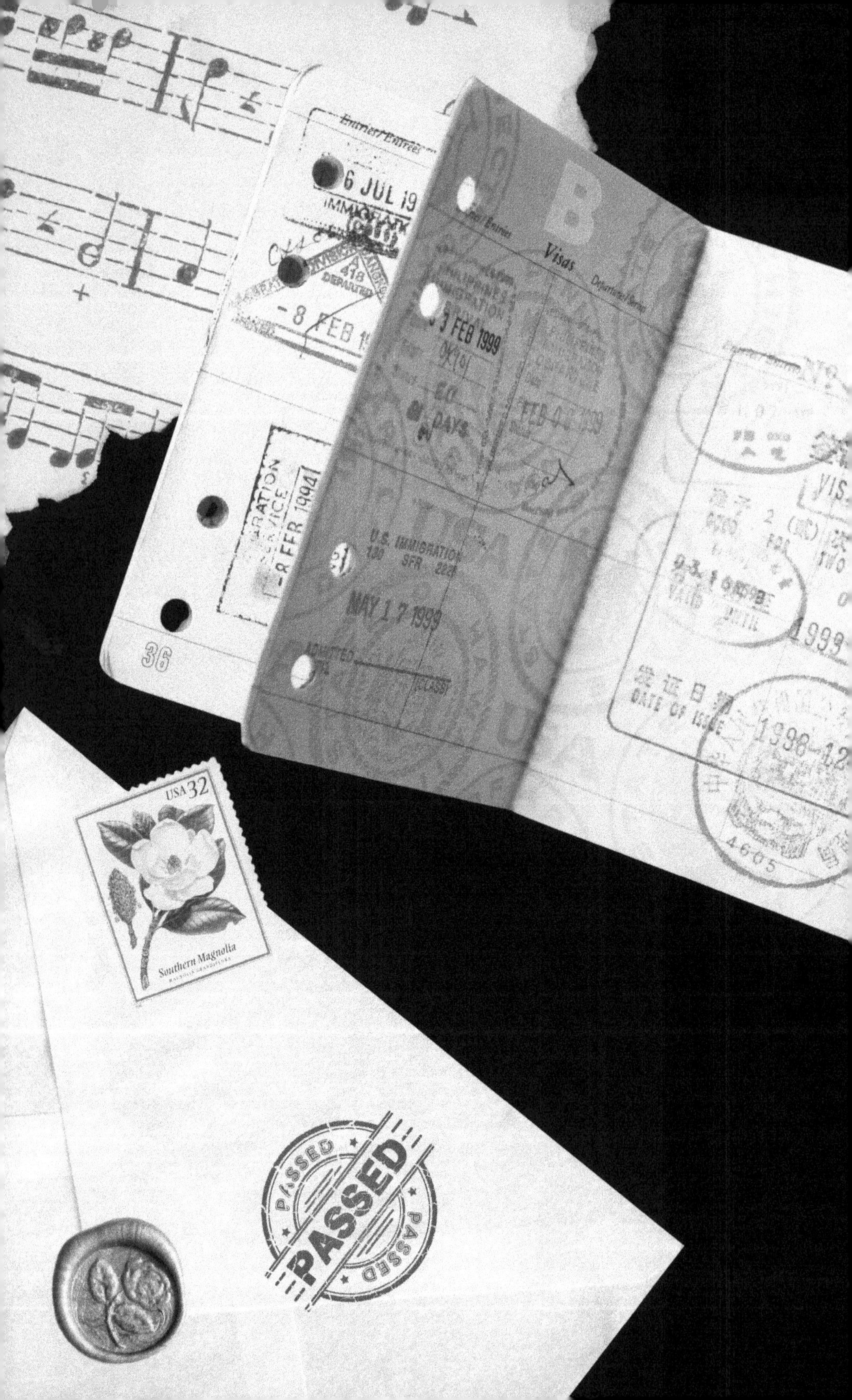
Entrées/Entrées
6 JUL 19
IMMIGRAT
418
DEPARTED
- 8 FEB 1
Visas
Départ/Sortie
B
Visas
PHILIPPINE'S
IMMIGRATION
3 FEB 1999
60
DAYS
GRATION
ERVICE
FEB 1994
U.S. IMMIGRATION
130   SFR   226
MAY 1 7 1999
ADMITTED
36
VIS
TWO
VALID   UNTIL   1999
DATE OF ISSUE   1998-12
4605
USA 32
Southern Magnolia
MAGNOLIA GRANDIFLORA
PASSED
PASSED
PASSED
PASSED

10

Zelda

I should be happy because I had gotten what I wanted, but I didn't feel that way. I felt like my heart was tugged in so many different directions, and I could no longer control my feelings. People at the party congratulated me on the proposal; I felt like my world was crumbling. James kissed my cheek, holding the conversation himself while people pulled my hand toward them to examine the diamond. A tear ran down my face.

"Are you okay, Zelda?" I raised my eyes to meet the speaker's.

"I…" I had forgotten how to talk. I swallowed and blinked a couple of times to try to relax.

"Babe." James glanced down at me as he rubbed my back. "You okay?"

"I need a minute."

I stepped away before answering any more questions. I rushed through the crowds of people dancing and chatting and headed toward the exit of the building for some much-needed air. The cool air hit my lungs like a sharp knife as I hunched over and pressed my hands into my face. This was all I wanted and begged for months. Yet here I was, having a panic attack.

I reached for my phone; I needed him. I needed to hear Edmund even if I should have been celebrating my exciting news.

It took one ring before I heard his voice.

"Hey, been worried about you," he said in a deep raspy voice. His voice calmed me. It sounded like he was asleep, and I instantly regretted waking him up.

"I'm sorry. I shouldn't have called."

"No, call me any time, Zelda."

"I-I got engaged," I said. Tears fell down my cheek.

Edmund didn't respond. He was quiet for a couple of seconds. It felt like an eternity before he finally said a word.

"Wow."

"Yeah…I…don't know what to do?"

"You're engaged, Zelda. You should be happy."

"Are you happy for me?"

"How could I be happy when I have feelings for you? All the letters, emails, texts, calls, we've spoken and gotten to know each other; I was hoping you felt the same."

"I do feel something for you. I…" I pressed my hands against my forehead. "I don't know what this is between us. I get excited talking to you, but I can't trust those feelings. It terrifies me if I pick you because I don't know the outcome. I don't know what to expect."

"What do you want to do, Zelda?"

"What can we do? You live in Scotland. I live here. How would we make this work? This is crazy! I shouldn't be doing this. You're just a bartender with no future!"

"Wow." His voice deepens, and I instantly my words.

"I'm sorry, I didn't mean that."

"I think it's best we stop all of this."

I froze at his words. "I…" I squeezed my eyes tight as I pursed my mouth, fighting the urge to scream.

"Maybe all of this was an accident." Edmund spoke, but I heard the pain in his voice. "Maybe this was not meant to be."

I leaned against the wall of the building and took a deep breath. "Goodbye, Edmund."

"Goodbye, Zelda."

I couldn't hold back the tears. All I felt was this pain taking over my heart. I should've been euphoric about this new chapter in my life, yet I wasn't.

Taking a deep breath, I wiped my tears. As I turned back to the entrance, I saw James walking down the steps. He saw me and knew that something was not right. I wrapped my arms around his neck, holding him like he was my only lifeline in this world. Maybe I had answered that letter to show me that I should be with James.

I was lying to myself so I didn't have to miss Edmund.

PART II

"Sometimes good things fall apart so better things can fall together." — Marilyn Monroe

Entrées/Entrées
6 JUL 19
IMMIGRATION
418
DEPARTURE
-8 FEB 1
Visas
Departure/Arrivée
B
3 FEB 1999
DAYS
U.S. IMMIGRATION
SFR
MAY 1 7 1999
ADMITTED
CLASS
FEB-4 0 1999
RATION
R FEB 1994
36
VISA
VALID
1999
DATE OF ISSUE
1998-12
4605
USA 32
Southern Magnolia
MAGNOLIA GRANDIFLORA
PASSED
PASSED
PASSED
PASSED

11

Eight months later…

Zelda

"You are making the biggest mistake of your life." You would think that someone who loved you might try to keep their thoughts to themselves. Not my mom. She encouraged speaking out when needed, which was right now as I had my first dress fitting.

Throughout any given day, I think about Edmund constantly and often contemplate messaging him by staring at his number in my contacts despite knowing it is not the best decision. My thoughts revolve around him.

I'd let myself go. Clara had called me a walking zombie. Here I had been given everything I wanted, and I couldn't stand it. I was walking around in my sorrow, dreading every minute of the day.

"What?" I faced my mom who was sitting in a chair. Her arms were across her chest, and her dark chestnut brown hair draped around her shoulders.

She glanced at my wedding gown as she took a deep breath. "You heard what I said."

The seamstress pinged-pong her gaze between us as we had this conversation again for the fiftieth time. "Mom, James is the one. Why can't you get that through your head?"

"Listen, I won't live long. I don't have a lot of years left in me. For you to stand there and pretend that all of this is right is truly a mistake." She reached for the complimentary champagne, and she shot it back like it was water.

"Mom, you're being ridiculous. You're not dying. You're not changing my mind." Releasing a frustrated breath, I cradled my head in my hands. "Why are you so dramatic?"

"I am?" She pressed her hand to her chest, pretending I had shot her in the heart. "I want nothing but the best for you."

"James is the best for me; why don't you see that?" I rebutted her statement. I tried my best to keep this appointment under control, but control was gone before we walked in. Clara should have come.

"No, he isn't!" Mom's voice pitched high as other brides and their families gasped around us. "I will die wishing that he was not my son-in-law."

"I would listen to your mom if she's saying that," the seamstress responded as she worked on the hem of my dress.

"Oh, for the love of—" I smacked my hands to my side. "You can't talk. You don't even know who my father is. I am not living a life where I'm all alone. I want stability, love, and devotion." By the time I realized what I'd said, the harm was done, and my mother's eyes told the consequence.

Mom stood and exhaled forcefully, then shut her eyes firmly. "I made my mistakes…" She paused as she gazed at me. "I'm not proud of them, but understand that I did it all for you. I would do it again and again, knowing how you turned out. A mother will do anything to make their child happy. But I see you, Zelda. I see how empty your eyes are. How you aren't that wild soul I created. No, you're a sad, selfish child who thinks money and stability are the route to a perfect life." Mom reached into her purse, pulled an envelope out from her bag, and handed it to me.

"That's your wedding gift; let me know what you want to do." Before I could speak, she abruptly grabbed her purse and left the store. I stood there, mortified by how I had talked to her.

Stepping off the pedestal, I moved toward the chair and planted myself there. "I need a minute," I mouthed as if I had forgotten how to speak. The lady walked away as others began whispering about what had happened.

I turned over the envelope with Zelda written in my mother's handwriting. I flipped open the flap to find a small note with a ticket I hadn't expected to see.

My love bug,
Consider visiting Scotland to explore the world and discover what fills your heart before life becomes too occupied.
Love always,
Mom

I took a deep breath and pulled out the next piece of paper; it was a ticket to Scotland for a couple of days from then.

～

CLIMBING the steps to my mom's apartment, I knew I was at fault for giving her attitude and making her feel terrible when all she wanted was what was best for me. I had to make it right. She was in my corner, trying to keep me strong through all my darkness. I knocked a couple of times before I called out, "MOM! I know you're in there!"

"I'm not talking to you," her muffled voice called from behind the door. She could be childish.

"I'm going to go," I called. It was the stupidest thing I could do. "I will go to make you happy."

The door swung open.

That didn't take too much effort. I felt my mother's arms wrap around me. "I'm proud of you."

"What am I going to say to James?"

That was when Mom told me the plan she had constructed with Clara.

～

By nightfall, I was headed to the studio to tell James I wanted a bachelorette celebration with only my best friend and Mom, and no other bridesmaids. James might question my decision, but I had to show him my confidence. Mom said I had to bullshit my way through it.

As I entered the studio, I was greeted by music blasting from the speakers. A group of people gathered around an art piece while James explained something. I hung back and waited. Riley saw me and gave me a concerned look. Ever since that time at the art studio, Riley had treated me like I was the enemy. James told me that she wasn't a fan of mine, but I wasn't quite sure why.

She rushed toward me, blocking my view.

"Hey. How are you?" I asked politely.

Riley rolled her eyes. "Zelda, you managed to come to visit at a busy time." She responded bitterly like I was the worst person in the world, ruining everything for her.

"James didn't tell me; I'm sorry. I can come later," I mustered out as she stormed off. I took a deep breath, held the strap of my purse, and walked over to the piece.

That was when I noticed my naked body displayed for the world to see. A couple of months back, James insisted we go away for a weekend to a beach resort down to the Keys. On our first night, we got intoxicated and had sex all over the room. It felt like we were back in a good space. The following morning, I lay there naked under my sheer blanket, and he took photos of me. We both did. It was erotic. Sexy. Now, I felt disgusted.

I saw an intimate moment I had shared with James, and it was being used to gain status.

"Are you fucking kidding me!" I screamed as everyone turned to face me.

I recognized the look James gave me; it was his rage that surfaced the minute he made eye contact. "Excuse me for a minute." He hurried to me, then gripped my arm so tight that it hurt. "What the hell are you doing here?" he hissed as he pulled me away from the crowd. I jerked my arm away from him.

"Why am I on display for the world to see? That was a moment between us!" He said the moonlight was beautiful on my bare body.

He'd made me feel sexy, stunning. In reality, it was an opportunity for him. He could make more money, be famous, and showcase what he could do for the art world while disrespecting his future wife.

"I'm done!" I pulled off the ring. "I'm done! You go back to your fucking art!" I whipped the ring at him as hot tears rushed down my cheek.

"Wait! You're being ridiculous! Stop!" James was calling out to me, but I wasn't giving him the benefit of the doubt. If that was my sign, I would gladly take it.

I was going to see Edmund.

FOLLOWING James's unexpected behavior that night, I packed my belongings and went to my mom's house. When I arrived, I couldn't hold back my tears. And upon seeing my distress, my mother immediately condemned James for what he had done to me. Clara had expressed her willingness to cut him into pieces thanks to her binge watch of *Dexter*. I couldn't help but agree with her sentiment. The wedding was a month away, yet my life was in shambles. James had called everyone to reach me, but I told everyone that I didn't want anything to do with him. He was not to know where I was.

The following morning at work, I went to Marissa's office and told her I needed a week off. I knew my career was on the line, but I needed to go.

"He did what?" Marissa smacked her hands on the table as I sank into the chair across from her. I couldn't hold back information regarding what had happened. Part of me thought I was overreacting, but nobody thought I was—especially Marissa.

I took a deep breath. "I need space. I need to get away before I explode."

"Why Scotland?" She scrunched her face as she tapped her pen against her lip.

"My mom has a good friend there that I knew as a child. She said she would gladly give me a space to relax. So my mom arranged it all." I hated that I couldn't tell the truth. But I couldn't say that I was going to see a man. A man I'd written letters to and who probably didn't want anything to do with me. But I was haunted by him. I had been stupid to think I wouldn't think about him for eight months. I'd remembered.

"I would love to meet a Jamie Fraser!" She leaned back in her chair. "Make sure you come back, you hear me?"

"Really?" My voice cracked. "You're okay with it?" I was stunned she was allowing me to leave.

"I like you, Zelda. I truly do. It eats me inside to know that a man who was supposed to love you, be committed to you, and shower you with goodness and respect decided it was worth showing your body to make a buck. I would have buried him." Marissa made her way around the desk and wrapped her arms around me. "Go take some mental health time. If he comes in, I will make sure he knows nothing." I held her for a second before releasing her with a weak smile.

I felt like the weight was slowly lifting from me.

Entrées/Entrées
6 JUL 19
IMM
418
DEPARTED
- 8 FEB 19
GRATION SERVICE
R FEB 1994
36
PHILIPPINES
IMMIGRATION
5 FEB 1999
60
DAYS
U.S. IMMIGRATION
180   SFR   2228
MAY 17 1999
ADMITTED
CLASS
B
Visas
Departure/Nation
VISA
TWO
VALID UNTIL
1999
DATE OF ISSUE
1998-12
4605
USA 32
Southern Magnolia
Magnolia Grandiflora
PASSED
PASSED
PASSED

12

Edmund

Since my last chat with Zelda, my life turned in ways I hadn't expected. Our band started to become a local hit. *Letters to Augustus* was born. Tom had insisted we create a name. Andrew had just lost his granddad, and we decided to pay tribute to him. It was a little thing, but it was a hit. Tom insisted that I put in the word letters —because of my obsession.

Crowds poured in every night as if we were the biggest and hottest band in Scotland. Lines formed and tickets sold. We were adequate enough that one of our songs even made it on the radio.

That triggered my parents to reach out. Mum was proud of me, while Dad insisted that it could fail. As usual, I needed to be better for him. Andrew insisted on forgetting about the noise and focusing on being part of it.

"Be in the moment," he stated like a motivational speaker. Andrew had become our man for everything, including managing us. He quit his studies and decided to work full time with the band. His parents were full of disappointment when he told them about it.

I started sleeping with Grace to occupy my mind. Music and sex got along well—too well. Grace helped us whenever we needed something. She was fitting in enough for us to have a relationship. About three months ago, we made it official.

"Look at what we have here; we got ourselves a fan of sweet and sexy Eddie." Tom pointed at me as I flashed him a cocky glance. I watched a bunch of women near the stage giggling and trying to catch my attention. It was common, and according to some local magazines, our golden retriever of a singer was the second most attractive man in the band. Unfortunately, the twins, Billy and Cole, didn't make it on the list.

I bowed, then sat back in my chair as I checked the corner where Grace stood at the bar. I gave her a wink while playing the melody of our latest song, "Love to Lose." Tom and I wrote the majority of the songs. We worked on this one a while back, and it was our ticket to the big leagues.

"We love you, beautiful people, and thank you for making tonight the most wonderful fucking night ever." The crowd roared as Tom clapped and tapped his foot while the drums kicked in, and my keys took hold. "Here's our last song of the night! Here's 'LOVE TO LOSE'!"

The screams. I couldn't forget that sound. It was an addiction. My body vibrated as the beams of light were on us. I could feel the sweat soaking me as the adrenaline took over. It was euphoria, an out-of-body sensation. Tom's voice was raspy, deep, and hit all the notes like it was a dagger to its victim.

The high slowly eroded, and I leaned back as I cheered and clapped with the crowd while Tom finished the song's final lyric. The words that still spoke to me.

"Let's forget the world, baby.

Let's submerge for a bit."

More screams. That is all we heard in that small venue. All of us came together on the stage and wrapped our arms around each other's shoulders for a bow. I knew that everything would be okay for a moment.

After performing, I helped the equipment guys pack our stuff into our Volkswagen van, which Tom had insisted on buying. Grace walked out the back door wearing a fitted red dress and her hair in loose blond curls.

"Babe, you were brilliant." She rushed to my side and wrapped her arms around my neck to kiss my cheek.

"Did you like it?" I winked as I cuffed her face, pushing the strands of her hair away from her beautiful face.

She nodded. "I love watching you play."

I wrapped my arms around her waist and kissed the nape of her neck. I could smell the sweet scent of the latest perfume she liked for the week.

"You coming by?" I still wanted to lean into this high as long as I could.

The bar we played at was outside the city, which was not that long of a drive. I figured I would take her back with me and probably fuck her brains out because I needed her right then.

"I can't. I have to stay at my mom's. Besides, we can see each other tomorrow. I'm actually taking off now." She pouted.

This was the fourth time this week she canceled, which was frustrating, but I knew she was helping her mom out. She told me with what, but I had forgotten. "Let me know when you get home, all right?"

"Of course!" She kissed me one last time before heading toward the street. I watched her go as Andrew came toward me with my helmet.

"Where is she off to now?" He cocked his eyebrow as he handed me my helmet.

"Mum's."

He nodded. "Okay. The boys want to go out for drinks?"

"No, I think I need to relax. Tomorrow, though," I promised. I patted his chest.

I turned to the rest of the guys who were chatting about some woman's number. "It was a pleasure providing you my hotness for the band, but I need to retire," I patted Tom's shoulder.

"Oh, fuck off, you douchebag. That's getting to your head!" Billy snapped; he was a jealous guy.

Before I could hear more bitching and complaining, I turned around and headed to my Harley parked in the corner. I needed a drink and some peace from tonight's festivities.

As I made my way to my flat, I noticed someone sitting against the door. Sometimes a homeless person would trickle into the area, but this person seemed different. They had a suitcase sitting next to them. I removed my headphones and examined what looked like a woman who was probably asleep. I couldn't see her face, but I slowly touched her arm, trying not to frighten her. "Excuse me, love, you're in front of my door. Did you need any help?"

My mouth parted.

Zelda glimpsed back at me with swollen eyes and tears staining her cheeks. "I left him, Edmund. I left him because I made the biggest mistake."

My mental train derailed. And I was the only victim.

The woman of my dreams, who I'd fantasized about possibly every chance I got and wondered what I would do if I had a chance with her, sat in front of my door.

Zelda came, but it was the wrong time.

My brain disconnected from my willpower because my arms wrapped around her body for a hug. It was the first time I'd ever held her or felt her. My face burrowed into the nape of her neck as her arms wrapped tightly around mine. I could smell her scent, a hint of lavender. Her hair was dark under the golden light of the streetlamp. If it were possible, the world would've suddenly slowed at that moment. This feeling was unexplainable. Leaning away slightly, I cradled her face in my hands. The gold hues of the streetlamp darkened her eyes, but I could see a sliver of her green eyes. "You're real?" I read her face. God, she was so fucking captivating. She was more than I expected in ways I couldn't explain. I wanted to kiss those lips. I wanted to taste her, but I couldn't.

Her lips parted as her eyes went heavy. "I needed to come here. I didn't book a room, but I can. I-I didn't know what to do."

"You did the right thing." I kissed her forehead, and I felt her body weaken under me. "Come in; it's chilly out tonight."

Zelda nodded, so we headed into my apartment. But an emptiness hit me when I didn't feel her body against me.

Zelda wrapped her arms against her body as she walked around the space. She examined everything while I stood against the door. I placed my helmet and her suitcase in the living room. I didn't know what to do then. So I watched her as she kept exploring the apartment.

"Zelda, I'm at a loss for words," I admitted and scratched my beard. She looked over her shoulder with a small smile. The room's light gave me a better view of what she looked like. She was mesmerizing. I was tempted to touch and feel her, but I had to hold back. I needed to tell her that I had Grace now. That was when I felt anger storming in my heart.

"I know we haven't spoken in a while." Zelda turned to me, and she watched me step closer. She swallowed hard. "But I couldn't stop thinking about you."

My chest tightened with a cluster of emotions, and my hands held the back of my head. "It's been months; you made it clear you didn't want anything."

"I know what I said." She pressed her fingers on the bridge of her nose. "I'm sorry. I wanted to have a chance again."

"I have a girlfriend," I confessed as I watched her eyes soften.

Zelda's lips parted, but no words came out. She stood there, and with each step, I knew there was no turning back if I reached her. I wanted nothing more than to touch her and feel her against me. "Maybe I should go," she suggested when I stood before her.

"No, it's late. You can sleep in my bedroom. I'll take the sofa."

"No, this is your space —"

"Zelda, please," I pleaded.

Her eyes glossed over, then one tear fell down her cheek. I reached for it and wiped it with my finger before pulling her once more into my hold.

"I don't know why, but you've always been in my head," she said against my chest. "Now you're real. Standing in front of me, I'm fighting the urge to kiss you. I want you to hold me."

"I can't do that." I cradled her head as her hands caressed my chest. My body begged to have her and finally be able to kiss her. As much as I wanted it, I had to remember that my girlfriend was in the picture.

"Let me get you set up, and we can talk tomorrow. You probably had a long flight." I ran my hands through her chestnut hair. She was a perfect fit against my chest.

"Okay. We can talk tomorrow."

I got her set up in my bedroom, but before I closed the door, Zelda reached for my hand.

"Thank you." Her voice was weak and filled with sadness, but I couldn't help myself. I brushed her cheek and kissed her softly.

"This is the best thing that has ever happened to me. We'll figure it out in the morning."

Entrée / Entrées
6 JUL 19
- 8 FEB 19
RATION SERVICE
-8 FEB 1994
36
Visas
B
3 FEB 1999
60 DAYS
FEB
U.S. IMMIGRATION
SFR
MAY 1 7 1999
VISA
TWO
VALID
1999
DATE OF ISSUE
1998-12
4605
USA 32
Southern Magnolia
MAGNOLIA GRANDIFLORA
PASSED
PASSED
PASSED
PASSED

13

Zelda

I was in a foreign place, embracing the scent of a man who had lived in my dreams for months. There wasn't any sleep as I lay under his thin sheets. Sitting up, I could see my phone buzzing with a call from New York. I ignored it as I swung my legs to the side of the bed.

The minute I heard the word girlfriend, I had wanted to vomit. I was too late. I didn't want to be a home-wrecker. I wasn't going to ruin someone else's happiness. So I got up from his bed and looked around to get ready to leave.

I studied some old photos on his shelves of Edmund as a clean-cut man with no beard or long hair. He was much younger. My fingers touched his face, and my lips curved into a grin. Edmund's sadness started to take over his eyes. It must have been the time he had lost his friend. He had confided in me all his struggles, and now I could see it through the years of photographs. There was a photo of him and two others standing together, laughing in school uniform. "You looked so happy," I whispered.

My finger traced along the books on his shelves. His room was exceptionally organized. I got changed quickly and placed my suitcase down, but I bumped into his desk. That's when I saw the letters.

There was our story, resting out in the open neatly placed on his desk; I lifted them. There was my writing, my words to a stranger. The feelings I had created for this man pulled me into an abyss I didn't think I could escape. I didn't expect to have such a range of emotions because I didn't think it would end up this way.

I heard a slight knock on the door, and I turned over my shoulder to find that Edmund had walked in. My hands cradled the letters. His chest was bare, and his hair was curly and loose. I felt heat blanket my cheeks from staring too long.

"I couldn't sleep," he confessed, stepping into the room and closing the door behind him.

I felt flustered. Words seemed too distant because as I parted my lips, I couldn't speak. My breath became heavy as the temptation of his presence took over. He stepped a little closer, but I backed up against the desk. Swallowing hard, I confessed, "I feel the same."

Edmund stood in front of me. *Touch me,* I thought. He hovered above me as his finger graced my cheek. "You're so beautiful, Zelda. You've occupied my mind all these past months. I told myself I'd get over you, but something in here, I wanted you." He pulled my hand to his chest. "You feel that?" His voice deepened as my fingers spread against his pec. "My heart is racing for you."

The still light of the morning sky lingered. I could smell the scent of his cologne and smoke. His eyes blackened, but I could see their fire. It was the same as mine. Edmund pressed against my forehead with his.

"I can't do anything until you end it with your girlfriend. I can't." I squeezed my eyes shut as his breath sent goose bumps down my spine.

"I know." He took a deep breath, and I felt his chest rise. "I want to end it for you."

Edmund broke away from me for a second to kiss my cheek. A small explosion rattled my bones. Temptation and desire drew us in as I closed my eyes, feeling his lips touch my skin. My fingers embraced his chest, and I crawled up to his neck to wrap my arms around him.

Edmund's lips parted from my skin, and his hands tugged my waist closer. And I wanted nothing more than to devour him, but it was a losing battle. "Edmund," I whispered as my fingers touched his cheek. "We can—"

Edmund growled as he pushed me gently onto his desk. He traced my thighs, and I wrapped my legs around him. I felt his hardness against me. "I finally have you here. I feel your body against mine, yet you're so fucking far away from me. You're too far from my reach." Edmund kissed the nape of my neck, and my fingers dove in his hair.

"I need to go. I can't stay," I pleaded with him.

Edmund leaned his head back. "No, you're not leaving. I want to be with you."

"How can we? You can't just end it with your girlfriend. That's wrong. Maybe this is a sign."

Edmund backed away, looking frustrated as his hands cradled the back of his head. "Signs! Signs! Always signs—maybe we go for what we want. I'm tired of giving up my chance at being happy. I don't want to force myself into something I'm not."

I wrap my arms around my chest. "So what do you want to do? How are we going to do this?"

"I'm going to talk to her and tell her we need to end it."

The guilt I felt was heavy for his girlfriend. I felt like the worse person alive, taking away her happiness for mine. "What's her name?"

He scratched his chin. "Grace."

"Where did you meet?"

"At the pub I work at." He licked his bottom lip.

For a couple of seconds, we stayed silent. The tension between us was strong. I couldn't help but wish that I could give in to it. My eyes trailed from his to his bare chest, to the band of his pants. My body begged me to have him, but I fought it.

"I have somewhere I'd like to take you today if that's okay with you," he said.

"Okay," I responded.

"I'll let you get ready." He turned and headed out the door. I finally caught my breath after being submerged in my emotional sea.

～

As we emerged onto the bustling street, a cool breeze touched my skin while I waited for Edmund to lock up. "Follow me." He reached for my hand, and we trailed down an alleyway.

"You're not going to kill me, are you?" I teased.

"If I did, I would have done it before." He looked over his shoulder, flashing me a cocky smile.

"You're terrible." I squeezed his hand, catching up to him. He scratched his beard as he winked at me. I never thought a wink could be so attractive that it sent my lady parts into a tizzy.

We made it to the parking area where he stored his bike. "I've never been on a motorcycle." I felt my heart beating faster.

"I like being your first for something." He straddled the bike as he reached for my hand.

The wind blew by while I clutched Edmund's body as he drove through the winding roads. My eyes watched the beauty of Scotland as I rested against his back. His body was broad and firm, much different from James's. It felt good to hold him. I imagine his hands on me, feeling him explore it in ways I'd never felt before. It was a feeling I'd never expected to have, and maybe I was worthy of someone who can love me that way.

We pulled to a makeshift parking area to Loch Muire. My legs felt like jelly, after the forty-minute drive, but the scenery was worth it. Edmund turned off the engine, then he gave me his hand to help me off. He helped me take my helmet too, and I let out a giggle. He surprised me by gripping my face with his hands and kissing me deeply. The cliché comparison would be butterflies, but it felt like that. Tasting him for the first time was like thunder on a hot day. When I came up for air, I leaned away and saw his hooded eyes staring back at me.

"I-I..."

"I broke up with her," he confessed.

"You did?" I was dumbfounded. "What? How?"

"Listen." He pushed my hair away from my face. "You mean more than anything in this world. I want to make this happen. With you."

"What did you say?" I demanded.

"Everything is fine now."

Edmund reached for my hand, and I felt a thrill shoot through me, but knew this would lead to a hurricane waiting for us.

14

Edmund

I took Zelda on the path toward a lake that I tended to hide out at. Glancing over my shoulder, I flashed her a smile. She was the most beautiful woman I'd ever seen. I watched how her eyes sparkled in the sunlight that peeked through the trees above us. *I would never be good enough for her,* I thought. I tried to fight that voice because I had her. I finally had that, and it felt so right.

"We have to climb," I confessed as we took in the massive rocks blocking the path.

Zelda crossed her arms. "Where the heck are you taking me?"

"Do you trust me?" I reached my hand for hers. She was hesitant, but she moved toward me. I gripped her waist and leaned in, smelling that sweet sunshine in her hair that drove me insane. She placed her head against my shoulder, and I lightly kissed her neck.

Zelda let out a giggle. "Are we climbing?"

"Yes, but you're distracting me," I confessed. Her eyes widened with desire. I did that to her. I made her feel this fire we had. Lifting her over the boulder, I felt a tad bit of excitement at touching her full ass. I fought the urge to touch her in other places too.

I watched her as she made her way to a little rocky patch of beach in the distance. The highland mountains and forest surrounded this. "I can't believe this." She pressed her hands behind her head. "This is like a painting. Edmund." She turned toward me with her lips wide. "This is breathtaking. I could stay here forever."

With my hands in my pocket, I walked toward her. "I knew you'd love this."

"Why here?" She beamed. "Why bring me here?"

"I wanted to show you the place where I escape and forget everything. I know you said you had the fire escape, but this is mine." I walked closer to her. "When I moved here, I decided to take up hiking. I needed something that would not turn into a bad addiction. So this was it. I would come swim or just sit here for hours." I marveled at the massive landscape. "Hold up—" I turned toward the boulder wall and pulled out a box I kept there from a bunch of trees. There were some blankets and essentials inside.

"Did you plan this?" Zelda asked as I placed my box down.

I shook my head. "I come here at least twice a week. I managed to find a hidden spot to keep my stuff in if I forget." Shrugging, I pulled out the blanket and laid it out.

She took off her shoes and placed them at the edge, then she started to take off her shoes. I shot her a questioning look as she dropped her jacket. "What?" She laughed and shrugged.

"Too chicken?"

"It's probably freezing, love." I crossed my arms and shook my head.

"My mom and I used to do this when we were younger. Come on." She unbuttoned her jeans and stripped down to her pink undies, and I felt my chest tighten with desire. Her body was curvy, with thick thighs and a narrow waist. She was breathtaking. I took off my leather jacket and threw it on the blanket without holding back. She took off her shirt and stood in her mismatched bra. She wrapped her hands around her body.

"Hurry up!" She started to dance around to keep warm. There wasn't such a thing as a hot day here. Maybe occasionally we had a couple of good days, but it was May. It was still chilly.

"You're bonkers, woman!" I howled as she ran to the water like it was a mission. She dove in, shattering the stillness of the water.

"It's fucking cold!" she yelled as she treaded. I pulled down my jeans, exposing my fitted briefs. Zelda watched me.

"I'm coming in!" I sprinted, and the icy water covered my body as I submerged with full force. I came out, sucking in breaths, and whipped my hair back. "Fuck! You're truly mental!" I swam to her, laughing.

"We will probably die of hypothermia," she remarked as I got closer to her.

"I'm blaming you in the afterlife." I was breathing faster while treading water. Her eyes darkened, and her cheeks were rosy. I was getting hard just seeing how incredibly sexy she looked all wet. I wanted her, so I pulled her close. Her lips trembled as she wrapped her arms and legs around me. It was freezing, but my body blazed from her touch. My lips crashed against her in a way that felt inhuman. I finally felt like my world was complete. She tugged me. There was a feeling of a fire around us; it was the flame of hunger absorbing everything.

She pressed her forehead against mine.

"I want to taste you all over," I whispered hoarsely, threading my fingers through her hair.

Zelda's chest expanded rapidly, which made her breasts press against my chest.

"Take me," she moaned.

The animal in me didn't hold back. I devoured her swollen lips the way it should be. I lifted her body out of the water while she straddled me, and I didn't break our kiss as she whimpered against my lips. As I lowered her on the blanket, her body trembled as she giggled.

"I want to kiss you all over your beautiful body," I growled when I hovered over her. My hardened dick pressed against her pussy.

"Edmund." She squeezed her eyes shut. I dragged my lips down her neck and cupped her breast before pulling down her bra and gently biting her nipple. Her hand gripped my hair tightly. "Touch me," she begged.

"Aren't you demanding?" I flashed her a devilish grin, then trailed my lips down to the hem of her panties.

My dick throbbed as I kissed her hemline. Zelda was panting. "I wanted to feel you cum on my face," I said, pulling the hem of her panties and dragging them down her damp legs. Then I tossed them away. "I've dreamed about this so many times. You screaming as I make you come."

I couldn't wait any longer, and my lips devoured her pussy like it was my only meal.

"Edmund!" Her voice was music to my ears. Her legs tightened with every lick, so I put my finger into her folds. Her raw and melodic voice pleaded. She arched her back as I devoured her like she was my air. She tugged on my curls when I licked her folds with my tongue, which made her body shake. I hit the spot as I pushed my finger inside because I watched her screaming in ecstasy.

"You are mine, Zelda. Always." I sucked her clit once more and felt her legs quake.

"Don't stop! Edmund, I'm—" I drove my finger harder and faster, working her while I tasted that sweet pussy. That was when I felt her walls tighten, and her legs squeezed my head. Her hands gripped my hair tight while her body convulsed as my hands gripped her hips.

Trailing my lips along her bare stomach, I kissed the valley of her breasts, as Zelda was catching her breath, so I cupped her face and kissed her deeply.

"I want you to taste yourself," I rasped. I gripped her hands and threw them above her head, resting my body against her shaking one. My mouth crashed into hers, feeling her moan vibrate as our tongues collided into each other.

Our breaths synced, and we stared at each other, hungry for more. "No one has ever made me feel this way." Zelda swallowed hard.

"You make me feel ways I never felt before too." I squeezed her hands, but my dick was pulsing against her pussy. I couldn't stop kissing her. Nothing in this world mattered other than us.

Zelda started to giggle, and her eyes looked brighter. "I have to confess; I've never had this happen to me at a lake."

I released her hands. "I will do this every time I come here with you."

~

ON THE DRIVE back to my apartment, I wanted nothing more than to have my hands on her every chance I got. At every light, I reached for her hand and kissed it. As I felt her breasts push on my back, I fought the hardness of my dick. I wanted to focus on her and give her all the love that she deserved, even if I had blue balls. It sounded farfetched, but Zelda was what I'd always wanted in my life. My heart was full, and I didn't want anything to interfere with it.

When we arrived, we had a mini make-out session in the back alley of my building, which led to people hollering at us to get a room. "I would… gladly." I cradled her face in my hands, and she smiled deeply.

"I don't want this to end. You are my person," Zelda confided.

"I waited too fucking long to lose you now." I kissed her once more, then we headed into the apartment.

Entrées/Entrées
6 JUL 19
- 8 FEB 19
418
DEPARTED
GRATION
SERVICE
8 FEB 1994
36
B
Visas
3 FEB 1999
60
DAYS
U.S. IMMIGRATION
190   SFR   228
MAY 1 7 1999
ADMITTED
VISA
TWO
VALID UNTIL
1999
DATE OF ISSUE
1998-12
4605
USA 32
Southern Magnolia
MAGNOLIA GRANDIFLORA
PASSED
PASSED
PASSED
PASSED

15

Zelda

"He sucked you dry?" Clara whispered into the phone as I stood outside the pub where Edmund played. He was finally back at McCandless before he headed north on their small tour.

Today was a perfect day. There wasn't any other way of describing it. After returning from our adventures, I jumped in the shower as he trailed. We made out, washing each other. The muscles in my lips hurt from smiling, feeling this flutter in my heart I never felt before. Edmund was good to me in ways I never thought I could have.

James had never made me feel sexy or ravished me when he'd had a chance. We'd always felt planned and organized. With Edmund, it was wild, free, and new like I'd been reborn. When he looked at me, I felt like I was the only girl in the world. I felt beautiful in my own skin. I was never the girl men were all over. I hid behind the boy I was dating because I had never allowed myself to be me.

Maybe my mother was right—I needed to feel fire.

"Yes, he did." I let out a laugh from the pit of my stomach. "I want to be with him, Clara. Maybe this is the endorphin high, but he feels so right." I fanned my hands because I was still heated from his kiss.

"Did you make it to home base?" she joked.

"What? Who still says that?"

"I'm at work. What do you want me to say? Did you get on his dick?"

I snorted so loud that people walking by gave me a weird glance. "Clara! No, I haven't yet."

"Well, we are all rooting for you and your sexcapades."

"Sexcapades?"

"Yeah, like when you do it for a solid twenty-four hours straight. It's fun. You need a lot of water, and your vagina is going to hurt like a motherfucker," she said matter-of-factly.

I choked on air.

"How is that possible? My, um… downlow would die."

"Oh, my little, innocent friend, get on his dick tonight, and you will see. James and you didn't do that?"

"No! We used to schedule it."

"Oh…" Clara sounded gutted by my statement. I could picture her eyes piercing me with disappointment. "We won't talk about that."

"Has he tried to call?"

"Call? Girl, he practically sent the Navy SEALs. He's been trying everything in his power to find you. He sounds desperate. James came to the office and asked around but Marissa threatened everyone if they said anything. He's been to your mom, and she wouldn't answer. He's going crazy. You'll have to face the music at some point."

I partially felt guilty for doing this to James, but he brought this onto himself. Before I could respond, hands wrapped around my waist, and I turned to feel wild curls against my face. "Darling, I need to head to the stage," Edmund whispered in my ear as he kissed my neck.

"Is that him?" Clara hollered.

"Clara says hello," I lied.

"Can I talk to her?" he requested. He reached for my phone, and I gave it to him.

"Hello, Clara?" He waited. "I promise to make—" He scratched his head as I watched him talk to my best friend. "I will. It was great chatting with you." Edmund kissed my cheek. "Your friend loves you."

"I know." I rolled my eyes, then put the phone to my ear. "Clara?"

"I'm drooling over his voice. Does he have friends?" she begged.

"I will talk to you later. Love you."

"Love you too."

Backstage, I got to officially meet the entire band including Andrew. He was similar in height to Edmund but with blond hair and dark brown eyes. He had a very broad body and a cleaner cut to him. He was an attractive guy, but my heart was clearly for one man. *Clara's type*, I thought.

"Lads, this is the famous Zelda." He presented me as he held my hand tight.

"Hi." I waved.

"Well, holy shit! You are real and not a creepy old man in his basement." Tom rushed me and gave me a bear hug. "I'm the attractive one in this group." Tom leaned away and winked at me.

"It's a pleasure." I grinned.

"Those are the twins"—Edmund pointed—"and this is Andrew." His friend stood with an expressionless face and his arms crossed, watching my every move.

"Hello, Zelda." He reached for my hand, and I shook his. His voice was deep, and his accent was very predominant. He didn't seem pleased. Something didn't feel right. I was getting the impression that I shouldn't be there.

"Boys, it's showtime!" Andrew cut the conversation short as he called for them.

Edmund reached for my cheek. "I got a spot right in front for you to see me." He winked.

"Did you? I guess I can look at the hot guy playing the piano," I teased.

We kissed before he left with the rest of the band. I felt so cold when he stepped away. I walked toward the side of the stage where I'd have the perfect view of Edmund as he was getting ready at the piano. He wore a black graphic tee and had his hair tied away from his face. He glanced at me and winked, which caused me to melt inside.

The pub filled with fans cheering as the drums set the beat of their hit song. That was when I saw Edmund start to play. He was so into it, as if he were making love to that piano, hitting those keys like his touch could devour them. I was almost jealous of those keys because I wanted his hands on me again, touching me like he had at the lake today. I was getting aroused at the thought of him, a soaked, mountain man coming out of that water.

"Need a drink?" a bartender asked as she came over to me.

"Uh…" I broke away from my trance. "Yeah, can I have a cider?"

"Sure, give me a second." Everyone was cheering and singing to the music, and it felt addictive.

"Here you go." She passed the cider to me.

"Thank you." I took it from her.

"Are you the Zelda?" she asked as she leaned against the bar.

"Yes." I nodded. "Have you worked here long—"

"Listen, you ruined my friend's relationship when you showed up and took what was hers. You're a fucking whore."

I stood there like a fool as I watched her go to another woman. They laughed and mocked me. My heart pounded. But I took a deep breath and turned to face the stage.

"GOOD NIGHT, MY BEAUTIFUL PEOPLE!" Tom screamed through the microphone. The crowd went wild while the last notes of the song played. I screamed when the guys stood and wrapped their arms around each other and bowed. It was incredible to see the power their music had. I was so proud of him and how he followed what he was passionate about. Women were reaching for him, and he took photos before he rushed toward me and stole a kiss. He then grabbed my hand and led me backstage.

"You were amazing out there! You're so talented. I'm so proud of you!" I pressed my hands to his bearded cheeks.

Edmund flashed me his wide grin, and I saw his hidden dimple. "I thought about you the entire time."

Biting my bottom lip, I felt myself blush, but the memory of the bartender took over.

"What's the matter?" His eyes narrowed as he held my chin.

"Um…" I swallowed hard. "The bartender was not happy that we were together."

Edmund scanned the bar. "Who said it?"

"Don't worry, let's drop it." I responded.

"Zelda, I do not tolerate bullshit." He released me and headed for the bar. No one had ever stood up for me this way. I followed quickly but wasn't fast enough. I saw Edmund already yelling at someone behind the corner. When I reached his side, all the things I thought would happen ceased.

"I'm pregnant, Edmund! I've been at the doctor's the past few days trying to figure out what to do. Then you broke up with me to be with that whore." The petite blonde stood there in tears with her hands pressed against her face.

"Edmund?" I was dumbfounded. Andrew rushed toward me.

"Let's go," Andrew demanded, reaching for my arm.

"No! Edmund? What is happening?" I pleaded.

"Zelda, please go with him. I will talk to you soon," Edmund snapped but continued talking with the woman standing in front of him. My world was crashing, and I couldn't comprehend what to do. I followed Andrew like a lost puppy, hoping it was all a dream.

Why was it every time I took a chance, something got pulled away from me?

Entrée/Entrées
6 JUL 19
IMMIGRANT
DEPARTED
8 FEB 19
GRATION SERVICE
8 FEB 1994
36
PHILIPPINES
IMMIGRATION
3 FEB 1999
60 DAYS
U.S. IMMIGRATION
190   SFR   22E
MAY 1 7 1999
ADMITTED
CLASS
B
Visas   Departure/
VISA
TWO
1999
VALID
发 证 日 期
DATE OF ISSUE
1998-12
4605
USA 32
Southern Magnolia
MAGNOLIA GRANDIFLORA
PASSED
PASSED

16

"**Y**ou are a piece of shit, Edmund. I knew you would do something like this!" Grace had yelled on the phone. I knew I was a complete asshole, so I had agreed to everything she called me on the phone. Messy was an understatement for what had happened. It was catastrophic. There was something to be said for someone who could do such a thing to someone. In my heart, it ate me alive, but I knew I could never live up to what Grace wanted.

I hadn't wanted Zelda to hear what was happening at the bar. It was why I had had Andrew get her out of there. Grace was making a scene, and fans were watching.

"Can we please talk about this somewhere else?" I begged her, pleading to have this conversation without cameras trying to record us.

Grace took a deep breath and bit her bottom lip. "Fine." She headed out to the alleyway, and I held the door open for her.

"You lied to me, Edmund. You told me you weren't in contact with her," she screamed, and her eyes were swollen and red. Her face looked full of despair. I'd had a day full of lust while she dealt with the news. I couldn't believe all this was happening. We were always protected, and she was on the pill. This was too much; I couldn't process any of it.

"I had never lied to you, Grace. But I won't say that I didn't still have feelings for her," I confessed.

"It was some letters! It's not like you dated her. How could you be attracted to a girl through words?" She spewed her hate and crossed her arms over her chest.

"I'm sorry, Grace. What would you have me do?" I begged, reaching for her arm. "I will do anything to make sure you and this baby are my priority."

"She needs to go. If you want any part of this baby's life, you need to end it with Zelda."

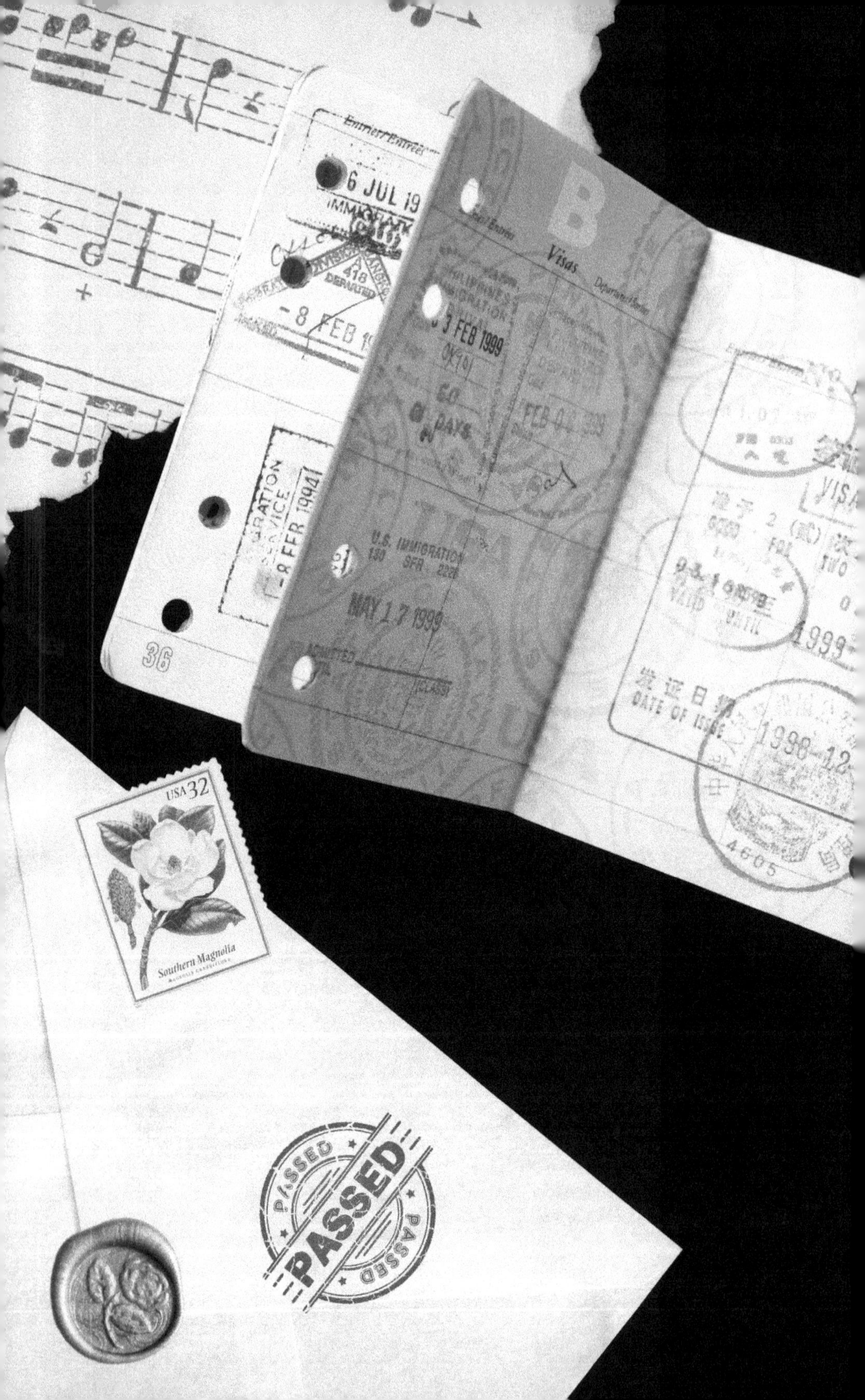
Entrée/Entrée
6 JUL 19
IMMIGRATION
418
DEPARTED
- 8 FEB 19
IMMIGRATION SERVICE
- 8 FEB 1994
36
B
Visas
Departure
PHILIPPINES
IMMIGRATION
3 FEB 1999
60 DAYS
FEB 0 1999
U.S. IMMIGRATION
130   SFR   226
MAY 1 7 1999
ADMITTED
CLASS
VISA
GOOD FOR TWO
VALID UNTIL
1999
DATE OF ISSUE
1998-12
4605
USA 32
Southern Magnolia
PASSED
PASSED
PASSED
PASSED

17

Zelda

I tried to feel worthy of love, but deep down, I knew I would never have it. I felt stupid for believing that taking a chance was worth it because I knew I would be left to pick up the broken pieces in the end. Running away from my life in New York to try something with a man whose heart was not mine was the red flag, but I had persisted. It was karma. I was broken and alone. The only thing I knew to do was to go.

After the pub, I wept. I played a part in ruining everything for that poor woman. I felt disgusted with myself. So when Andrew took me back to the apartment, I grabbed all my things and decided to leave. I needed to go back home, to my life and salvage what I had left.

"Don't leave," Andrew begged. "Edmund needs to talk to you. You can't leave now."

"I can't be here." I paced as I searched the apartment for my things. "I can't be here for him to break my heart." I held back the tears. "He belongs to her." Andrew knew I was telling the truth. He needed to be a father to her baby. I couldn't come between them, not when I knew their lives were about to change.

Andrew swung his hands behind his head and let out a deep breath. "Do you want me to say anything?"

My chest tightened. What was I going to tell him? What was I going to say to the man I had fallen for? "Do you have pen and paper?" Andrew nodded.

Andrew offered to walk me to my taxi, but I insisted it was not needed. I managed to find a hotel that could take me for the night near the airport because I was able to change my flight for the morning. It was last minute, so it cost extra, but I had to get out of there. Once I climbed in the taxi, my tears started.

I took out my phone and hovered over James's name. I was going to get married. I was going to be a wife to someone; I could be happy with him. I could make things work and fix it all. But I needed to speak to someone who could be a voice to guide me from the darkness.

"Mommy," I cried into the phone.

"I'm here. What is happening? Darling, are you all right?" Her voice was weak as if she'd been sleeping.

"Are you okay?"

"Of course. Enough about me, what has happened?" she pleaded.

"Edmund had or has a girlfriend, and she's pregnant with his child. I left, and I'm trying to come home, but I need you. I feel so stupid. I shouldn't have done this. You told me to go, and I had my heart shattered. I feel guilty for hurting her, and I wish nothing more than to take the pain away." I word vomited my emotions into the receiver as my sobs got louder. I didn't care if the driver could hear. I needed my mom.

"I will pay for your ticket home. I wish I was there to hold you in my arms. But I'm proud of you, darling" she confessed.

"Why?" I leaned against the window.

"Because you followed your heart. It will get easier with time, but I'm so proud of you. You deserve love."

"That wasn't love, Mom. This has been breaking me into a million pieces. I've had a fiancé use me as artwork, and a man who can't be with me because of his obligations."

"You don't think I've ever been in your shoes, Zelda? You don't think I ever felt what you're feeling? As much as it sucks right now, you were better off doing it than wondering what-if. Those haunt you more."

"I have nothing, Mom." I sobbed.

"Stop it. I didn't raise a daughter who gives up. Stand up straight. You're allowed to feel pain. That pain will only be there for a little while because, one day, you will find someone who truly loves you for you," she said.

The taxi driver pulled into the hotel and came to a stop. I took a deep breath. "Mom I'm here. I'll keep you posted."

"I love you so much." Mom's voice was a balm for me, but it was only a Band-Aid for my broken heart.

"I love you, Mom."

"Come home. We will work this out together."

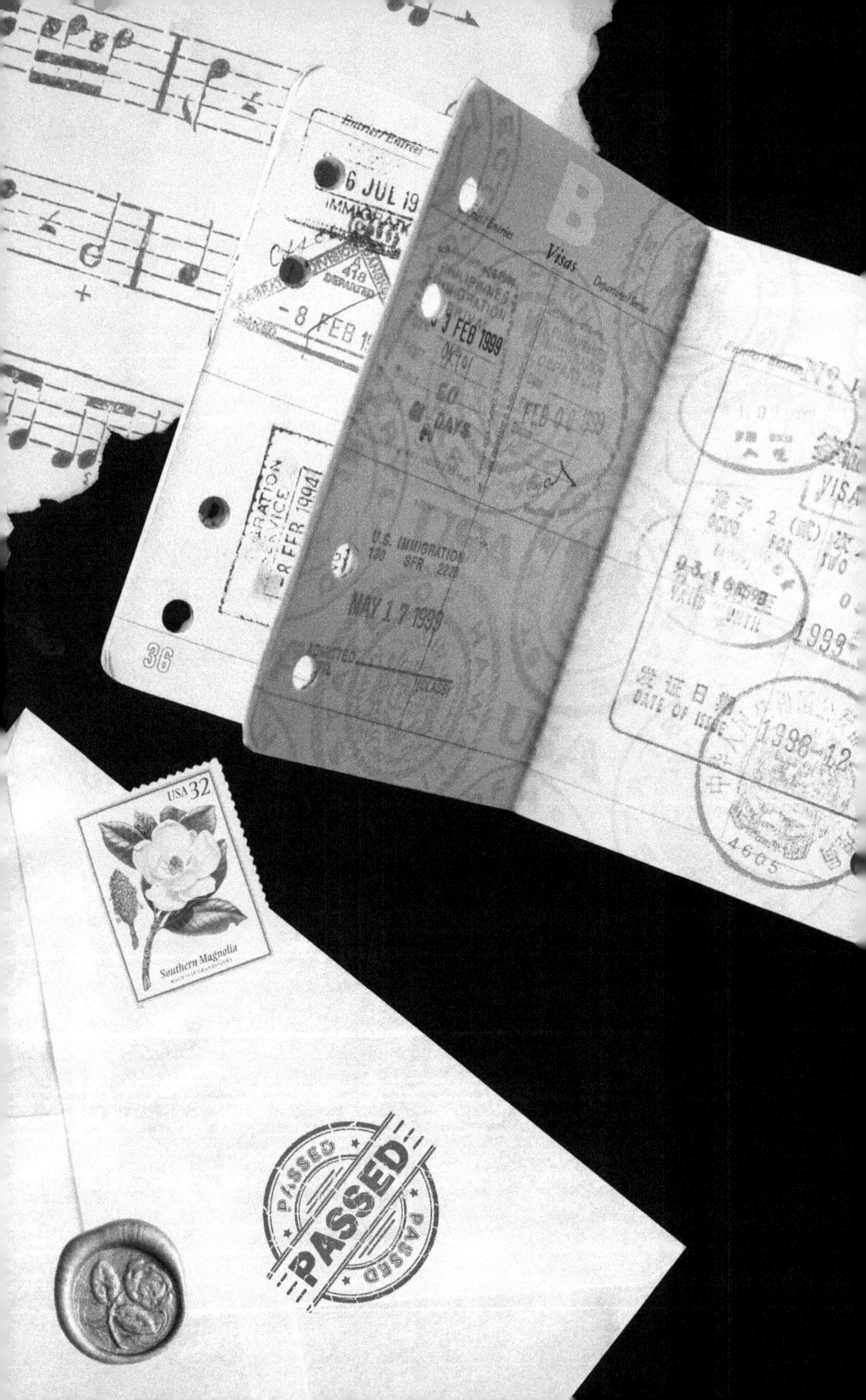
Entrier/Entrées
6 JUL 19
IMMIGRATION
418
DEPARTED
8 FEB 19
RATION SERVICE
R FER 19941
36
Visas
B
U.S. IMMIGRATION
130   SFR   222
MAY 1 7 1999
3 FEB 1999
60
DAYS
FEB 0 2 1999
VISA
TWO
VALID UNTIL
1999
DATE OF ISSUE
1998-12
4605
USA 32
Southern Magnolia
PASSED
PASSED
PASSED

18

Edmund

I held Grace while she cried into my shirt. I wasn't going to be the person to let her do this alone. She held my arm tight, and I felt my world slip through my hands.

"Please stay with me tonight," she begged, but I didn't stop thinking of Zelda. I needed to explain everything to her.

"Not tonight; I need a moment." I pulled my hand away slowly.

I was torn between loving someone and taking responsibility for my actions. The bar was suffocating. I needed to see Zelda.

"You're going back to her," she snapped. "Why? I need you," she demanded as she screamed into the night sky. And like her cries, the heavens roared above us.

"I need a minute! I need to figure out what all this is for me. Just give me time. I need to tell her goodbye." Anger oozed out of me. I was stupid to believe I could be happy. I fisted my hands, and my heart beat rapidly from the irritation. "I need to let her go." My voice was drained, and an ache flooded my heart.

Grace studied me with her hands on her waist. "Fine. But I will make it hard for you if you change your mind."

"Are you threatening me? Is this how you want things to be

between us?" Her tone pestered me. The way her gaze shifted to darkness left a bitter taste in my mouth.

My heart pounded as I felt my breath strain from this conversation. "I need to go," I demanded as I walked away, not looking back. I didn't care about her shouting behind me. The only thing I needed to do was speak to Zelda before it was too late.

I called Zelda repeatedly. Her phone went straight to voicemail. When I got home, I decided to call Andrew. Zelda had left. She was gone. She'd slipped through my fingers, and I never got to talk to her.

"Fuck!" I screamed; I needed to find her. I needed to speak to her before it was too late. That was when I did the stupidest thing I could have done. I looked up flights heading to New York. One was leaving in the morning, so I went to that airport to tell her I couldn't let her go. I couldn't just let this end before it even started.

SITTING near check-in for the flight, I waited for six hours, watching every person who passed by. My eyes grew heavy, but I fought them by going to a coffee shop. I drank three cups of espresso as I waited for her. I tried to figure out what I was going to say. How was I going to make it all work? *Zelda deserved better*, I thought. Grace could be vindictive and keep my child from me.

My eyes finally saw who I've been waiting for.

Zelda with her suitcase, looking broken. I had driven her to feel that way. Standing up from my seat, I approached her as she scanned the screen for her destination. My thoughts dragged me to the lake at the smell of her perfume. For a moment in time, we had enjoyed each other. Nothing around us mattered, just her and I.

Zelda swung around and stepped back clutching her chest. Her eyes widened, but she looked exhausted. I felt the need to kiss her, to tell her I wanted nothing more in this world than to be with her. "Don't leave." That's all I managed to say as an ache in my body spread like wildfire in my soul. "Please, don't."

Zelda's eyes were swollen from the tears she'd wept. I did that. I had hurt her, no one else but me. I reached for her cheek, but she pulled away.

"I can't, Edmund. I can't be with you. You have a girlfriend who loves you. She's pregnant with your child," she snapped. "You have a life. What are we going to do? You have obligations you need to focus on before us."

"Don't…" I pleaded, "don't do this."

Zelda stared at me wide-eyed and broken.

"You can't let her go through it alone. I can't be the person who takes you away from them. I had no father, and I begged for one."

"I know, baby!" I reached for her, but she threw her hands in the air; people were starting to notice as I tried to calm the situation.

"I'm sorry. We can't be together." Bitterness flashed across her face as the tears fell. "It's over, Edmund. We can't keep this up, knowing that our world will crash. You made me feel things I'd never felt before. I deserve love, but I can't be here while you deal with your life. We need to let it go. Maybe in the future—"

"Don't fucking do that. Don't give me your petty crap about how we need to focus on our lives. You know me. You know that feeling in your heart is the fire of us. We can't ignore it." I gripped her hand and placed it on my heart. "This will always be yours."

Tears ran down our cheeks. "I can't do this."

"Yes, you can! You can love me."

"I could love you, but I could never be enough." I pressed my lips to hers. We melted for a second. I didn't want to admit this was the last time I would be with her. She crumpled in my hold as we had our last breath together. I tasted her salty tears as I held her face, using her as a lifeline. A little moan released as I rested against her forehead; this was the moment I knew I would regret.

I had to let her go.

"I will always have you in my heart."

"Maybe we will love each other one day." She pressed her hand to my cheek. "Maybe we could finally have our happily ever after."

I rubbed my mouth as I tried to take a breath. "I want you to be happy, but please don't go back to James."

Zelda looked away as rage flashed across her face. "You don't have a say in what I choose. Same way, I don't get a voice in yours."

She pushed me away before I could try to hold her again, leaving me in pain and misery. How could you fall for someone so much yet have it all end? I stood there a coward. I wanted to run to her and beg for forgiveness. I told her we could make it work, but my father's voice told me I had to be a man. I had to take care of what I'd done. Sometimes life gave us consequences we had to deal with. I needed to make things right with Grace, to make a life worth living with her.

Entrées·Entries
6 JUL 19
- 8 FEB 19
RATION
FEB 1994
36
Visas
B
PHILIPPINES
IMMIGRATION
3 FEB 1999
60
DAYS
U.S. IMMIGRATION
SFR
MAY 1 7 1999
VISA
TWO
VALID UNTIL
1999
DATE OF ISSUE
1998-12
4605
USA 32
Southern Magnolia
MAGNOLIA GRANDIFLORA
PASSED
PASSED
PASSED
PASSED

19

One month later

Zelda

"We can pull a Thelma and Louise, honey," Mom suggested. It was my wedding day, and here I stood, trying to remain strong while my mom tried everything she could to stop me. I loved my mom, but she could ruin any moment with her terrible advice.

"Mom, I love James. This is happening," I admitted as I squeezed her hand tight.

The day I arrived back in the US, James got word that I was heading to my mom's place and was waiting at the door. He begged me to forgive him and give him another chance. A part of me wanted to confess to him what I'd done, but I wanted to keep those couple of days hidden. Edmund was my past; there was no need to remind myself of what I couldn't have. So I said yes, again. Clara and Mom couldn't hide their disappointment at me accepting James's apology. They thought I was terrified of being alone, but I told them that my life was beautiful before the chaos I had provoked. All of this was worth it because I knew my life would be great with James. Mom was convinced that I was making the biggest mistake in my life. I could forget Edmund. I could forget the feeling I had with him. Mom felt like I needed to stay with her. She'd pleaded with me not to go through with the wedding. But it was happening.

I wished desperately that I had Edmund, but the stars hadn't aligned.

Mom touched my cheek with a weak smile. I watched her look all over me as I tried to keep my nerves down. "As long as you are happy. That's all I want," she said. I knew that was what she wanted, but I knew Mom saw the truth.

I hadn't been able to stop myself from mourning a love I would never have. I attempted to hide it. I reminded myself that I was happy before Edmund came into the picture. I had a good relationship with James. We had it all, and I had just got lost in something that wasn't real. I knew what we had for that short time couldn't take over me anymore. I had to let him go.

"Here is the veil!" Clara came into the room. I smiled and took a deep breath. "You look beautiful." She beamed at me, but it felt forced. I knew my best friend was hiding something.

"What's up?" I asked. "What's wrong?"

"Uh…" Clara swallowed hard as she glanced at my mom. "Do you mind if I have a moment with Zel?"

"Of course, I will get us some mimosa." And she headed out the door. Clara looked anxious as if she was frightened of something.

"What's the matter?" I asked.

"Don't be mad," she said. "I got a letter from Edmund. You don't have to read it. You can burn it if you want."

"What? He sent you a letter?" I croaked.

"Yes, but he wanted me to give it to you on your wedding day."

"Why? Why did he have to do this?" I threw my hands in the air. "Why would he do that?"

"He wanted to say something before it was too late?" Clara suggested. She watched me sitting on the edge of the bed in my long lace gown with tulle and crystals. She pulled her hand from behind her back and handed me a green letter.

"Read it and consider his words. I will give you a minute." She kissed my forehead before leaving the room.

The green letter rested on my lap and a rush of tears overtook me. A single tear landed on the envelope, exploding into a water stain. My hands were clammy, and my heart beat roughly as I clutched it. I slipped the paper out and unfolded it, then I read his words.

Dear Zelda,

I wake up every day wishing life were different, but it isn't. When you left, a part of me went too. I won't ask you to come back. I won't ask for you to talk to me. But I want nothing more in this world than to have you in my life. You mean so much to me. You always will. I will be right where you left me. In another life, we can be together. It can be in our dreams; I hold on to that.

Your wedding date is close, and this is the last thing I want to talk about because I wish it was me. I wish you were marrying me and not James. It sounds crazy, but in the short time I held you in my arms, I knew you were the one. In my heart, the feelings I had were once in a lifetime.

You were my perfect storm, and I will forever remember it.

I never got a chance to say it, but I think I've fallen for you,

Edmund.

I stood and looked at myself in the mirror, wiping away tears as I took a deep breath. "I had fallen, Edmund," I whispered to myself, knowing he would never hear it. I placed the letter in the pocket of my bag and fixed my veil. The show had to go on. I had to become the woman I aspired to be and toss my past aside.

I climbed down the stairs with all eyes on me. With each step I took, I felt my breath slip away. I watched a man who was madly in love with me through the veil covering my face, thinking I'd been stupid to complicate things. I felt foolish, standing on the very bottom step and gripping the bouquet like a lifeline. My mom reached for my hand, and when I turned to see her, the pain I saw behind her beautiful eyes weakened me more.

Then I took my next step toward James. He stood, clean-cut and handsome, as he smirked. He'd made mistakes, but I did too. All these feelings I had didn't make any sense. I should be showing him I loved him, and I should stop thinking those thoughts because life wasn't like that. You couldn't always have what you wanted in life. All we were doing was holding a raft, hoping to survive through the horrors we might face.

So I stood straight, held my head high, and told myself Edmund was gone. He was a figment of my imagination, and I had allowed it to take over. The man I invested in was James. We would make it happen, and I would hide the pain in my heart.

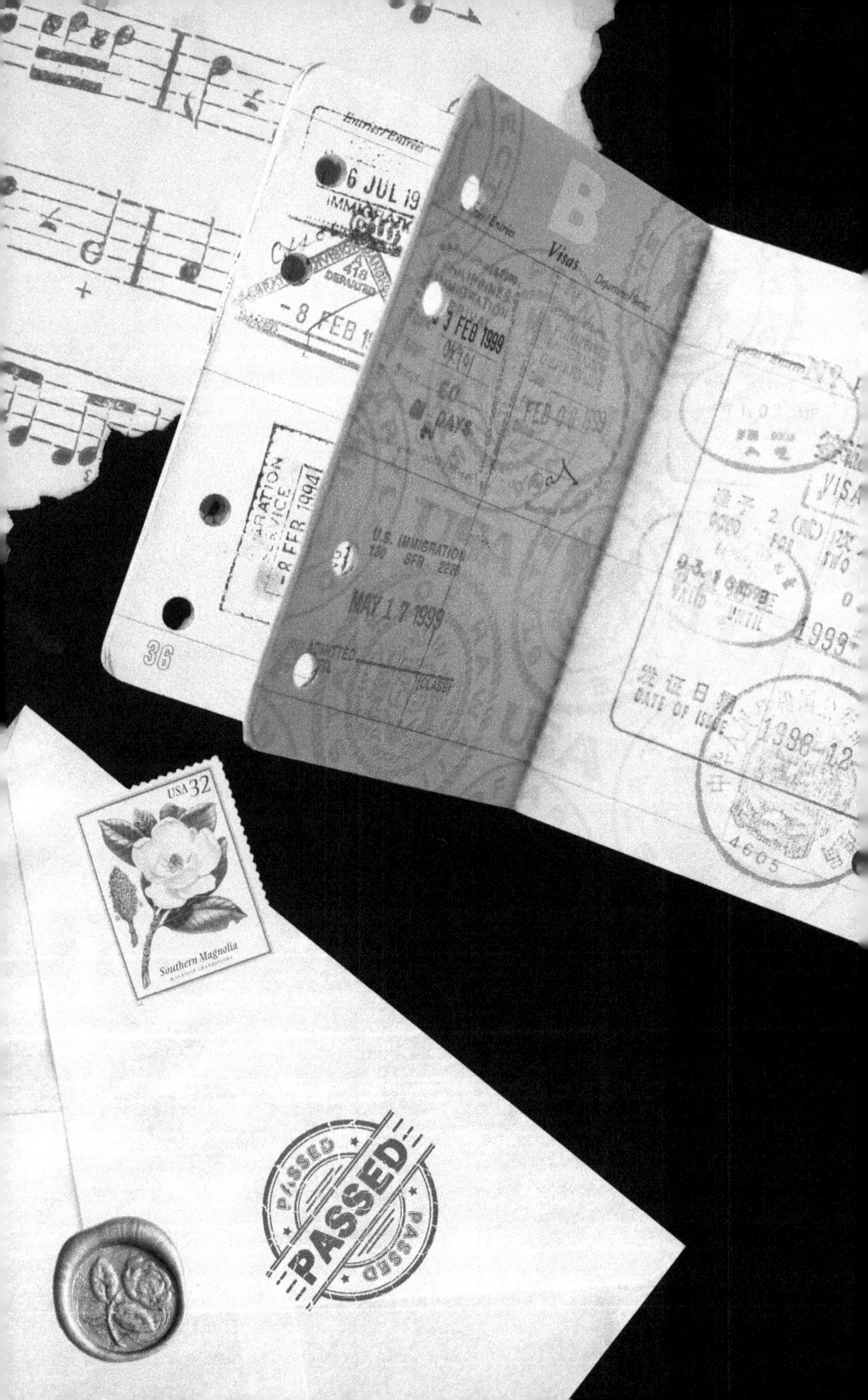
Entrées/Entrées
6 JUL 19
- 8 FEB 1
Visas
Départ/Uscita
B
PHILIPPINE
IMMIGRATION
3 FEB 1999
60
DAYS
FEB 0 6 1999
U.S. IMMIGRATION
MAY 1 7 1999
ADMITTED
RATION
SERVICE
- 8 FER 1991
36
VISA
GOOD FOR TWO
VALID UNTIL
1999
DATE OF ISSUE
1998-12
4605
USA 32
Southern Magnolia
MAGNOLIA GRANDIFLORA
PASSED

To: zelstclaire11@hmail.com
From: eddie_h2020@hmail.co.uk
Subject line: Ghost from the past

Dear Zelda,

It's been a while since we've spoken. Three months to be exact. You probably don't want to hear from me, but I wanted to reach out. I found out I'm having a little girl. Fuck, I'm going to be a dad. It's been hard to focus on this relationship without thinking of you. I know you told me not to contact you, but it's been hard. I keep thinking, what if I had said yes to you instead of this? I was raised to be a gentleman, but what the fuck does that even mean?

I think about you being married now and what that looked like. You must have been so beautiful walking down the aisle. I contemplated crashing it, and being the guy who screamed for you not to get married. I even thought about holding a boom box over my head and blasting a song to you.

I've written more songs, and somehow all of them belong to you. Zelda, I try every day to keep going, but you're in my head. Please, can we be friends? If I can't have you, I want to have a friendship.

I want to tell you also that Augustus has been signed to a label, and that the local radio plays my music. Fuck, I was so excited to hear it for the first time when I was in a store. I cheered and danced with some old man. It was ridiculous, but you would understand. I wanted to call you that night and tell you. But I was terrified you would ignore me.

I'm trying to be the boyfriend Grace wants by doing everything she needs during this time and helping the guys with the band, but I need help. If you don't answer, it's okay. I needed somewhere to escape. This was the only place I had.

Forget me not,

Edmund.

To: zelstclaire11@hmail.com

From: eddie_h2020@hmail.co.uk

Subject line: Zellie answer me

Hey Zelda,

I'm lying on the tour bus in the small bunk bed, hiding from the guys as I type this email. I wonder why I try to reach out when you don't respond. I figure one day you will. I have hit a dark place. I should be happy because we are going on tour. But the darkness hasn't been letting me accept it.

It's weird; the noise seemed to silence when I was with you as if you were the calm to my storm. I never had that happen to me before.

Andrew has been on my case about my drinking. I need to slow down, but it's been helping me fill the void in my heart.

Grace and I fight all the time. She has me on a tight leash. She doesn't want me on tour because she thinks other women will come after me. We had a big fight before I left, and she threw a bottle at me. The following day, she apologized for her behavior and blamed it on the hormones.

Every night I'm on stage, I try to get out of my head. The music allows me to have short periods of freedom before I'm swarmed by reality.

I can't take it—I can't be with her. But I can't leave her alone either. It is ingrained that I need to be a man in this situation, but I can't deal with it all. I'm fucking done with it. Andrew is convinced I need to break up with her before it worsens.

I miss you. I returned to the lake to see the fall colors, and all I could think about was us jumping into the water and touching you. Seeing those big, beautiful green eyes staring back at me, I wish I could hold you. I wanted to show you my world when you were here. I wanted to take you to places like that library I discussed. It frustrates me every day that I didn't fight harder for you.

How are you? What have you been doing lately?

I want to hear from you.

Love,

Edmund

To: zelstclaire11@hmail.com

From: eddie_h2020@hmail.co.uk

Subject line: Please don't block me

Dear Zelda,

I'm on the rooftop of the hotel where we're staying. We're playing in London, and I swear I saw you in the crowd of fans. I even rushed after the concert to find you, but it wasn't you. I sound like a nutjob for telling you this. It's like you're haunting me.

So as I stand watching the city lights on the roof, the cold winter nights aren't holding back. I had a bottle of whiskey to ease my mind. It's been three months since I sent you an email, and I'm still waiting for your reply.

Grace and I barely talk. She's at the end of the pregnancy and wants me to stay away. I don't get it. I'm worried for her. I've done everything for Grace, but she keeps pushing me away. I kind of want her to end us. She keeps telling me that I can't leave because she won't let me into our daughter's life. I feel lost. Everything feels so heavy lately. My heart is breaking.

Please answer me — I need you. I want to hear from you. Even if you tell me to go fuck myself.

Please don't forget me,
Edmund

To: eddie_h2020@hmail.co.uk
From: zelstclaire11@hmail.com
Subject: hi.

Edmund,

I read your emails, but what do you want me to do with them? You picked Grace, and I can't compete with that. She's the mother of your child.

I can't lie and say I haven't thought about you. Every time James kisses me, I think about you. Every time I lie in bed with him, you're all I think of. But the thing is, you're my past, Edmund. Nothing more. I poured my heart out, thinking we could do something, but we didn't. I've thought about you, but I've tried to forget you.

I'm afraid to say too much and fall into our rabbit hole again. You're making this hard for me. I walked down the aisle. I married James.

Is it a fairy tale? No, it's not. Nothing is.

I sound bitter, but all I think about is how much pain I had walking away that morning at the airport. You made me feel like I was worthy of love. The kind of love people talk about in books. The kind where you are the most important thing in the world.

Edmund, you're going to be a dad. You will be a figure in her life that needs to show her what love means. Grace will always be in your life. You can't drop everything because you're on a different path than I am. I know you may think being friends would be easy, but I can't.

I'm so proud of you for finally seeing your potential. Don't fall down the drinking path. You're stronger than that.

Z.

To: zelstclaire11@hmail.com

From: eddie_h2020@hmail.co.uk
Subject: My last email

Zelda,

I was sitting in a rocking chair holding my sleeping daughter, Chloe, against my chest, and I wanted to send you a message. She arrived the second day of the new year. She is the most beautiful human being I've ever seen. I love her so much; my heart feels so full for her.

After your email, I thought about what you said. I stopped messaging you. It's been three months, and I wanted to tell you what has happened.

Grace and I called it quits. After the delivery, she thought it was for the best. I guess it was my fault. I kept pushing her away, and now, she wants to just be a co-parent.

I get Chloe on the weekends, while Grace gets her during the week. I miss Chloe all the time. Next week we are going on tour, and it's going to be hard not having my little girl with me. Sometimes I wonder if I should quit being in the band so I can focus on her. But we need the money.

My parents finally met Chloe, and they were thrilled. I can't help but feel madly in love with her. She's my comet, my world, and I don't ever want to lose her. I don't even know why I'm emailing you, knowing you won't answer. I just wanted to tell you that I think I'm finally feeling this balance in my life.

E.

To: zelstclaire11@hmail.com
From: eddie_h2020@hmail.co.uk
Subject: I need you.

Zelda,

Chloe isn't mine.
E.

. . .

To: eddie_h2020@hmail.co.uk
From: zelstclaire11@hmail.com
Subject: I'm sorry.

Edmund,

I'm so sorry, my heart hurts for you. I know you love her so much and want to be her dad. You still can. You don't need to be her blood father to be there for her. I hope Grace lets you be there for her. You sound like a good dad.

I quit my job. I hated what I was doing. I was tired of doing the same things all the time. James was mad because I didn't "consult" with him first. He's been mad a lot lately. We got into a really bad fight the other night, and I ended up sleeping at Clara's. He's not talking to me again. I'm trying to make our marriage work, but all he does is get mad at me constantly.

I'm in a dark place.

Your song has made it across the ocean. I heard it today on the radio, and I lost it. I cried. I am so happy for you, and I couldn't even tell you. I wanted to call you right then, but I didn't. I'm sorry. I'm so sorry about all that is going on.

Maybe we can talk?

To: zelstclaire11@hmail.com
From: eddie_h2020@hmail.co.uk
Subject: Now?

Zelda,

I'm sorry he's treating you like shit. Thank you for the support.
E.

To: eddie_h2020@hmail.co.uk

From: zelstclaire11@hmail.com
Subject: Please talk to me.

Edmund

Please. I called you a couple of times and got no answer. I know you're dealing with a lot. It's been a week, and I haven't heard from you. I'm sorry.

Z.

PART III

"Déjame quererte, entrégate a mí" – *"Disfruto"* by Carla Morrison

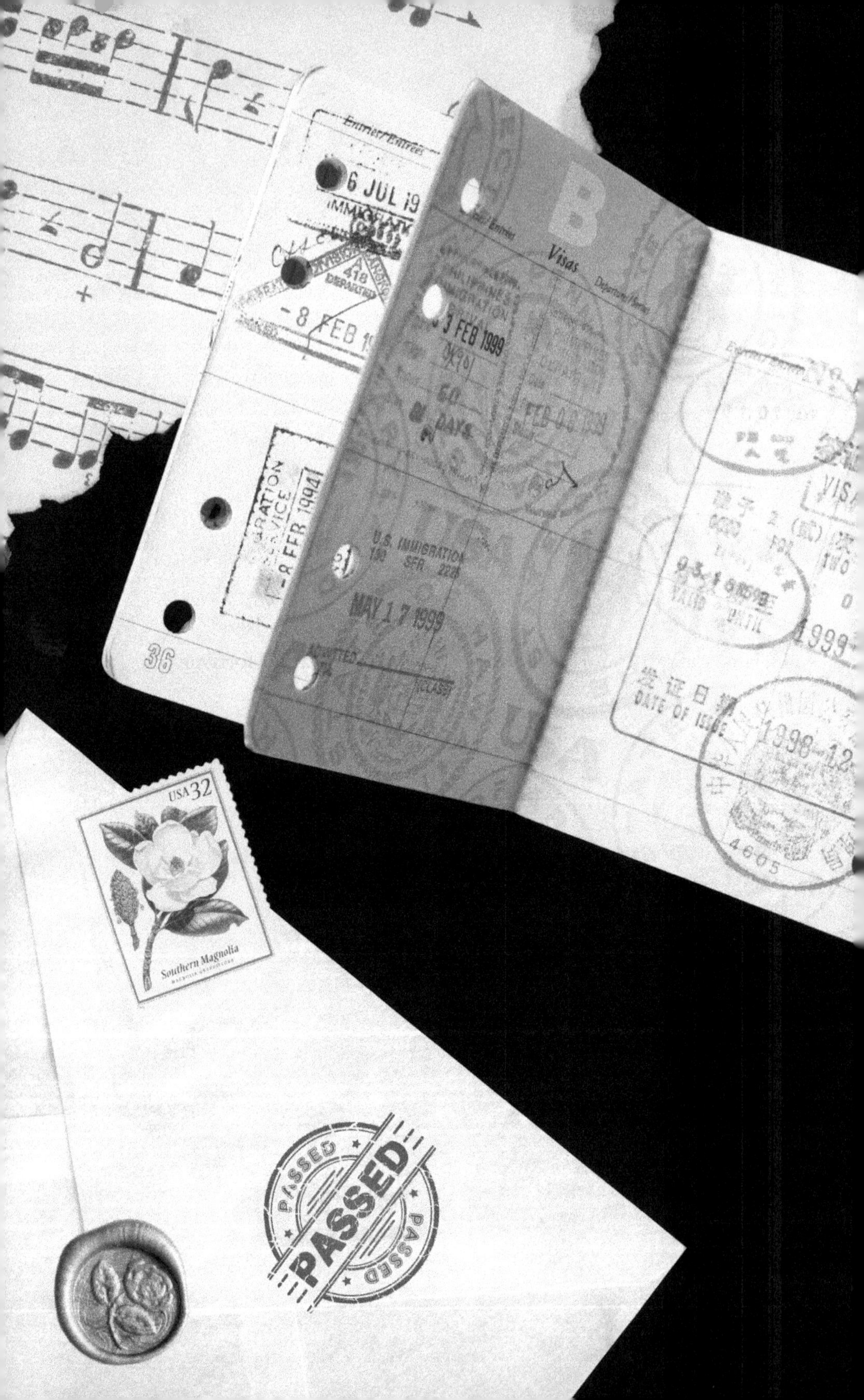
Entrée/Entrées
6 JUL 19
- 8 FEB 19
GRATION
SERVICE
8 FEB 1994
36
Visas
Departure/Same
B
3 FEB 1999
60
DAYS
U.S. IMMIGRATION
SER   226
MAY 1 7 1999
FEB-08 1999
VISA
TWO
VALID UNTIL
1999
DATE OF ISSUE
1998-12
4605
USA 32
Southern Magnolia
MAGNOLIA GRANDIFLORA
PASSED
PASSED
PASSED
PASSED

21

Zelda

My life has become the movie *Groundhog Day*. Every day, I was a zombie awoken by James's manhandle; I lay there as James had sex with me, then got up from bed once he finished. It was like I was just a sex doll for him, allowing him to release onto me. He'd then get out of bed to take a shower while I stared into the distance, feeling depressed.

I was dying inside.

I pulled the pillow over my head when I heard the shower start and released my screams from my lungs. The numbness overpowered every part of my body.

Four months and I have had fourteen interviews with no job offers. James reiterated how stupid I was to leave my job without a plan. He was furious. I was stupid to think he would've supported me in the darkness.

During my meeting with Marissa, I sat across from her while she was talking about the latest trends, and I saw the email from Edmund come in. That fire he had created in me took over, and before I knew it, I told her I quit. I packed everything at my desk and left that day. I was tired of having to do the same shit all the time. It felt like James was allowed to express himself every day, but I couldn't.

That night, I went home in tears and thought James would support my struggle, but it hadn't been like that.

"You're so fucking stupid, Zelda!" He smacked his hands on the kitchen counter and took a huge breath. His words were repeated over and over like a broken record.

It was weird how you can't remember fully what happens in an argument because of how heated it can get, but the one thing I remembered was when James said, "Zelda, you don't think! You're like your mom. You do things without a care in the world. You're so fucking dumb."

A couple of months ago, he decided, with the help of the new studio girl, Melody, (who seemed to be too fond of my husband) that he wanted to expand the space for future art shows. I hesitated because it was a lot of money, but James insisted we would be fine.

Well, we weren't. His ragging on me was really a constant battle with himself.

Most nights, I wished he'd stay away. He had continued to stay at the art studio some nights, and deep down, it felt better to be free of him.

That morning, he asked me how many interviews I had and how many jobs I had applied for as he walked out of the shower. It was like a sergeant checking off a list to ensure I stayed in line. James threw his hands in the air, frustrated when I said I didn't have any interviews.

"What is your problem? I won't support you financially if you're going to be lazy. Get out there. You're in bed! Move around. You gained weight, and you barely fucking look good."

"James, stop yelling at me!" I snapped back. "What do you think I'm doing? I'm trying!" I cracked. "You are making me feel sick with all this yelling! Leave me the fuck alone!"

James reached for his clothes and changed. "I'm not taking this shit anymore." He turned away. "I need to get away if you're going to complain about everything."

"Fine! Leave! Run away to your art studio!" I yelled at him as he walked out.

I HATED MY LIFE. I needed to escape from the four walls that confined me. What made it worse was that there had been silence after my last email to Edmund. All emails had stopped.

Staring at the café board to figure out what I wanted, I kept asking myself, "What do you want?" The lady behind me tapped her foot while releasing frustrated breaths. I'd been spending my time at this café looking for a job search. Nothing was happening even after I'd revamped my résumé about a hundred times.

"Excuse me, if you don't know what you want, can you let others go?" The lady finally snapped as I turned to face her.

"Of course!" I sarcastically gestured as I bowed to her like she was some queen. She gave me a dirty look but headed to the barista and asked for a complicated drink.

Once I finally ordered, I went to sit at the window and watched people pass by, then opened my laptop. I typed a sentence about who I was and deleted it. *You're an idiot,* I thought. I kept typing when I saw I had a text from Clara.

CLARA

Did you hear that Letters to Augustus is coming into town?

My eyes widened.

ZELDA

What do you mean?

CLARA

The band! They're coming! Edmund will be here!

I stared at the message, speechless as I reread the words on my phone.

ZELDA

When are they coming?

CLARA

Next week! I just found out from a coworker.

ZELDA

Is it my replacement? The one who took my position.

CLARA

Stop it! She isn't doing well. Marissa wants to fire her.

I felt bad that I quit at a time when it was important for Marissa, but I was just over it.

I distracted my thoughts by typing the band's name into the search engine. I clicked on their website, and there he was, posing with his bandmates and looking incredible. I managed to stumble onto his Instagram and looked at him in his photos. I wanted to write a message and see if he would respond, but I knew he didn't want to talk to me. If he did, he would have reached out. One photo—a view of the lake— caught my eye.

My memory of that day came like an uncontrollable wave. My cheeks felt hot, from the thought of him kissing me. His face would flash a cocky smile as I kissed his cheek. His dark eyes deepened as he sent my body in pure arousal. *A person should be loved that way*, I thought.

ZELDA

I'm buying us tickets.

CLARA

Girl, I beat you to it. I've already convinced Marissa to let me go and check them out. Guess who my date is? I even have backstage passes.

The cloud I had over my head had disappeared.

It'd been almost a year since I'd seen him, and I didn't know how I would react in front of Edmund.

~

As I LAY dead on the floor at Mom's yoga class, everyone waved at me while I took the restoration section too seriously. Mom waved to her fellow yogis, and I turned my head to watch her. She closed the door before leaping in the air like a ballerina. I wished I could have seen my mom when she was younger. She was a brilliant dancer.

She sat down, lifted my head onto her lap, and traced her fingers through my hair. I giggled as I felt for a moment like I was four again. "I don't like how James treats you," she confessed.

"Mom, what am I going to do? I can't just end it," I said. My entire body told me I should. My mind already planned my escape. James emotionally beat me down every chance he got.

"Honey." She released a deep breath. "James has been a complete asshole to you. He's a boy, spoiled and rotten to the core. The way he treats you is unacceptable, especially after what he said to you today."

"It's my fault because I did complicate things for us." I felt sick to my stomach, realizing I had only a couple of hundred dollars to my name.

"Stop. Life is too short. Sometimes we need to pull the trigger and make ourselves happy. You've been creating this 'perfect life,' but eventually, it was going to crack. Zel, you were not listening to your heart," She looked down at me sternly. "You keep creating something that you're not. You thought at the time it was the right thing to marry James. You made a mistake. We all do. You thought that life with him was right, but it wasn't. Stop forcing everything to work."

"So why do I feel like a terrible person?" I pleaded as the urge for tears started.

"No." She wiped the tear that fell down my cheek. "I didn't raise a weak girl. I raised a fighter. You are going to get what you want and deserve. Life is messy and complicated. Pick yourself up. Live for me because I don't know how long I have left in this world. I want to see you happy, even if it involves being messy."

"Why are you so convinced you're going to die soon?" I snapped. "Why do you make sense?" I fought the tears.

"Because I want you to be happy." She smiled as she pulled me into her hold, and I fell onto her shoulder. I held her as tight as I could.

"Edmund is coming to town," I confessed.

"Are you going to see him?" she asked as I leaned away from her.

"I want to." I shrugged, wiping away tears. "Mom, I really want to."

"Then you better pick yourself up and tell him how you feel about him."

Entrée / Entrées
6 JUL 19
IMMIGRATION
- 8 FEB 19
B
Visas
Départ / Sortie
PHILIPPINES
IMMIGRATION
3 FEB 1999
60
DAYS
FEB O.C. 1999
U.S. IMMIGRATION
130   SFR   226
MAY 17 1999
ADMITTED
RATION
SERVICE
R FER 19941
36
VISA
TWO
1999
DATE OF ISSUE
1998-12
4605
USA 32
Southern Magnolia
PASSED
PASSED
PASSED

22

Zelda

The week dragged on. Even worse was that James kept finding everything that I was doing wrong. He was at the point that everything I did was just another reason to hate on me. I was walking on eggshells, and I couldn't hold back any longer.

The night before the concert, I finally had the courage to tell him I needed space. James decided that he wanted to tell me how he truly felt.

"Why can't you be more like Melody? You are nothing like her," he snapped as he picked up his bag. "She thinks I deserve better than being with someone like you. Zelda, I'm tired of always pleasing you. You want your space? Take it. I'm fucking done."

I looked at him with such fury. My body was boiling from his words, "Go then! Go with her! I don't want you anymore!" I screamed at him. "I deserve better than you."

James looked at me and chuckled. "You can't survive without me."

How could you love someone so much but hate them in the end?

∼

THE FOLLOWING DAY, I sat on Clara's bed, showing her what I had for outfit options. She shook her head, disappointed. "You're telling me that you want to win the heart of the man you adore, and you're going to show up in granny panties and a prairie dress?" She eyed me up and down.

"I'll have you know that modest elegance can still catch the eye," I presented. She rolled her eyes.

"Who do you want? A man from *Bridgerton* or the guy who looks like a budding rock star?" She threw her hands onto her waist.

"What does it matter?" I narrowed my gaze. "He likes me for who I am."

"Yes, but sometimes, you need to remind him how worthy you are."

"Will you stop if I wear something of yours?"

"Fuck yes." She had a devilish grin.

Clara scrambled in her closet, then she screeched with delight. She threw something at me. "Wear this!"

I opted for a tight black skirt, which showed my tone legs and a band tee that scooped down my shoulder. My hair was wavy with some glitter, my lips were red, and my heels were towers. The idea was that I was going to show Edmund what he was missing.

I've had the confidence of a model as I walked the streets like a catwalk. With each step, my heels struck the ground authoritatively. I wanted to be with Edmund, so everything was riding on that night.

Clara clung to my arm as we walked along the street. A crowd swarmed the concert hall where Letters to Augustus was in bold letters in bright lights above the doors. I let a deep breath escape as my nerves kicked in.

"You okay?" Clara nudged me as she reached for our VIP badges in her clutch.

"Yeah, I can't believe he became big," I said as I watched the bold lights shine. He did it.

"Listen." Clara reached for my chin, and I finally attempted to make eye contact. "You walk in like you own this fucking shit. Show him that even though you both stopped talking, you can't fight these feelings. Edmund could say he has no feelings, but we know that is a lie. That man sent emails to you for a year, pleading to talk to you."

"I know. It feels wrong being here because of James," I confessed. "I just feel so complicated."

"I'm drop-kicking James. He's a piece of shit! Who cares? He's nothing to you. He was okay with the separation. He's probably with Melody, Zelda. I hate to break it to you, but you are not right for each other. I know it, and your mom does too. You need to figure out what you want. If it is with Edmund, then go for it. I will be here to the end." Clara flashed me a small smile as she hugged me tightly. The word separation scared me. I had been thinking about it for the past few months. I knew it was the right thing to do in my heart because I was tired of being someone's doormat.

"Why are you much wiser than me?"

"Because you make stupid choices thinking it's right, and I need to get you back on track. Now, let's get Edmund drooling over you."

We released each other, and Clara took the lead while the venue workers checked our VIP badges. When we walked into the concert hall, I suddenly felt anxious. I listened to all the women walking by talk about each band member like they were theirs.

"I want to try to sleep with Edmund! He looks so fucking sexy in the new photos," a blond woman wearing a very low-cut shirt announced.

"Yeah, he's good with his fingers," her friend said, and they both laughed. I felt ill.

"Ignore it," Clara whispered as I tried to focus on my goal. I didn't even know what I was going to do. Try to start again? Make something happen? He was famous now. Why would he even want to talk to me anymore? After his last email, Edmund was cold. I couldn't blame him because I pushed him away.

"Welcome to the VIP area! You will be in the front row of the concert but will be given backstage access after the show. You will get to take photos and chat with the band at that time." The woman holding the clipboard seemed to work for the band management company. "Head on in."

I took Clara's hand as we walked down the aisle toward the front of the stage. It was an old theater converted into a concert hall, so all the seats except those in the balcony had been stripped. When we reached the stage, we saw the band's logo draped over the backdrop.

My heart pumped. My palms grew sweaty, and my chest tightened at the thought of him. I was reminded of his narrow eyes, cocky smile, and hands. I could still feel his kisses on my neck and how the smell of his cologne triggered full-blown ecstasy. He was my perfect storm, and my heart was in the eye of it.

After half an hour, Clara insisted on drinking two beers for my nerves. That was when the roar of the guitar thundered from behind the curtains. Tom sang as loud as he could when the drapes spread open. The lights flashed around us as the bass vibrated underneath our feet. That was when I saw Edmund putting his energy into the keyboard, but something was different. We stood closer to his side as I noticed more details about him. The girl next to me screamed his name as he tapped his feet and dove into the music.

Edmund was sexy. His beard was much shorter and trimmed, and his curls were in a loose bun. His tattoos were exposed in his fitted black Henley T-shirt and dark wash jeans with his combat boots. I noticed a new tattoo poking out from the collar of his shirt. Clara kept looking over at me, and I tried my best not to fall weak, but there he was.

I wanted to feel his touch. I was so close to him that I could trace the bead of sweat down his neck. My eyes closed, and I pictured him standing in his room shirtless. I was already wet at the thought of his lips on me. Nothing compared to his eyes when he was starving for me.

Hearing their music and the crowd roaring their names made me incredibly proud of them. Even though we weren't together, I was so happy they were making it.

"Thank you, New York, for an amazing time! Thank you for being our first spot on our very long tour! You will forever be in our hearts," Tom uttered, out of breath. The rest of his bandmates stood next to him. They all wrapped their arms around each other's shoulders and bowed as the fans shrieked. The amount of panties and bras thrown at them made me feel worse, knowing that I wouldn't be able to compete with that.

"Come on! We need to head in first before the rest of the women come along." Clara grabbed my hand, and we rushed through the crowd toward the dedicated section for VIPs. Security stopped us and held us off until the band walked off stage. Tom and the twins were coming off while Edmund proceeded down the stairs. He didn't look my way as he went straight into a room.

"Ladies welcome; come in and enjoy the drinks. The band sits in the back. Feel free to go and chat." The same lady who had greeted us at the beginning was hosting as we walked into a room filled with people. There were couches throughout, music playing, and drinks being sent around.

Finally, I saw Edmund sitting in the corner with a woman on his lap. They were close, and he kept rubbing her back, and she laughed at something he said.

"I want to go," I confessed to Clara. I felt overwhelmed, but she gripped my arm.

"No! You can't. You're finally here."

"What am I doing here? What is this all for?" I argued.

"You don't get to take off without saying anything." Clara bustled over toward Edmund with my hand in hers, dragging me to my fate. I wanted to leave; I needed to breathe. I wanted to escape.

"I can't." I pulled my hand from her hold. "I can't!" I cried as an ache overtook me.

Forcing my way through the crowd, I sped to the front, seeking the doors to freedom. I swung it open and took my first breath of the night air. I cupped my mouth, and tears rushed down as I succumbed to the ache I couldn't recognize in my heart. A weight I knew all too well made me collapse as I pressed my hands to my face. I tried to hide it for as long as I could, but it was too late.

I walked down the street, trying to escape, when I felt a tug on my arm. Panic kicked in, and I tried to pull back. I turned to see who it was, and my heart dropped.

"Why did you come to see me?" His eyes were dark like he was tortured, and his jaw was tight. His chest heaved, and I could see the anger written all over his face. "Why are you standing here when there is nothing between us?"

"I missed you, but I guess you didn't miss me," I cracked.

"You're fucking married! Playing house! Why bother to come here when you have a fucking husband? You can't come to me whenever your husband decides he hates you."

Tears slid down my hot skin as rage overtook me. "What is wrong with you?"

"Nothing."

"I'm not the one who said I couldn't be with you in Scotland, remember? I came for you! I wanted to be with *you*! I left James!"

"Don't fucking do that!" He pointed at me. "You made it clear you wanted nothing. So go back to your pussy of a husband who uses you. Because you're just a trophy wife. Nothing more."

The sting in my heart was unavoidable. "How can you say that to me? You said you wanted to love me! Now, I'm nothing? What is wrong with you, Edmund? I was nothing to you? Look me in the eyes, and tell me I was just a groupie to you?"

Edmund rubbed his lips with his hand. "It's over." He couldn't look at me, so I reached for his chin and tugged it toward me.

"You want to tell me it's over and say I was nothing? Then look me in the eyes, or you're no better than James."

His dark hooded eyes watched me, and I felt this anger as I dug my nails into his shirt. His breath tattooed my skin. I felt his heat and lust. I felt his desire and pain like I was in the darkness with him. People began watching us. They were taking photos, but Edmund's eyes never left me.

Edmund then pushed my hand off his chin. "Go back and play house. James is going to be mad at you." Before I could respond, Edmund walked away and headed back inside while people attempted to get autographs from him.

I couldn't breathe. My hand held my mouth, feeling an explosion of sadness. I didn't deserve to feel love.

Entrées / Entrées
6 JUL 19
IMMIGRATION
8 FEB 19
418
DEPARTED
IMMIGRATION SERVICE
R FER 1994
36
Entrée / Entrée
Visas
Départ / Départ
B
PHILIPPINE
IMMIGRATION
3 FEB 1999
60 DAYS
FEB 04 1999
U.S. IMMIGRATION
190   SFR   226
MAY 1 7 1999
ADMITTED
VISA
GOOD   FOR
TWO
VALID UNTIL
1999
DATE OF ISSUE
1998-12
4605
USA 32
Southern Magnolia
PASSED
PASSED

23

Edmund

I was a piece of shit.

Holding the tumbler of scotch in my hand, I leaned against the sofa while the guys partied at the club where we ended up. I was next to some chick who was trying really hard to get more than an autograph while I sipped my drink. It didn't take long for me to make out with the blond fan in the back closet, letting myself forget Zelda. I had no sensation, and my heart was numb.

I'd become bitter over the months, and I couldn't fight the anger. It was all I knew. When life decided to fucking ruin you, there was no point in saving yourself. After finding the truth out about Grace and how she knew I wasn't the father of Chloe, my world was flipped upside down. She'd been jealous of my love for Zelda, so she lied about the pregnancy being mine. She wanted to be famous and have money. That was also when I found out about the other man she was still with. She'd tried to use me like every fucking person in this fucking life. That was when I knew that I was not worth being loved.

When I finished with the woman, she tried to have sex with me, but I brushed past her and left the closet. I was an asshole. The world felt more balanced when I drank it away.

Tom rushed over and wrapped his arm around me, skunked. "Fuck, man! We are killing it! These women are all over us!" he screamed into my ear as I leaned my head away.

"I get it—I already fucked the blond one in the back," I said, flashing a cocky smile. I sounded like a douchebag.

"For fuck's sake, you couldn't wait?" Tom nudged my chest. "No wonder you smell of sweat and pussy!"

Andrew approached us as the only sober one and said, "What is going on? The twins are drinking shots off some woman on a table, Tom looks like he is about to die, and you look miserable. What is happening with you all? I can't leave you alone."

"You're not my fucking father, Andrew," I snapped.

"I have to be with the way you idiots act. You have a show tomorrow, so let's wrap this up."

"Whatever." I exhaled a deep breath of rage. I needed to punch something.

Screw Zelda. I can't do this again, I thought. I won't let myself go down that path with her.

"After seeing Zelda, you lost yourself. She was crying her eyes out. What did you say?"

"I'm tired of people using me. I'm tired of people thinking they can play with my emotions."

"How was she doing that?" Andrew narrowed his eyes. "She was here for you."

"Zelda won't leave James for me. She won't leave that relationship for me. No one would. No one will ever want to give up something good for a man like me. I'm not worth it."

Andrew looked defeated. "I'm on this road of music, holding whatever life brings me." I reached down toward the table and downed the shots someone had ordered. "Bottoms up." The liquor burned my throat, and I let out a growl.

"What Grace did was unforgivable, Edmund, but you don't get to piss on everyone that fucking cares for you," Andrew snapped, getting in my face.

"Fuck you, Andrew! I don't need you to start this."

"Start what? Saying that you're a coward? Or that you need a pity party because you were hurt? Too many bad things happen in this world for you to be a prick about them. You are in a band that has gone global, and you decided to be a bitch about everything."

"Fuck you." My fingers dug into the palm of my hands, and I got into his face. Andrew didn't hold back.

"Bring it, Edmund. I know who you are, you fucking prick!" He yelled in my face, then he shoved his finger into my chest.

That was when I saw black; the rage ambushed me in a way I didn't expect as I threw a punch at his face. We gripped each other, fighting like we couldn't hold back what had built up these past months. He sucker-punched my gut, and I fell to the ground. The reaction to the situation was screams. Tom tried to pull Andrew off, and the bouncers pushed the crowd aside. The security guards pulled Andrew off while I fought to be free while trying my best to swing at him.

"You fucking pussy," Andrew snapped as he wiped the blood from his mouth. I felt intense pain in my head as security dragged us out of the club like garbage.

"Don't ever come back to this bar! Get out of here!" The security was the size of The Rock. He gave us a glare that was the most frightening thing I'd ever seen. Andrew and I were literally on the ground looking at each other before we snickered.

"You hungry?" Andrew asked.

"Fucking starving."

Tom came out with the twins. "What is wrong with you two? I was about to get a fucking blow job!"

Andrew and I glanced back at each other with bloody, swollen faces and laughed.

～

LYING IN MY HOTEL BED, I couldn't sleep. I wanted to call her. I couldn't help but feel guilty for how I treated her. I had been mad; lately, I felt so unstable. I wanted to hear her. I wanted to touch her. Maybe it was the liquor I had polished off, but I wanted to have her back.

I pressed her phone number, and the first call went straight to voicemail, which I had expected.

The second did the same.

The third as well.

Then I left her a voicemail.

"I'm sorry, Zelda. I'm sorry for everything that happened. I've been so broken these past months, and all I feel is pain. Please answer me. Please talk to me?"

I threw the phone on the edge of the bed and ran my hands over my face. I released a frustrated breath, then took off my shirt and pants. While climbing into bed, my phone's vibration caught me off guard. When I looked, it was Zelda.

"Hello?" I answered after the first ring.

"Why did you call me?"

"I'm so fucking stupid."

"Yes, you are."

"Please, Zelda, listen to me for a second," I begged as I sat up in bed.

I could hear her exhale into the receiver. "What do you want? You made it clear, and I can't be doing this."

"Do me one favor, please. Tomorrow, come see me in the morning. I will wait for you." I sent her the address of the hotel where I was staying. "Let's make this work. Come on tour and be with me."

There was a long pause before she responded, "Good night, Edmund."

"Please." I cradled my head in my hand. "All I think about is you every minute of my day. You're the one I could never truly let go of."

She hung up.

Asking her to come with me was too much for her, but I wanted her in my life. I wanted something to happen. The whiskey had given me the courage to make it happen.

Entrées/Entrées
6 JUL 19
IMMIGRAT
418
DERAITED
- 8 FEB 19
Visas
Departure/Depar
B
FEB 1999
60
DAYS
U.S. IMMIGRATION
180   SFR   226
MAY 1 7 1999
36
GRATION
RVICE
FER 1991
USA 32
Southern Magnolia
MAGNOLIA GRANDIFLORA
VISA
TWO
VALID UNTIL
1999
DATE OF ISSUE
1998-12
4605
PASSED
PASSED
PASSED

24

Love was bold and courageous, but it was also devastating and destructive.

I could only think about being with Edmund. I was in my apartment, living a life I hated and needed freedom from. I sat in the bathroom, on the cold tile floors, holding my phone in my hand with tears in my eyes. I didn't understand why I felt this way for Edmund. I was ruining everything in my life for him.

I wiped my face with a tissue and fought to remain quiet as I stood and checked myself in the mirror. Who was I? What was I doing? It hadn't been right that I had read that letter. But if I was so happy with James, why had I wanted to reach out to a stranger?

Of course, it was. I needed to end it. I needed to come to terms with the fact that James and I weren't right for each other. Swallowing hard, I took a deep breath and rinsed my face with cold water.

Swinging the door open, I watched Clara pacing on the phone.

"What is happening? Can you let me know where she's at? Of course, we will be there shortly…Bye."

I shot her a confused look. "What happened?"

"It's your mom."

"My mom?" I couldn't comprehend what she'd said. "What do you mean about my mom?"

"Don't panic." Her calmness made it worse.

"What happened to my mom?"

"She was at a restaurant and fainted, but they are doing a test—" Before she finished, I was reaching for my track pants and a hoodie. "They said she's going to be fine."

"No!" I snapped. "That is the only family in the world that I have. I'm going!" I cried with shaking hands and anger in my heart.

"Alright, I'll come with you."

"No. I'll go on my own." I turned away from her and headed to the kitchen to grab my car keys and left.

∾

CALLING my mom's phone again, someone finally answered, "Hello?" a man's voice replied.

"Hi? Um…this is Eloise's daughter, Zelda. Can you tell me where she's at?"

"Oh, yes! She's at Mount Sinai. This is, uh…Bobby…her boyfriend," he said awkwardly. Boyfriend? Mom would've told me that. She would've told me about this man.

"Oh…okay." I exhaled, not arguing with the newfound information. "I will meet you there."

Everything felt like it was moving quicker than I could comprehend. I rushed to the hospital with my hands gripped tight on the steering wheel, and my heart beat so fast. I couldn't handle anything else right now because all I needed to do was reach for my mom.

I parked in the emergency area, rushed toward the doors, and begged the attendant to find my mother. I reached the nurse and panted, "Hi, I'm Eloise St. Claire's daughter. I don't know what happened, but can I see her?"

"Yes, she's in room 431," the nurse answered.

"Thank you." I gave her a small smile and walked quickly down the hallway to the elevators.

I walked into the room, and she lay in bed, holding the hand of this Bill or Bob?

"Mommy!" I rushed toward her and wrapped my arms around her.

"Baby girl? What are you doing here?" She wrapped me tight in her arms as I cried. "What happened?"

"It's nothing, sweetie. I fainted." She flashed a smile as she held my face.

"You're lying to me," I said, and she became flustered.

She shook her head and kissed my cheek. "I love you so much, but you don't need to worry. This isn't your battle."

I shot a confused look and turned to face her boyfriend with his head in his hands. "What aren't you telling me?"

Mom pushed my hair away from my face. "Sweetie, I have a mass in my head."

"A tumor? What?" I couldn't breathe as my vision blurred. " When did this happen?"

"I've known for a couple of months."

"What? And you didn't tell me?" I snapped. "How could you?"

She pressed my hands together while I shook my head. "Because it isn't your battle. It's mine. You have taken care of me enough." She smiles with glossy eyes. "You can't save me this time. I was told about five months ago after having memory loss and terrible headaches. The doctor found out I have glioblastoma. It was too late for treatment because it had progressed quickly. Unfortunately, I didn't catch it in time."

"No! That's not fair…we can get help. You can do treatment, Mommy, right?" I begged her to do it. "Mom, I need you. You are my life," I cried as I crashed into her chest.

"Baby, I will always be there, no matter what happens. I will be there. But there isn't anything we can do at this point. The doctors have said that it has progressed to the point that I need to look at possible hospice options."

Her boyfriend looked up and flashed me a smile. "I've tried to convince her for a while, and she hasn't listened to me."

"I don't—I can't believe you have a boyfriend."

She rolled her eyes as she let out the tears. "Let's change the subject. I was going to have you meet this week. But cancer blew that." She shrugged. "Bob, this is my beautiful daughter, my sweet little girl, Zelda."

"Mom, this isn't the time for it."

"I know." She shrugged, "But you know I don't like sad situations."

Her arms wrapped around me like all those nights as a child. It was just me and her in this world, and nothing mattered but her and me. I was losing her. I couldn't imagine living without the one person who mattered the most to me.

"Mom, I need you to fight to stay."

"Baby"—she kissed my forehead—"there isn't anything to save me. I've hit my dead end. I wish I could stay longer, but I can't. Let's make the time I have left the best."

"I love you," I said, crawling onto her like a toddler who had gotten hurt. I wanted to smell her and hear her voice next to my ear. I wanted to feel like I was that little girl who only wanted her mommy to protect her.

My mom rubbed my head as she sang, "And I will always love you," while I cried into her chest, wishing this was a bad dream.

Growing up, my mom and I watched *The Bodyguard* so often that we had to get a new VHS tape. My mom would sing Whitney Houston as she put me to sleep, and she would sing that song when life was hard. She always reminded me that I needed a bodyguard one day because she wouldn't always be there, but I kept telling her it would be hundreds of years before she'd leave me. Yet here I was. My body-guard's life was coming to an end.

Then I asked, "How long do we have, Mom?"

"Baby, I only have a couple of months."

"Then I will spend every minute of every day with you until you take your last breath. I will be your bodyguard."

"Oh, sweet babe." Mom squeezed me against her chest and kissed my forehead. "I have the best daughter in the world."

THE FOLLOWING MORNING, I sat in the chair across from Mom while the doctor explained the next steps. I tried my best to focused on the conversation, but my mind was gone. I feared what life was going to be like without her. I felt overwhelmed because I didn't care about anything or anyone else.

I couldn't leave my mom, but the nurse nudged me to go get some breakfast. I walked out of the rooms when I saw him in the hallway. "James," I mouthed as I paused in the hallway. He wrapped his arm around me, and I felt his embrace as he kissed the top of my head.

"I'm so sorry. Clara told me when I went to the apartment. She was there getting your things, and I figured I could swing by here." I looked at him with swollen, tired eyes.

"Thank you if you want to see her," I said as I rubbed my forehead. He nodded.

James walked into the room while Mom and Bobby were chatting. Mom stopped mid-conversation and teased, "Oh, look who showed up," as James headed toward her.

"Hey, I'm so sorry." He patted her foot.

"Stop it! Oh, my heavens, you all sound like I'm dead! I want us to have fun in the next couple of months!" Mom was way too cheerful for someone given a death sentence.

"We can make that happen," James responded.

"Bobby and I have something to announce," Mom confessed. "We're getting married."

I was dumbfounded as James watched me while we glanced at the soon-to-be newlyweds.

"Mom, this is crazy," I was overwhelmed by it all.

"I've never been a bride, so I want to do it before it's too late."

USA 32
Southern Magnolia
PASSED

25

Edmund

"Get your shit together!" Andrew called to the band as we headed to the bus. I was tapping my foot at the hotel entrance, wondering if Zelda was coming along. I was wrong to demand she come back to me and run away. I collapsed my face into my hands.

"Eddie, let's get going. We need to be on the road to make it in time for Nashville," Andrew snapped. Ever since he decided to quit as a doctor, he had become the most demanding manager. He had become more in tune with us and the business than we had expected.

"I asked Zelda to come," I said into my hands.

"Are you kidding? You did?" He slapped his hand against his side.

"I know. I'm a fucking idiot." I looked up at Andrew shaking his head.

"After all you have done to that poor girl? I'm not surprised she didn't come." He continued," I can't help you with this one, Eddie. You're on your own." He walked toward the hotel's front entrance.

I waited. My knee shook, and my palms were sweaty, but I had to make a choice because it was time for me to go, so I stood and grabbed my backpack. Walking through the bus doors, I put on my sunglasses as I watched the band shove their stuff into compartments. Then I heard something that gave me a chill.

"Edmund!" For a split second, I thought it was a figment of my imagination. I turned to see Zelda running at me. I dropped my bag and ran toward her, and she entered my arms. I embraced her and kissed her lips like they were the only thing in the world. I felt her arms wrapped around my neck, and she held me like I was her life vest, keeping her from drowning. The taste of her was something I'd craved for so long. I could feel myself crack like stone as my hands raked through her hair, touching her soul with mine.

"You came! I won't ever leave you. I want you forever, Zel." I pressed my hands to her cheeks and kissed her lips. They were mine. I would caress them every minute I got. "You came," I said again as I leaned against her forehead.

"Edmund"—she ran her fingers through my hair—"I would drop everything to be with you, but…" She paused. "I can't."

I stood there watching her with narrow eyes, feeling the same pain I had in Edinburgh.

"What do you mean?"

"I just can't." Her eyes were red with a hint of tiredness behind them.

"Forget about James and come with me. Be with me. Zelda, we can have the life we want," I pleaded, holding her face in my hands. I couldn't let her go. I needed her. I needed to feel her heart for as long as she let me.

"Edmund, please don't make this hard." She let go of me, wiping her tears.

"What do you expect me to say? I'm pleading for you to come with me. Let's start our lives together. Let's make this happen," I begged, rubbing her cheeks.

Zelda let her crying take over. "My mom is dying," she admitted. Her beautiful green eyes swelled into a deep emerald pool of color as I felt the breath in my lungs escape.

"I can't go. She only has a couple of months left. I can't leave her."

I pulled her into my hold as she cried. "I'm so sorry, my love." I kissed her head and held her tight. I wanted to be strong for her, but I couldn't. I knew what would be next. I knew that she would have to go. She couldn't come with me, and I wouldn't beg her to go anymore. She needed to be with her mom as long as possible.

"Listen," I said as I tried to release her, but Zelda wouldn't let go. "Listen to me, Zel. Stay with your mom. Make her happy. I will drop anything if you need me. I will come and hold you like this until you tell me to let go. You hear me?"

"You don't have to do anything," she asked into my shirt, which was drenched from her tears.

"You matter to me. If I must drop everything, I will."

"You're insane to give up everything for me."

"Zel, I waited too long for someone like you. I can't just let you go." I flashed her a cocky smile as Zelda looked at me. Fuck, I wanted her so bad. I finally had her in my arms, but she was about to be gone again.

"Can you keep talking to me? Chat with me every minute of the day? I want you…" Zelda pressed her hands to her temple.

I pressed my hand to her cheek. "We'll make this work, you hear me? But I don't want to make things complicated with James."

"We are separated. I chose you." Zelda's eyes locked onto mine, and I felt my heart explode in a million pieces. *I am worthy of love,* I thought.

"I'm in love with you Zelda." I pressed my lips to her, feeling her crumple from my touch. Breaking away from her kiss, I mouthed, "You don't need to say it."

Zelda nodded as she watched me with those eyes that seemed to weaken and disappear. She was lost in her darkness, and I was going to come for her and pull her back to the light.

I kissed her forehead. She fit perfectly under my chin. "I will be here whenever you need me. I will come to you if you need anything with your mom."

"I know." She pressed her hand to my cheek. "How long are you in the US for?"

"For a month, then to Toronto, and we leave back for London after that. I will come back after London and spend time with you."

Zelda's gaze fell and she looked down at her feet.

I lifted her chin. "I will come back."

"Maybe it's another sign."

"What's a sign?"

"Every chance we get, we somehow manage to be unable to be together. What if the universe is telling us that we aren't meant to be?"

I licked my bottom lip, then exhaled. "I…" I didn't know what to say to her because, secretly, I wondered if she was right. Why had we never happened? I shook at the thought because I couldn't allow that idea of that ruin our chances of having something that could be great. I pulled her into me one more time and wrapped my arms around her, inhaling in her scent, feeling her warmth, and trying to remember every detail of her before I got onto that bus.

"Edmund, let's get a move on!" Andrew hollered. I glanced over my shoulder, then looked back and flashed Zelda a weak smile.

"Call me tonight?" Zelda bit her lip, but the tears kept falling.

I kissed her cheek. "I will. Keep me up to date with your mum."

"I will."

I walked to the bus, but each step felt like I was being sucked into quicksand, barely being able to progress. I took a final glance at her before climbing the steps of the bus. I watched her from the window, not caring what my bandmates or Andrew were screaming about. I saw her give a small wave before she stepped away. The bus started, and I pushed my face to the window to get one last glance at her.

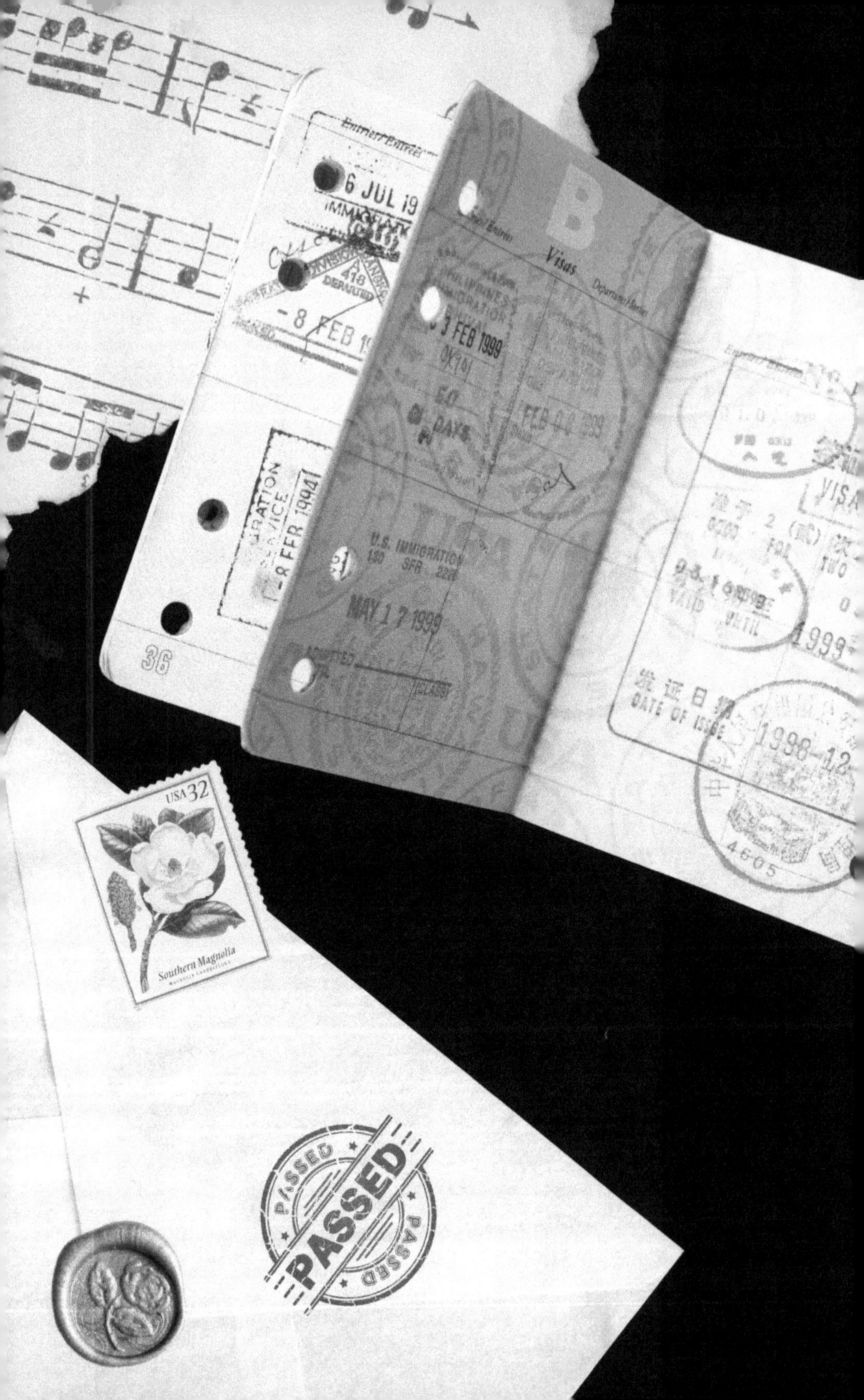
Entries/Entrée
6 JUL 19
IMMIGRATION
418
DEPARTED
- 8 FEB 19
RATION
SERVICE
8 FEB 1991
36
B
Visas
Departure/Départ
PHILIPPINES
IMMIGRATION
3 FEB 1999
60 DAYS
FEB 09 1999
U.S. IMMIGRATION
190   SFR   226
MAY 1 7 1999
ADMITTED
CLASS
VISA
TWO
VALID
UNTIL
1999
DATE OF ISSUE
1998-12
4605
USA 32
Southern Magnolia
PASSED
PASSED
PASSED
PASSED

Zelda

I was going down with this imaginary ship with no chance of survival. I walked home in a daze. All I wanted was someone to take charge of my life because I was tired of trying. My mind was slipping into a mental grave.

When I trudged into my apartment, James sat on the island, and he lifted his head with worried eyes. James came and wrapped his arms around me, but I pushed him away. I felt surrounded by loss.

"I am so fucking sorry." He crossed his arms against his chest from my rejection. "I canceled my appointments at the studio. I'm such a terrible husband," he confessed. James wasn't a person who thought about others. I knew that.

"It's okay. You have a lot going on right now." My words came out harsh because deep down, I had wished he wasn't here. Something was going on with him, like he was holding something back. James had checked out before, and we had held on to each other, thinking it was worth it. I pressed my fingers against his cheek. His hazel eyes narrowed, and a small smile crossed his face.

"I can take time to help you with your mom. It is a lot."

"No, I want this separation. I want us to come to the realization that we are not meant for each other. Live your life, James."

That's when it hit me that I was taking advantage of him. He had potential to be with another person. He had married someone who couldn't give him the love he deserved. I'd tried to be the woman who was perfect for him, but I was tired of it.

I wanted to be free.

"James…" I stepped away from him. "I think we should divorce."

He shot me a look of confusion as he pinched the bridge of his nose. "What? Where did this come from?"

I couldn't tell him about Edmund. I was ashamed of what I'd been doing. "My mom has months, maybe weeks, to live, and I felt like all of this didn't fit. I am not the woman you should be with. I don't bring in enough, I waste food, I waste money, I don't clean enough, I don't make your food. I'm constantly being belittled by you. Why? I can't live like this. I shouldn't have taken you back." The rage was building. "I pleaded with you. You're never home. You're never here. I can't do this. I thought I could play the part, but I can't," I confessed, defeat swarming my body.

"I never asked for you to be a fucking trophy wife. You think that little of me?" he yelled as he tried to reach for my hand, but I stepped away.

"Yes! I do! I don't feel like we even love each other. We're convenient. We wanted this to make our lives feel complete." I pressed my hands against my face.

"Is there someone else?" He slammed his hands on the counter and leaned closer. "Is that it?" He cocked his head to the side angrily.

"I need a break. I need to find myself. I-I don't want you to be waiting for something that may not exist anymore," I confessed. "You deserve more than me."

James ran his hands down his face. "I don't know what the fuck to say, Zelda." He crossed his arms and headed to the bedroom. I stood alone in the kitchen, pressing my hands to my face, crying about what I'd done. I couldn't be his wife. Freedom slowly slipped into my vision.

Within ten minutes, I saw James walk out of our bedroom with a duffel bag. He passed me as I watched him go to the door. He stopped at the door and turned to me. "Please come back to me, but if you can't

—just let us go." Looking into his swollen red eyes, I nodded, and he walked away.

When death pays a visit, you realize life is too short to waste time.

~

I STOOD at the door to my mom's apartment, swallowed hard, and knocked three times. I opened my eyes when the door swung open, and there was Bobby, my soon-to-be stepfather.

"Hey, Zelda! Come in." He was a tall fellow with broad shoulders and a lean body. He had salt-and-pepper hair, a full beard, and bright gray eyes. He was the type of rugged Mom would never go for. She'd always been attracted to men who seemed a tad crazy. Bobby wore combat boots, plaid, and jeans that had seen better days. He had tattoos on his arms, and a demeanor that said, "I probably belong to a motorcycle club and not the good kind."

"Thank you. How is Mom doing?"

"She must have stolen some drugs because she is on a high. Your friend, Clara, is here with her. Come on in and get settled." He made room for me as I walked into the narrow hallway filled with photos and art.

Mom had always been a powerhouse who couldn't be held back. That was why she had been on her own. Seeing her now, being catered to by a man who was literally at her beck and call, was unusual.

In the living room, was my mother on her green velvet couch with my best friend resting her head on my mom's lap. She considered Clara another daughter. Clara loved my mom in ways that I couldn't explain. She sat up quickly and came over. "Zel!" I wrapped my arms around her.

"Girls!" Mom snapped at us both as she observed us in disbelief.

"Mom? What do you want us to do? How can we not?" I replied. Mom rolled her eyes as she looked out the window.

"I want to make the next few months the best ones yet. I don't want to worry about the end because that's a drag."

"Well"—I took a big breath as Clara looked at me—"I will be solo because I asked for a divorce from James."

"It's about fucking time," Mom said with her hands in the air.

"Pardon?" Clara glanced my way. "And are you going to try with Edmund?"

"Edmund? Why does that name sound familiar?" Bobby asked from the antique chair my mom had stolen from her neighbor.

"Oh yeah. It's definitely for Edmund. Clara showed me what he looks like, and I would climb him like a tree."

The three of them chuckled, enjoying my ruined life.

"It's not about him," I lied. "I'm tired of trying to be something that I'm not." I was ready to take my life back. My feelings were pointing me in the right direction more than ever.

"She's in love." Mom watched me as I took a deep breath.

"My life isn't important right now. Yours is."

"Honey, you're my life. I want you to be happy."

Even though Mom was dying, I was the one disappearing in this situation.

"Bobby, pull out the sangria. I need to chat with my daughters." Mom reached for my hand and tugged me next to Clara.

"This man is yummy," Clara admitted as she pulled out her phone.

"No wonder she wants to bang him," Mom said.

"I haven't," I admitted. Bobby walked in with the sangria.

"What is wrong with you?" Mom clutched her necklace in mock fear.

I ignored her and said, "That is a discussion for another day. We need to create a list of what you want to do for—"

"My last hoorah!" She flashed her hands as if she had spirit fingers.

"No! That's terrible."

"We can call it you going out with a bang list," Clara replied.

"This is morbid," I responded, shaking my head.

"I couldn't agree with you more," Bobby said as he handed us sangrias.

"Anyway, I have a list." Mom pulled out a leather book from the side of the coffee table. "This is what I want, and you better accept it." She handed the book to me as I looked over the words she'd written down.

1. To get married.

2. *To go to a music festival.*
3. *To die seeing the ocean.*

I expected more to be on the list, but as I read each one, Mom reached for my hand and leaned in. "I didn't ask for much." I knew it would still be the hardest thing I'd ever do.

Entrée/Entree
6 JUL 19
IMMIGRATION
418
DEPARTED
- 8 FEB 19
RATION
SERVICE
FEB 1994
36
Visas
Departure/Sortie
B
PHILIPPINES
IMMIGRATION
3 FEB 1999
60 DAYS
U.S. IMMIGRATION
SFR 226
MAY 17 1999
ADMITTED
CLASS
VISA
TWO
VALID UNTIL
1999
DATE OF ISSUE
1998 12
4605
USA 32
Southern Magnolia
MAGNOLIA GRANDIFLORA
PASSED
PASSED

27

Zelda

"She doesn't want to talk to you, James!"

Sitting on the guest bed in my mom's apartment, Clara paced while she shouted at my future ex-husband on the phone. It had been a week since I'd seen James, and he wouldn't stop with the calls. He was trying everything in his power to change my mind, but it did the opposite.

"I get that it felt random, but you knew this was going to happen, James. You pushed her away. It's over. Listen, I need to go, but I will pass along the message to her." Clara pinched the bridge of her nose. When she hung up, she released a breath, and Mom walked into the room.

"What's going on?"

"James is losing his shit because your daughter decided to end their marriage."

"I pulled the rug from under him, but I can't give him what he wants. I'm not that person," I confessed.

"We know." Mom leaned against the doorway. "You're like me." She winked at me, but it felt more like an accusation than a confidence booster. Mom walked into the room with her cane as she slowly sat on the edge of the bed before she continued, "Listen, I need to have a talk with you."

My eyes narrowed, and I glanced at Clara. "What do you need?"

"I…" She paused as she ran her hand through her hair. "We need to talk, and by we, I mean Bobby and I."

"Okay? What do you want to talk about?"

"I think it may be best if it's just you and I, Zel. Sorry, Clara." She glanced at my friend, but I reached for her hand.

"She's family. Anything you need to say, you can say in front of her," I said.

"Zel, I can leave." Clara kissed Mom's cheek. "We will start that bucket list." She winked. "I'll talk to you later." Mom and I waved, then we finally looked at each other.

"So…" I took a deep breath. "What did you want to talk about?"

Mom bit her bottom lip. She did that when something serious needed to be communicated. My gut clenched as fear crept through me. "Mom?" I pleaded because the suspense was destroying me.

"Bobby and I go way back," she said matter-of-factly. "*Way* back."

"Okay? What does that have to do with anything?"

"He was my first love, to be honest. We met in high school, and he was the cute jock. I was head over heels for him."

"Rekindling past relationships is normal, Mom," I responded. If this was the most significant thing she wanted to say, it hadn't been necessary to kick Clara out.

"It's not just that…" She closed her eyes and exhaled a deep breath before opening her eyes to look at me, and a single tear ran down her face. "I got pregnant." She reached for me. "And I ran away. I was scared. I didn't think he wanted a baby, and my parents were terrible, so I left, and I had you."

Bobby was my father.

There are moments in my life when I could pinpoint my heart shattering, and that was this. I couldn't speak, couldn't comprehend what my mom was saying. "You told me my father died, and he was a one-night stand. You told me he was a prick. You made me hate him! What the fuck? Are you kidding me? That man in the other room is my father?" I stood abruptly, and my hands cradled my head, feeling outraged. The walls seemed to be squeezing out the air because I couldn't breathe. Mom was trying to reach for me, but I brushed her away. "No, stay away from me."

"Zelda, please! I wanted to tell you, but I was afraid!"

"Afraid of what, Mom? That we could have had a normal life? That we didn't have to live above a strip joint? I was so embarrassed to have people over because of you! It was why I wanted a normal, boring family! That man is my father, and you tell me now? Now that you're dying, it's convenient for me to start a relationship with him?"

"It wasn't like that, Zelda. I want you to have a family. I want you to have someone who will be there for you when the darkness comes."

"I just proof my point! You're doing this for convenience! I don't need anyone but you!" I yelled as the tears poured down my hot skin. "My world is crashing, and I don't know how to put all these puzzles together, Mom. I love you so damn much, but I can't stand you right now!"

"You don't think it's hard for me? You're the only love I've ever had. How could I let you live a life where you have no one? Look at you," she cried. "I want you to have someone when the world gets too dark.

"When I found out I was sick, I reached out to Bobby. I wanted him in your life. I wanted him back in my life. I found out he didn't have anyone either. He doesn't have kids or a wife. He loved me too much, and I hurt him."

I pressed my hands against my chest, feeling like I couldn't breathe. "I need air—I need a moment," I said, ambling out of the room. Then I sped out of the apartment while my name was being called by my mom and now my *father*.

I rushed up to the apartment's rooftop. I needed to scream at the heavens and ask why they fucked with my life. Swinging the emergency door open, I felt the embrace of the cool night air touch my skin, and I breathed. I reached for my phone and tried to call Edmund.

It only took one ring.

"My sweet Zel, how are you? I've been dying to hear from you," he confessed. It'd been a couple of days since we were able to call each other. After the situation with James and me permanently moving in with Mom, we barely could call. I closed my eyes tight and pretended he was standing before me. Sliding down against the wall, I wrapped my arm around my legs and pressed my phone to my ear.

"My mom confessed that her boyfriend is actually my dad," I said.

"What? Wait—Bobby? He's your dad?" He sounded like he was processing it. "Zelda, I'm sorry. I can catch a flight to be with you." During the past week, it had been challenging to make time for each other. But Edmund managed to message me every chance he got. So I tried to fill him in on the hot mess I was dealing with.

I exhaled. "No. You have a show in a couple of days. You need to focus on that. It's more important."

"Babe, nothing is more important than you. I can get the others to fill in while I'm off."

"Your groupies will be disappointed." I laughed.

"I don't give a fuck about anyone other than you. You're my heart, and I will be there."

I secretly wished he could be here holding me and making me feel better, but I knew his concert was a big deal. There was a US label interested in them, and I couldn't take that away. "No, please don't come. We can FaceTime." I touched my phone and waited a couple of seconds for him to appear on my screen.

Edmund sat against the headboard of his room; his curls were sporadic, and his beard was thicker. He wore a fitted sweater. "Hey, baby." His raspy, low voice and British accent always weakened me. I felt sudden heat on my cheeks.

"Hey, babe." I pushed my hair back.

"I wish I was there to hold you. I don't know what else to tell you because I've never experienced this, but darling, I will be there."

"Being there is more than anything I need in this world."

"I know I shouldn't change the subject, but I want to kiss you so much."

"Stop." I hid my lips, but my smile peeked out.

"There is your sweet smile. I know your world is upside down, but it will get back on track. I will do anything in my power to make that happen. I know what your mom did was hard, but I promise it may be good for you."

"I don't believe in promises. No one ever keeps them, remember?"

"Zelda? Stop thinking that way. Bobby is your father. He is trying."

"He didn't. He's here now? He could have tried harder," I confessed as I watched his eyes narrow. "If he loved her so much, why didn't he come for her?"

He let out a breath. "I don't know why. We all have our own mistakes to live with. Just try to give him a chance?"

"I will try." I nodded.

We stared at each other for a couple of seconds.

"Fuck, I really want to kiss you now."

My smile widened, feeling the freedom finally coming alive. "Oh, on a happier note, I'm getting my divorce papers soon."

"I'm proud that you're taking control of your life." Edmund held my gaze, and I felt butterflies take hold of my soul like I shattered. "I'm not perfect, and I'll make mistakes in this relationship, but I'll keep holding on to you like you are my lifeline. I love you, Zel. As for your mom, she loves you. She doesn't want you to be alone in this world. She wants someone to love you as much as she does. Yes, it's terrible fucking timing, but it's better than never."

I wiped the tears away. "I don't want to lose her."

"You will never lose her, darling. She will be in the stars, the air you breathe, and those big beautiful green eyes. Your mom will be there when you have babies and when you grow old. She'll be there every step of the way."

"I'm terrified."

"It's normal to be scared; everyone is. Don't let this pain take away the days you have left with her. Go back and make amends, Zelda, before it's too late."

I sniffed back more tears. "You're right."

"I know." He winked. "Now go give your mom a big hug and tell her that even though you're mad, you still love her."

"Okay," I said.

"Hey, before you go." He scratched his chin. "Go grab a star."

"What?"

"Look up to the stars and grab a star, make a wish, and throw it back."

I shook my head, but I looked above me. The world seemed so

small when I looked at the stars. We are just a speck of dust compared to what is up there. I reached out my hand and pretended to grab a star and place it against my chest.

"Make a wish," Edmund encouraged as he watched me from the screen.

I wished to come out of the depth of the deep emotional ocean so I could swim to shore.

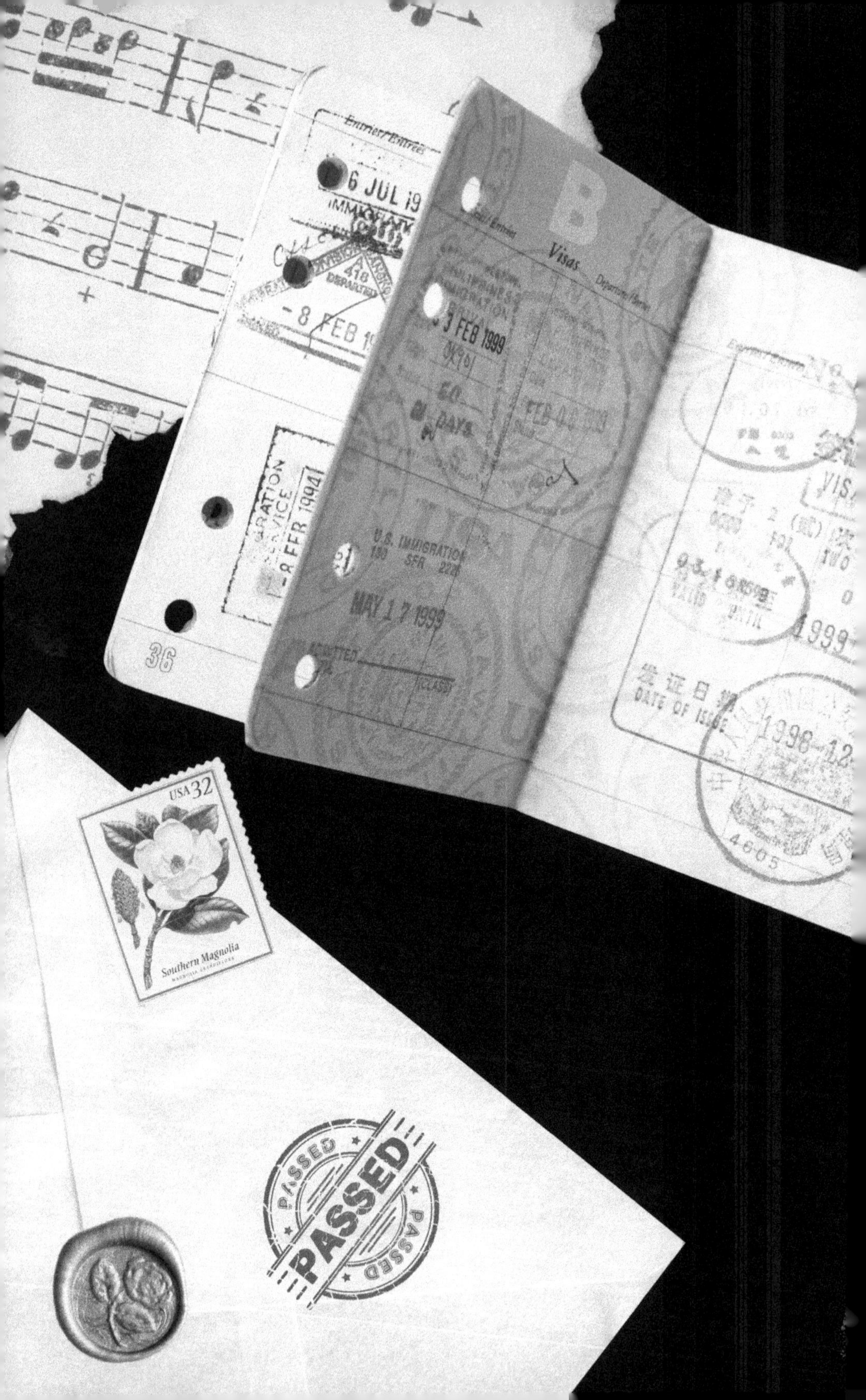
Entrier/Entrée
6 JUL 19
IMMIGRATION
418
DEPARTURE
- 8 FEB 19
GRATION
SERVICE
FEB 1994
36
Bel/Entrée
Visas
Departure/Départ
PHILIPPINES
IMMIGRATION
3 FEB 1999
60 DAYS
U.S. IMMIGRATION
190   SFR   226
MAY 1 7 1999
ADMITTED
CLASS
B
VISA
TWO
VALID UNTIL
1999
DATE OF ISSUE
1998-12
4605
USA 32
Southern Magnolia
MAGNOLIA GRANDIFLORA
PASSED
PASSED
PASSED
PASSED

28

Edmund

Another city, another round of shots. After that call with Zelda three nights back, I wanted to jump on the next flight to see her. She was alone, feeling her world slip away while I lived freely. What made it worse was that I was becoming a household name. But all I wanted to do was go to my girl who needed me.

"Look at you, Eddie! You made it onto Zlock!" Tommy scrolled his phone as we chilled backstage waiting for our show to begin.

"Let me see!" Andrew rushed to Tommy's side, looking over his shoulder. "I don't think your girlfriend will be happy to see that."

We hadn't made it official because we didn't know what we were. Zelda's life was complicated, and I didn't want to confuse it more. Yet I wanted to be with her—just her. After she told me about James, I knew she would be mine.

As I stood and grabbed the phone from Tommy, I felt a sickening feeling crawl over me. I was in a photo, and a woman was cozied up on my lap. *Fuck*, I thought. "That fucking woman literally jumped me at last night's show."

"Sure, sure." Tommy winked at me.

Both twins sat in the corner, playing some video game without a care in the world. I swear, even though they were part of the band, they could go missing and no one would notice.

I shook my head. "It was not like that at all. I would not do that to Zelda."

Andrew crossed his arms. "You're in love with her."

I rolled my eyes and ran my hands down my face. "Let's prepare for tonight's show."

"No. Is Eddie in love? Holy shit!" Tommy gripped my shoulders. "I was beginning to think that we would never survive another tour. Boys, he's found his fucking muse."

"Should we tell him that Zelda has been our muse since the beginning?" Andrew whispered as I shook my head and watched Tommy parade around the room triumphantly.

"Boys, let's drink!" Tommy started to pour tequila in shot glasses and handed them over to us. We cheered, and I let the liquor burn down my throat. My phone started ringing, and the boys sang "Lover Boy."

I headed to the back corner and answered my phone.

"You saved me," I said.

"I needed to hear your voice before you went on stage," she whispered.

"Why are you whispering?"

"My mom is trying everything to make things better. So any time I'm up or doing something, she swarms me like a bee. I'm currently hiding under my sheets."

"Don't tease me because I would love to be under those sheets with you." The thought of having sex with her was overwhelming because I still remembered tasting her.

"I know you would. Maybe later, you can show me what you would do under those sheets."

"Are you trying to get me hard before I get on stage? Because let's face it, that'd be bad."

"Why, is another woman going to hop on your lap?" She knew. Fuck, I had wanted to tell her, but she figured it out.

"I just saw it," I confessed, exhaling a deep breath from my chest.

"Listen, I get it. You're a celebrity. Women are going to be all over you. And we aren't really—"

"Do you want me? Because I want you. I want all of you, Zelda. After all this time, I'm still right here. I don't want anyone else."

"I know." Her voice was soft. "I-I want that too… there is so much going on, and I need to be with mom… and the divorce with James… and trying to figure out a job—"

"Zel, I will be waiting for you right where you left me. I'm not going anywhere. I promise." I felt my heart tighten in my chest at her words. I never understood how anyone could fall in love with someone until I fell for her. Zelda was not some groupie who wanted to sleep with me because I was a celebrity. She saw me. The real me. I couldn't escape that. It felt like I was losing control of my car over a cliff, and it scared me.

"Guys, five minutes to stage!" One of the staff rushed into the room as the boys were bounding with pure adrenaline.

"My sweet Zel, I've got to go. I'll be thinking of you, you hear me?"

"I will be waiting for you. Call me whenever it is done," she pleaded.

"THANK YOU FOR A WONDERFUL NIGHT, Nashville! Thank you for letting us crash this place! See you next time!" Tommy moved as if he was Mick Jagger, and he sang like Axl Rose, but he was genuinely soulful. He was a unique piece of art.

As we all stood next to each other and bowed, the crowd roared, "Augustus." My body was sweaty, my heart was pounding, and all I thought about was Zelda.

We headed to the after-party, and Tommy and Andrew embraced me with some shots in their hand while a bunch of women stormed the room, ready to partake in whatever Tommy had going on. I wondered when a good time to leave was when a woman beelined toward me. She had determined eyes and a desperate air about her. Her big eyes, big boobs, and fitted outfit were even more reason to look away.

"I think you're the sexiest guy out of all of them," she said, then quickly sat on my lap before I could move.

"Thank you." I felt uncomfortable. She was beautiful, but I needed to step away.

"Your accent is so fucking hot! I've been thinking of doing this to you all night." Before I could stop her, she kissed me on my lips. I was dumbfounded. Not a single part of me wanted this. Seconds went by, and the only thing I wanted was to hear Zelda's voice. I pushed the woman off, and anger took over.

"What the fuck is wrong with you?"

The woman whimpered as I got up aggressively.

"Where are you going?" Andrew was in mid-conversation with some random woman, trying her best to come onto him. She was pressed into his chest, and his arm was wrapped around her waist.

"I'm heading back to the hotel," I snapped.

"Why? We are having fun!" Andrew rolled out a laugh, then took a swig of his beer.

"I want to see Zelda. I will see you in the morning," I shouted, my eyes narrowed at him as the music increased in the speaker.

Andrew nodded and returned to the woman and the liquor. I surveyed the room, watching my bandmates indulged in booze, women, and possibly drugs. I wanted to check out of this place. I had to break free from it before it took hold of me.

ONCE IN THE HOTEL ROOM, I kicked my shoes off and took a shower. After getting into my track pants, I glanced at my phone. I was one hour behind her, and it was already midnight. She said I could call her, but I felt terrible. I debated it for a few seconds, but my finger hovered over her name.

"Fuck it," I muttered.

It took one ring to hear her voice.

"Hey," she whispered with a slight tiredness. I didn't blame her. Zelda was probably in her eighth dream when I rudely interrupted.

"Hey, go back to sleep. We can talk later."

"No, I missed you."

God, I wished I was there, I thought. "I miss you too." Her voice was arousing, even with a trace of sleep.

"I was thinking of you."

I closed my eyes, thinking of how her lips felt against my lips.

Memories poured in, and I felt my cock throb against my track pants. "I'm not going to lie. I'm thinking of the first time I tasted you."

Zelda moaned. "I'm not going to lie. I'm trying to remember when we were at the lake. Remind me?"

"I remember picking you up and touching you for the first time. I slipped those panties off. I watched your eyes, and fuck, baby, I remember how hungry you were for me." I lay on my bed, closing my eyes tight as my hands took hold of my cock, stroking it to the thought of her.

"I wanted you to touch me so badly, and you did. You craved me as much as I craved you."

"My kiss covered your skin, and my lips embraced those perfect fucking breasts, tugging your nipple, and you let out a soft moan. Baby, are you touching yourself?"

"Yes," she moaned.

"My lips couldn't wait any longer, so I tugged your panties off and fucking devoured that pussy. Your hands tugged at my hair as I licked your core."

"I want you to fuck me so bad," she purred against the receiver.

"I need to feel you squeeze your thighs as each stroke of my tongue makes you explode." I remembered her body losing control as I held her waist tight, not letting her go. I stroked my cock while she kept moaning. I could picture touching and tasting her sweet pussy. "Let me devour you," I growled.

"Edmund!" Zelda called.

"Baby, come all over my face. God, I want to feel that sweet euphoria…" I said. My grip around my shaft was rougher and faster as I listened to her panting.

"I want to come with you. I want you to fuck me."

"You want me to fuck you with my big cock? You want me to unravel you as I take you hard?"

Zelda moaned in my ear, and I was on the verge of exploding. "I can feel that gorgeous pussy sliding up and down my cock as you rock your hips."

"Harder and harder." She moaned. "I'm coming."

"Better fucking keep touching yourself because I'm not done with you. I'm stroking myself harder, and I'm going to fill that tight pussy up with my cum."

"Edmund, I'm coming," she pleaded.

"Picture my dick exploding in you because my hand is pumping."

"Yes!" She moaned loud, and her breathing was heavy.

I exploded. My eyes clenched tight, feeling the satisfaction of her touching herself as she thought about me. My hands were filled with cum, and I let out a rough, raspy sound against the phone.

"I can't wait to do that to you in person," she said.

"Oh, we will be doing a lot more than that," I teased.

She would be the death of me.

Entrée/Entrée
6 JUL 19
IMMIGRATION
-8 FEB 19
RATION
SERVICE
-8 FEB 1991
36
Entrée/Entrée
Visas   Departure/Sortie
B
PHILIPPINE
IMMIGRATION
3 FEB 1999
60 DAYS
PHILIPPINE
DEPARTURE
FEB 08 1999
U.S. IMMIGRATION
100   SFR   2826
MAY 1 7 1999
ADMITTED
CLASS
VISA
VALID
1999
DATE OF ISSUE
1998-12
4605
USA 32
Southern Magnolia
PASSED
PASSED
PASSED
PASSED

29

I had missed phone sex or sex in general. It had been the Sahara Desert since the last time I had anything. James and I were intimate, but there wasn't any connection. It was more of a need for him than a want from me. But when Edmund had called me last night, I pictured him in my bed with me as we got lost in each other's embrace. I told myself to slow down, but Edmund was a force.

Mom had tried hard to get into my good graces while my "father" was making himself present. Bobby wanted to go for a coffee with me, and I told myself I would try with him. I was trying my best not to freak out and get mad at what my mom had done, but at the same time, how could I not?

Bobby had taken me to a local record joint to look for something for Mom. I stayed quiet the entire time while he tried to make small talk. He caught me looking at Fleetwood Mac, and he started to have a full conversation with me.

"That is the song that your mom sang at the talent show in high school." Bobby pointed at "The Chain." "That's when I fell for her." I glanced at him with his eyes glued on the record, scratching his chin.

"She sang each word with force. God, she was stunning onstage. She was a singer and dancer."

"Mom?" I narrow my gaze. "My mom? She's an alright singe—"

"She's an amazing singer! People were in awe of her. Especially with the high notes. That's what made me fall head over heels for her. I was so engulfed by her. Eloise had this fire that people wish they had."

"What was she like?" I asked. I'd never seen photos of Mom young because she didn't have much. She never talked about her parents or her early life. She kept moving forward.

"She was a firecracker. Still is. She never had an ounce of hatred for anyone except her parents."

"How were her parents?" I was curious. "She never talks about them."

"Her dad was a prick. He used to hurt her, and her mom was a drunk. Her family came from high society. Her father, Raymond, was a top judge or something like that. Eloise's mom, Simone, only cared about the high life. But, Eloise, she was so different from them. One night, I was driving home from practice, and I saw her walking alone in the rain. She was crying and had a bruise on her face. I knew, in my heart, I had to save her."

I froze at the idea of Mom struggling before I was in the picture. She was a rainbow after the storms. She fights for what is right, so to imagine my mom suffering all her life broke me. A single tear raced down my cheek as I looked up at Bobby. "Is that why she ran?"

Bobby took a deep breath, closed his eyes, and nodded. "When she found me, we talked, and she told me about you. I'm not going to lie to you and say I wasn't mad. I was furious. I've missed so much of your life. But deep down, I knew why she did it. Her parents would have ruined her. You saved her from the hell she lived in."

I glanced back at the records, trying to hide how I felt, but Bobby touched my shoulder.

"I know you probably hate her right now, but she had her reasons."

"How can you be okay that you were never in my life?"

"Because even though I missed those years and wished I could have been the father you should have, I knew she had to do it to keep you alive. Eloise isn't perfect and neither am I. Life doesn't have guidelines. I wish I had been present at your birth and seen you take your first steps. I wish I had dropped you off at school and picked you up after the broken hearts. Looking at you, I see a part of me in your smile and your sweet eyes. I know you're scared and afraid now, but we don't have much time with your mom. Don't let the anger cloud you. We have the rest of our lives to build a relationship. I love you."

My lips trembled as I watched him. "How can you love me when you don't know me?"

"Because you're my daughter. I will love you until my last breath."

"I have a hard time saying that to you right now," I confessed.

"It's okay; we can jump in together and figure it all out along the way." He grinned, and I gave Bobby our first hug. I held him close to my heart as I squeezed him, hearing his steady heartbeat.

"Now, will you tell me about Edmund? I overheard you mentioning him to Clara." I looked up at him and scrunched my face.

"He's just a guy."

"And I was once a guy too, so give me the details."

I released his hold. "I read a letter from the previous owner of my apartment, and we started to chat. After that, it turned into more of a relationship."

"While you were with James?" He tilted his head.

"Yeah. I feel terrible about that," I said.

"Hey." He reached for my hand. "There aren't guidelines. We are bound to make mistakes. So how do you truly feel about James?"

"That's it, I don't. I have no feelings toward him. I thought he was what I wanted because of the structure and feeling of comfort."

"Why?"

"Because of how Mom raised me. I shouldn't blame it on her, but I wanted something tangible."

"How did that work out?" Bobby cocked his head to the side.

"Shitty."

"James wasn't the right one. Forcing yourself to have a perfect life probably means you're terrified of following your feelings." He nudged me.

"I guess you're right." I shrugged. "Is that why you didn't marry?"

"I had relationships, but none of them came close to your mom. She made me feel something unknown. Is that what you feel for Edmund?"

"Yes. That's what I find attractive. What I want is to enjoy every second, not to predict what life will be," I admitted.

"Well then, you figured it out. If Edmund is the comet in your life, then go catch him," Bobby said.

"You're filled with metaphors," I joked.

"I have to catch up on those and dad jokes." He winked. "Come on, we need to plan a wedding. Let's get that album for Mom."

"Okay." I beamed, feeling a comfort with him.

WHEN WE WALKED into the apartment, Mom threw us off by singing "We Belong" by Pat Benatar with Clara as her backup singer.

Mom belted into her remote as she lay on the couch. I laughed so hard, and Bobby nudged me.

"I told you," he whispered into my ear.

I watched my friend and my mom duet the song and embrace. I jumped into the group and we sang together.

"Oh my goodness!" Clara laughed as the next song played. "It's all coming back to me now!"

Mom hollered. "Bobby, get over here! I need to dance!" Mom reached for his hand, and he picked her up and cradled her in his arms. They were slowly dancing in the small apartment, and Clara watched them.

"We need to make her wedding perfect," Clara said.

"What about Vegas?" I replied.

Clara looked at me with wide eyes. "Yes! Vegas with Elvis. That would be perfect!"

"You think we should do that?" I asked.

"Fuck yeah!"

While watching Mom sing, I got a FaceTime from Edmund. I answered as Mom was hitting the high notes.

"Holy shit, who was that?" Edmund appeared on my screen, and I flipped the camera. Mom sang her whole heart out as Bobby twirled her around. I'd never seen her that way. Over the years, she was reserved with what she sang, but this was stunning. And it killed me inside to know that she was dying.

"Edmund, I have an idea." I flipped him back to me.

"Of course, babe." He flashed me a grin with his scruffy look making an appearance. I quickly left the room with Clara, and we hid in my room, not wanting Mom to hear what I said next.

"Would you let my mom sing a song at one of your shows?" I asked.

"I'll talk to the guys, but they should be fine. She's incredible."

"Maybe we can give her that," Clara added.

"Anything to help you." Edmund licked his lips. God, I loved this man.

"By the way, we are going to Vegas! Just in case you want to stop by." Clara leaned into the video.

"We do have a show in Vegas, strange." He winked. "I get to see you."

"Yay!" I cheered. "Send me the dates on how long you're there till, and we will plan the wedding."

"Perfect. I need to go practice, but I'll call you later."

"Of course." I winked, knowing all too well what that call would be.

As I hung up the phone, another call flashed on my screen, which instantly changed my mood—James.

I swallowed hard, knowing exactly why he was calling me. My lawyer had sent him the divorce papers. I pressed ignore because I didn't want to think of any of that right now.

30

Zelda

The last hoorah was in full force. Clara and I worked endlessly through the past two weeks, planning the ultimate wedding adventure for my mom.

Letters to Augusta had two shows left before arriving in Las Vegas. When I talked to Edmund about the plans for the weekend of his performance, he told me to leave the arrangements with him. I insisted that it would be too much, but he didn't accept no for an answer. The last thing in the plan was getting Mom a wedding dress and finalizing the details with Bobby.

Bobby talked to me privately about what happened at Mom's last doctor's appointment. "Eloise isn't doing well; the prognosis is getting worse. Maybe this trip will be too much for her."

"No, Bobby," I pleaded, clutching my necklace while my heart lodged itself in my throat. I couldn't find the right words to beg him not to change the plan. My emotions were in a tangled knot, making it difficult to grasp everything. "Mom never asks for much. She deserves to have the best."

Our new reality was a bitter pill to swallow. Mom's life slipped through my fingers as the days continued, and I couldn't stop it. Every day, I looked up information on how to deal with end-of-life care. Both Bobby and I created a watch, checking on Mom every night as she slept in the living room. The doctors had suggested a home care bed would be more supportive as she was deteriorating faster than we could keep up. The living room was a much bigger space for her, plus her plants and the sunshine surrounded her.

Most days, Mom wanted to stay in bed because she would pretend she wasn't up for anything when we knew she had no energy. I hated that I couldn't do anything to take away her pain and suffering. I fought the tears that welled up every time I saw her lay in that bed like she was being stripped of her freedom. But I had to stay strong for her. One of us had to.

That was why I knew Vegas was something she had to do before it was too late.

Edmund's arrangements helped us achieve two bucket-list items in one location, allowing Mom to marry the man of her dreams followed by her center-stage performance. With the support of Andrew, we arranged the most magical experience for her. To top it off, he booked a luxurious room at Caesar's Palace, and everything was paid for. I was going to pay for everything, but Andrew indicated that Edmund had paid for it already. No questions asked. This was the most significant gift I would ever pull off for Mom, yet she didn't know anything.

When I found out about Edmund paying for everything, I called him that night crying, but he insisted that it was the least he could do for me. I felt a weight lift from my shoulders because I didn't know how to I was going to pay for it. I told Edmund I would repay him, but he said he just wanted to make my mom happy. *I love him*, I thought.

The day before we were to leave for our trip, I lay next to her as she was reading an art book. "Mom, how are you feeling?" I leaned on her shoulder as she lightly touched my cheek.

"I'm feeling good, actually." She kissed my forehead, "What's up?"

"We did it, Mom." I felt the tears well in my vision. "We did it."

"Did what, honey?" I lifted my head as I looked at her confused glance. She closed her book. "What did you do?"

"You are getting married! In Vegas!"

Mom's eyes widened, and her mouth parted. "Wait! How?"

I pressed my hand onto hers and said, "Everyone helped plan this.

We leave tomorrow. Your bags are packed, we got you a wedding dress, and everything is taken care of."

Mom pressed her hands against her mouth as tears streamed down her face. Her mouth widened with excitement as I witnessed her sheer happiness. It was as if I briefly took her away from the darkness and got her to see the sunshine. Mom's eyes glistened as she pulled me into her hold, and I felt the overflowing love between us for a moment. Nothing mattered now, not cancer, my relationships, or the world. It was just our light that had bound us over the years.

"Let's go to Vegas, baby," she whispered in my ear.

MY MOM WAS the most beautiful bride I'd ever seen.

"Look at you, Mom." I watched her adjust herself in the mirror in her white gown. She was frail, bony, and barely able to stand as she sat in the wheelchair we had to get her. Her long veil was on, and her silky white dress fit her well. She had fair makeup with a deep red lip. I watched her pat herself while looking slightly nervous.

"Thank you, darling. I have the jitters," she confessed as she smiled. "It's like at your wedding."

"You're way prettier than I could ever be." It was the truth, and I hugged her tightly. I pushed her toward the arched doors and watched her fidget in her seat.

I kissed her gently on her cheek, but she stared at her husband-to-be. "Mom, are you okay?" I whispered as the piano started to play. I glanced at the altar to see Bobby and Clara waiting for us as we reached the doorway.

Momma looked at me as she fought the tears, took a deep breath, and released, "This is the perfect way to get married." She cuffed my face. "And I love you for what you did. This is so perfect! You make me so happy, baby."

"Mom," I replied as I felt the tears rush down, "I wish this was for forever."

"Oh, sweetie." She pressed her hands onto my cheeks. "It will be forever in the stars." She wiped her tears as I did the same. I squeezed her tight in my arms.

I never expected it, but I walked my mom down the aisle toward Bobby and an Elvis impersonator, and she giggled the entire way. Mom was having a bad day but didn't want to show it. She glimpsed me with her big green eyes. She was the perfect bride. Mom was fulfilling the dream that she'd always wished for.

"Let's get you married," I said, and everyone, including Elvis, cheered.

Bobby loved her. Mom had never had a man who made her smile or would love her how she deserved. I remember the nights when she cried in bed because she felt alone. I remember all her pain from the men who had hurt her. Standing at the altar, Bobby looked at her like she was the air he breathed. Cancer was a fucking bitch because she didn't deserve to die, not when she finally had her happiness. Elvis began, and I glanced at Clara. She winked at me while we listened.

Suddenly, we were interrupted by a commotion at the chapel entrance. Mom glanced at me with a broad smile, and I shot her a confused look. "What is happening?"

"Can you go check?" I asked Clara. She nodded and walked swiftly in her six-inch heels.

"As I was saying, my gorgeous couple, we are here to celebrate the love between Eloise and Roberto. If anyone has objections, speak now—"

"I'm sorry. We have more guests." Clara shrugged, then she walked in on the arm of Andrew, followed by the twins, Tommy, and the man I'd been waiting my whole life for, Edmund. I bit my bottom lip, and my cheeks heated at the sight of him. He smirked at me as he walked toward us. His hands were in his pockets, showing his ink. His hair was pulled away from his face, but strands of his curls were free.

He said, "Hi."

"Hi," I replied as I watched him slide into the pews with the rest of the gang. Edmund's eyes didn't leave me as he rested his arms on the bench in front and grinned at me with his hungry, dark eyes.

"Do any of you object?" Elvis asked.

"No!" The men all shook their heads.

"Edmund, nice to meet you, but you need to wait twenty minutes before you kiss my daughter. You hear me?" Mom instructed, pointing at him.

Edmund pressed his hands to his heart. "I promise." He nodded but looked back at me. "I can wait."

~

"I NOW PRONOUNCE you man and wife. You may kiss your bride!" Elvis belted the words as Mom kissed Bobby, who lifted her in his arms. The entire room cheered; the guys hollered from their seats. The older lady at the organ started playing the "Wedding March," and Bobby pushed the wheelchair with Mom in it as they walked down the aisle. I locked arms with Clara, laughing as the guys cheered and whistled. This was the most awkward wedding I'd ever attended.

Before I reached the front of the chapel, I felt an embrace as Edmund spun me around to face him. His hands gripped my neck, and he kissed me like I was the only thing he had left. My arms wrapped around his neck as I tensed at his touch.

He broke away from me and leaned his head against my forehead. "God, I fucking missed you." His deep, raspy voice sent a rush of blood through my body.

"I did too, so much!" I pushed a strand of hair away from his face, and his irises darkened. He gave me a cocky smile.

"I know I've been busy with the tour—"

"It's okay. I get it. How long are you here?" I asked.

"You have me all night. I told them that the next two days are about you." I looked at the guys crowded together. Clara was chatting with Andrew, who was definitely eyeing her in a way I had never seen before, while Tommy gave him dirty looks.

"We should have a fun night," one of the twins announced.

"I can't go too crazy. I'm here for my mom's wedding—" Just as I was about to continue, Mom and Bobby interfered.

"Well, if it isn't the man who destroyed my daughter's marriage."

I shot my mom a look, but before I could say anything, she reached for Edmund and pulled him into a hug. "Thank you. James was never right for her."

"Mom!"

"What? Someone had to tell you." She narrowed her eyes before returning to Edmund.

"I love your daughter," Edmund said.

"I see it in your eyes, but don't break her heart. Got it?" She pointed at him.

"I promise." He nodded, giving me his smile that made me melt. I crashed into his chest and looked up at those chocolate eyes staring back at me.

"I think I've had enough fun for today. Thank you for doing all this for me." Mom reached for Bobby's hand as she started to look tired.

"It was small. Tomorrow, there is a big surprise," Edmund confessed.

"What is it?" Mom flashed me a confused look, but Bobby interrupted.

"Let me take you. Have fun, kids! Enjoy your night. Make good choices!" Before they walked away, Bobby gave me a squeeze.

"I see now that you two are meant for each other." He winked before leaving the chapel.

"I'm not trying to kill a moment, but I want to go and drink and party!" Tommy hollered from the back. Andrew and Clara were in their own world.

"I will check in later," I whispered in Clara's ear.

"Don't worry." She pressed her hand on my face before heading out of the chapel. I stood there before Edmund. He made me feel weak in a good way. His eyes were hungry for me, and his pull on me made me think in ways I had never felt before.

Edmund licked his bottom lip and tugged my hand toward him. I wrapped my arms around his neck. His head dipped toward the nape of my neck, and I felt him suck in a breath before kissing my bare skin. I cradled his head, feeling a sense of drive, wanting nothing more than to be with him now. The world continued, but our little bubble was what I wanted.

Edmund pushed a strand of hair away from my face as his eyes darkened. "I would love to take you right now." His deep, raspy voice sent shivers down my spine. "But I promised the guys we'd go out together." He winked. "We can have alone time later."

I pouted as he planted a kiss. "We finally have alone time, Edmund. Really?"

"I know, but something is happening at this party we have to go to."

I let out a frustrated breath but had to accept this comes with the territory of dating someone in a band. "Okay."

"I promise, we'll have fun together."

Entrées Entries
6 JUL 19
IMMIGRATION
418
DEPARTED
- 8 FEB 19
B
Visas
PHILIPPINES
IMMIGRATION
3 FEB 1999
60
DAYS
FEB 04 99
BRATION
SERVICE
EFEB 1994
U.S. IMMIGRATION
130   SFR   228
MAY 1 7 1999
ADMITTED
CLASS
36
VISA
TWO
VALID
1999
DATE OF ISSUE
1998-12
4605
USA 32
Southern Magnolia
PASSED
PASSED
PASSED
PASSED

31

Zelda

Being with a successful band had its perks. The security rushed to our sides when the band created chaos at the entrance. Tommy jumped the line as women begged for his autograph, and I stood next to Clara as Andrew and Edmund talked. Women threw themselves at Edmund as he paused and took photos. I held a smile for him, but deep down, I felt off. I'd been trying to stay in a bubble with him, but it was bursting.

"You okay?" Clara leaned toward me, and I finally glanced her way. I was trying to cover the worry I had written all over my face.

I gave her a small smile. "A little overwhelmed by all of this."

Before she could respond, Tommy rushed over to Clara. He was so taken by her. She didn't acknowledge him, and he tried everything to get her to notice him. Yet Andrew was in the picture.

"Ladies, would you like me to escort you into this fine establishment where we will dance seductively?" Tommy said as he bowed in front of her.

"Are you trying to be like *Pride and Prejudice*?" Clara crossed her arms and let out a snicker.

"I think you like me." He winked.

"Just the accent," Clara said, and I swore Tommy almost fell backward. He was coming on strong, but I knew Clara could handle him.

The place was packed with people. We had a private section on the second floor. It was known as the "elite" section. To rent one of the booths was roughly thirty thousand dollars. I almost choked on my drink when Clara pointed it out on her phone. The guys were chatting with other people. The surrounding area was filled with rich people trying hard to get pictures of the band. I felt like I was just sitting there. Edmund attempted to make eye contact, and he would wink at me, but it would last for a second before he was sucked in once again in another conversation.

"Do you want to go dance?" I asked Clara as she swayed to the beat and sipped her drink.

"Yes, I'm bored! Let's have fun!" She reached for my hand, and we headed toward the stairs. I glanced back to see Edmund, but he was conversing with a woman.

Clara navigated through the crowded dance floor and found a small spot to call our own. We got lost in the music. I forgot about the noise momentarily and let my mind be at ease. My world was spinning, and I needed to figure out where the horizon was. I needed to come out of the deep sea and catch my breath for the first time.

"Let go!" Clara reached for my face.

"I'm trying!" I lied.

Clara reached for my waist and swayed my body as I lifted my hands into the air and closed my eyes. The liquor pumped my heart faster as the sweat glistened on my skin.

Four songs in, and none of the guys had come down from the booth. I kept glancing up, but all I saw was Edmund in an intense conversation with the same woman. My heart fluttered, an ache I couldn't comprehend.

Was it jealousy?

Maybe, because I was annoyed that he didn't want to hang out with me. I didn't want to sound needy, but for someone who said they missed me, Edmund didn't try.

"I want to go up there," I pleaded with Clara as I leaned into her. "I need to know what is happening."

"Okay." She looked up at the second floor and back to me. "Let's go see."

We walked through each group of people as I watched Edmund laughing with the woman. She kept touching him, and he kept smiling.

The smile that he gives me, I thought.

"Hi!" I said as I stood next to him.

The woman was gorgeous. She had rose-colored hair, dark eyes, and a dress that fit so perfectly I wished I could look that way. She was a model of some kind. I didn't recognize her, but everyone else did.

Edmund reached for my hand. "Babe, sorry, I've been chatting with Sofia," he said.

"Oh, hi." I reached for her hand. "I'm Zelda."

Sofia reached, but her eyes wanted to kill me. "I didn't know you were in a relationship, Edmund," she confessed as she patted her chin.

We had never defined what we were, but at the same time, we had a history in line with what would be considered a relationship.

"Yes, this is my girlfriend, Zelda." Edmund pulled my waist and placed me on his lap. "Newly." He winked at me. I took a deep breath, feeling emotions I didn't know how to handle.

"You two are cute. I must head back. It was so nice seeing you, Edmund." She stood and walked away. It was as if I had ruined him for her.

"What was that?" I asked, sitting on his lap as he sipped his whiskey.

He licked his bottom lip and rubbed his chin. "Nothing. She likes the band. Turns out she went to university with some mates I know. We were talking."

"You promise not to hurt me?" I asked.

Edmund narrowed his eyes and held my face. "I would never hurt you, Zel. You have my heart. I'm sorry I've been occupied. I'm trying to balance all of it."

"Am I too much? If this is the case, we can take it—"

"Fuck no!" He pulled me into a kiss, sending shock waves through my body. I thought my doubts had left, but I could feel them still creeping into my heart.

Entrée/Entrée
6 JUL 19
IMMIGRA...
- 8 FEB 19
RATION
SERVICE
FEB 1991
36
Visas
B
IMMIGRATION
3 FEB 1999
DAYS
FEB 4 1999
U.S. IMMIGRATION
SFR
MAY 1 7 1999
ADMITTED
CLASS
VISA
TWO
VALID
1999
DATE OF ISSUE
1998-12
4 6 0 5
USA 32
Southern Magnolia
MAGNOLIA GRANDIFLORA
PASSED
PASSED
PASSED
PASSED

32

Zelda

The muscles in my face hurt from smiling. I loved every minute of it.

His hungry eyes watched me everywhere I went in the club. I could feel him strip me mentally, which left my body aching for his touch. His fingers traced my bare back when I saw him, making me feel the fire of lust and leaving me wet with desire.

Edmund kissed the nape of my neck, and I was ready to drop my panties for him.

Clara was surprisingly cuddling close to Tommy, which I didn't expect to happen. She raised her champagne glass to me as Tommy whispered in her ear. I flashed her a devilish grin. Edmund placed his hand into mine and squeezed. I winked at Clara and nodded my head to tell her I was ready to go.

Trying to get everyone to walk toward the elevators was like herding cats. It took us only a short time to get to our floors since the club was inside the hotel. Edmund held my hand, and I watched him in amazement. Andrew held the elevator door for Clara as she said good night to the boys.

"Can you double-check if Bobby is doing okay with Mom?" I asked as I reached for her hand.

She looked at me like I was deranged before she hugged me back. "If there was an issue, Bobby would be calling. Go have fun." She squeezed me tightly before pointing directly to Edmund. "You — condoms!" she responded.

"I can do that." He winked at her before he reached for my waist and pulled me against his chest. The doors closed as the elevator went up one floor. Tommy stood beside us while the rest of the guys had already exited. We ignored him and headed in the direction of Edmund's room.

Edmund barely opened the door before his lips crashed on me with such hunger that I let out a whimper. He lifted me in his hold as my legs wrapped around his waist, then pushed me against the wall. I tasted him, feeling his beard on my skin as my nipples hardened against the thin silk material. It was a rough exploration with unspoken desires. Time became still as our mouths moved together, feeling our taste crash like a supernova. I held his body tight, pressing together as if it bridged the distances we had between us. His eyes met mine again, breaking our kiss as I took a deep breath. The city light's glow from the window shines against his face, and I could feel that magnet he craved for.

"Tell me I can have you." His forehead rested on mine as we panted.

"Have me, Edmund." Our breaths mingled with determination. We were lovers in an irresistible force.

He carried me to bed, and I rested on my knees. Edmund unzipped my dress and pulled it over my head, exposing my white lace panties. My breasts were displayed for him as his hands caressed them with his lips, and my thighs squeezed from his touch.

"Fuck, I just want to look at you." Edmund stepped away, and we gazed into each other's eyes, feeling this fire we had for one another.

The moonlight illuminated half of him like he was slowly creeping out of the darkness. He slipped off his shirt, baring himself in front of me. I felt my heart pound in my chest, feeling this ache in my body wanting him to touch me. With one hand, Edmund unbuckled his belt and pulled it off, then he dropped his jeans and boxers. I bit my bottom lip while he adjusted his impressive hard length.

I couldn't help but admire his sculpted body, as my hands traced the contour of his abs leading to the happy trail. That was when my hand stroked his erection as his forehead rested on mine. He let out a growl, and his hands gripped my waist tight.

"Be a good girl and let me ravish you." He pushed me back down on the bed as he lay on top of me. I could feel him pressed between my thighs.

He trailed kisses along my jawline before he tugged my bottom lip. "I can feel you throbbing for me," he teased before he sucked on my nipple while his hand gripped the other. My body trembled. The glow of the night lingered on us, and I saw a glimpse of his eyes. Fuck, I'd never been horny from someone watching me.

Edmund didn't wait to taste other parts of me. He pulled my panties down and bit my inner thighs lightly. I gripped the edge of the mattress, and he licked my clit. Each stroke touched my soul.

"I missed tasting you and feeling you throbbing against me," he growled. His hands gripped tighter on my waist.

"I'm begging," I breathed. "I need you in me."

"You want me to fuck this pussy like I own it?" Edmund kept teasing me as his tongue licked my clit. He lifted himself, pushing his cock between my legs. He looked like the darkness I pleaded to have.

"Condom?" I bit my bottom lip.

"Fuck yes." He kissed me roughly, then he got up and grabbed one from his nightstand.

"You thought you were going to get laid?" I watched him rip it open with his mouth before stroking himself with the rubber.

"I knew I was going to fuck you till tomorrow, so I bought a big pack."

I squealed as he jumped on top of me.

He pulled my hands away; he gripped my wrists with one of his hands as the other rubbed my clit. Everything became a blur pure of ecstasy. Edmund entered me with such force that I let out a cry of pleasure.

With each thrust, his lips bit my neck softly and my head drove into the pillow. "Fuck, you're so tight." He moaned against his lips as my eyes widened with euphoria. I broke free from his hold and my nails clawed his back as he thrust harder, rough, into me. It was a need. A fixation.

Our souls became one. With every thrust, I felt my heart soar, loving this man more. Edmund cupped my face as my breath hitched, and his eyes darkened with his craving. "I love you." His raspy voice deepened.

My eyes felt this familiar rush of emotion as I stared into his beautiful face. Edmund made me feel an electricity that thundered in my heart.

Our hands intertwined, and I could feel our pulse sync, beating as one. "I love you," I cried to the heavens. "Don't stop kissing me," he demanded as his lips devoured mine. My eyes squeezed shut as my heart quickened and my body jolted as I reached climax. Our tongues crash in a tender collision as the euphoria took hold of my body, feeling my orgasm spread through me as I moaned against his lips.

I tried to catch my breath. "I love you." Nothing mattered in this world. We were connected in ways that would never break. His head dug into my shoulder as he fisted my fingers tightly and released in me. His body shimmered with sweat, and I felt his clammy palms.

Love is not just an emotion; it's a choice. It's to be able to love someone whole through the darkness of moments to the brightest. It's to see them raw and exposed. Edmund allowed me to feel that. I trembled underneath him. He did the same.

I was his, and he was mine.

Edmund's lips dragged along my jawline. He laughed weakly. I couldn't stop staring at him as I brushed his curls away from his face, feeling the sweat on his forehead.

"I want to be able to make love to you like that as often as possible," he said. "God, you're perfect." He lifted himself from me, and my body hummed with adrenaline.

"You're not bad yourself." I winked and watched his naked body displayed in front of me. He discarded the condom before returning to the bed, crawling under the sheets as I did the same. He wrapped his hands around my waist and tugged me against his body.

"Is this what you want?" he asked. "Do you want to be with me? If you need to take a moment, I'll wait for you."

"I wanted someone who looks at me the way you do," I confessed as I traced his bearded jaw. "I wanted someone to think I was worth loving."

"If you let me"—he paused to kiss my neck—"I will love you until my last breath."

THE MORNING ILLUMINATED through the sheer drapes as I watched Edmund sleep. My fingers moved along the hair on his chest down his defined abs where the light danced on his skin. He had hints of freckles and a small birthmark on his rib. My fingers vibrated from his growl.

"Back down, woman," he barked, turning toward me.

After four rounds, our bodies were starved for food. "Is Edmund tired?" I teased as I ran my fingers through his hair.

"Of course, I am." He finally cracked his eyes open. "You had your way with me, Ms. Zelda St. Claire."

"I don't think you complained because, if I'm not mistaken, you said you loved when I was your dirty little slut." I bit my bottom lip, remembering him fucking me from behind as I screamed, then he tugged my hair. It was hot.

Edmund rolled onto me, and I squealed beneath him. "You are my dirty little slut. Especially when you suck my fucking—"

"You're terrible." I pressed my finger to his lips.

Edmund kissed my finger and hung his head. "I don't want to lose you again."

"You won't." I embraced his face.

I HAD to leave before my mom sent a search team. It wasn't a walk of shame because I held Edmund's hand down the hallway. He pushed me against the wall to kiss me every chance he got. We looked like two high school kids. We laughed. We giggled. It was like electricity had been jolted into our hearts.

I swiped my key at the door, but he gripped my waist. "Don't go." He pouted.

"You have set practice, and I need to help with Mom." I smiled at him, feeling my cheeks on fire at how happy I was.

"You're killing me." He winked, then pressed my hand to his heart and kissed each finger.

"I will see you later."

"Bye, darling." Edmund let go and walked backward while I held the door open.

Mom was right. This was a feeling I'd never felt before.

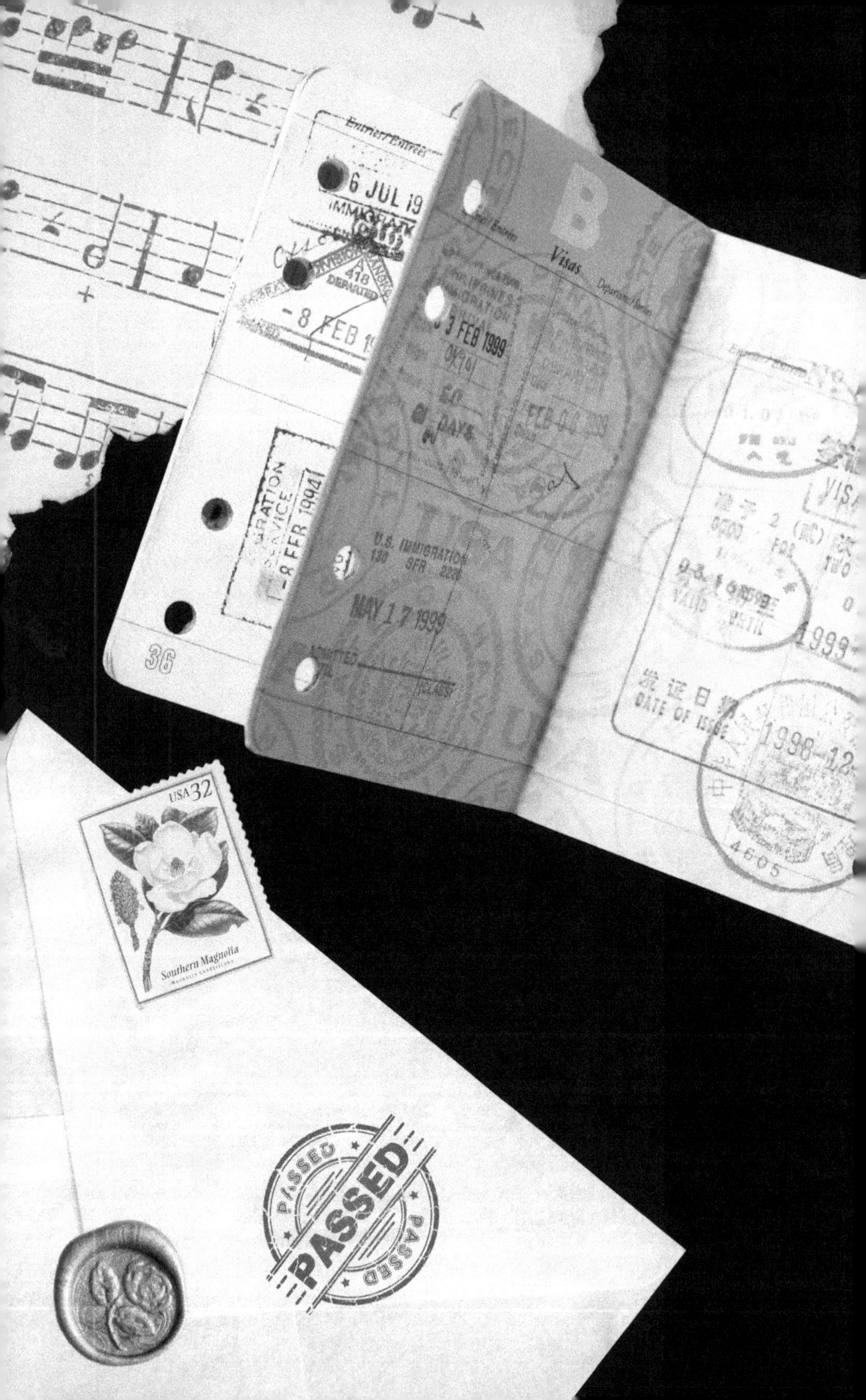
Entrer/Entree
6 JUL 19
IMMIGRATION
418
DEPARTED
- 8 FEB 19
GRATION
SERVICE
FEB 1994
36
Visas
3 FEB 1999
60 DAYS
U.S. IMMIGRATION
130   SFR   2220
MAY 17 1999
U.S. IMMIGRATION
FEB 09 1999
B
VISA
1999
DATE OF ISSUE
1998-12
4 6 0 5
USA 32
Southern Magnolia
PASSED
PASSED
PASSED
PASSED

33

Zelda

Tonight was for Mom, and that was what mattered to me. Clara, Mom, Bobby, and I stood backstage watching Letter to Augustus perform. I watched Edmund sing his heart out from the piano while Tommy got the crowds to roar. We cheered them on from the sidelines. Mom was in her element as she closed her eyes and danced. Bobby stood as close as he could, keeping her strong. Mom managed to hold herself up. She was trying her best not to let us see her weak.

After Bobby told me more stories about Mom and her singing, it killed me that she never got a chance to follow her dream. I didn't want her to lose hope with her lack of strength. That was how I knew I had to make this happen for her.

"You all are truly incredible!" Tommy screamed into the microphone. "But I must stop for a quick second. I have a special guest. There is this woman whose only wish is to get a chance to sing a song onstage." Tommy looked back at us, and Mom froze, but her mouth dropped to the floor. She glanced at us before looking at Tommy.

"What is this?" Mom asked as she looked at me and then back at Bobby. "What did you guys do?"

"Bobby thought it would be good to have a show just for you," I revealed, then I kissed her cheek.

"No! I can't–I'm rusty," she argued, shaking her head aggressively.

"We know that is a lie," Bobby divulged. "You were singing this morning."

"It's different when you're in the shower," she barked.

"I think we need some encouragement, my beautiful people. Can we get a chant going? 'Let's go, Eloise,'" Tommy repeated while the crowd mimicked his words.

"Let's go, Eloise."

"Let's go, Eloise."

"Let's go, Eloise."

Edmund stood from the piano and headed toward my mom. "You ready to take charge of the stage?" Edmund winked at me before reaching for her hand.

Mom stood from her wheelchair, overwhelmed by everything. "I don't know any of your songs," she admitted, breathing heavier.

"It doesn't matter. What song do you want?" he asked. The crowd got louder as Tommy waved for Mom to come onstage.

"Do you know 'Across the Universe'?" Mom requested.

"I do. It's one of my favorites," he said. "Let's get you going."

Mom placed her hand in his. Edmund led her to the stage, holding her waist as she stepped toward Tommy. The backstage crew rushed over to give a stool for her to sit on. The crowd cheered, seeing her beautiful soul. Her light shone then, and I felt Clara holding my hand and Bobby wrapping his arm around my shoulders.

"This is the moment," I cried as the tears welled in my eyes.

"Wow, I was blindsided by this," Mom said into the microphone as Tommy bowed to her. The cheers were still coming but had started to fade.

"I'm dying. I have a couple of weeks or so, and one of my wishes was to attend a music festival. This is cooler." She paused as the crowd cheered. "I didn't think I would get a chance"—Mom peeked at me—"but my beautiful daughter organized this. I will be singing 'Across the Universe.' I sang this song as she fell asleep in my arms." Mom fought the tears. "Hit it, Augustus, make me proud!" Mom looked back at the band as the familiar melody started to play.

Nothing could take away Mom's happiness as she held that microphone. She sang as hard as she could while the band performed. She was stunning performing on that stage. Mom was made to be in the limelight. Deep down, I felt like she could have been a singer if things had been different. She could have been something more. I hope in the multi-universe, she is the biggest star out there.

Mom belted into the microphone as the crowd sang along. The lights dimmed, and I saw this world slowly slipping away from her. But she was still a ray of sunshine bursting through the darkness.

Edmund started to sing with her during the last verse. He walked up to her as the drums began to pick up. The music got louder, and he stood before her as they sang together. I cried into Bobby's chest, and he held me tightly. My world was a mess, but I wouldn't change anything.

The crowds burst into cheers as the band came together, holding my mother's hand with theirs, and bowed simultaneously.

It would forever be my favorite memory of her, with her bright eyes, beautiful smile, and heart exposed to the world.

Sitting backstage, I watched my mom on a high as she kissed Bobby. I couldn't stop smiling. Clara chatted with some worker who helped the band when the guys entered the room. Andrew was the first to come in. We all stood and clapped. Each one walked in, throwing their hands with gratitude, but Edmund was the last one. He walked in slowly toward me, not stopping for anyone other than me. He came up to me with his little devilish smile and pushed my hair behind my ear. I kissed him, wrapping my arms around his neck. I tasted whiskey as he moaned against my lips.

"Baby, I just want to take you back to my room," he growled in my ear, and heat took over my body.

"No screwing in front of us! Especially Zelda's mom!" Tommy announced. Edmund leaned his head back and blew out a breath of frustration.

"I am not a fucking idiot." Edmund's English accent deepened as he rolled his eyes.

"On that note…" Mom stood; she lost her balance, and Bobby caught her. I rushed to his side, but she waved at me. "I'm just tired," she confirmed. "I'm not dying—" She threw her hands up. Then she fainted.

Suddenly, it felt like the world was spinning on a broken record player. I screamed for her, and Bobby cradled her head as Clara ran to call for help. Everything was in slow motion. I felt like I was underwater. "Mom!" I kept calling. "Mom!" I screamed.

Entrée/ Entrée
6 JUL 19
IMMIGRATION
418
DEPORTED
- 8 FEB 19
RATION SERVICE 1994I
36
U.S. IMMIGRATION
180   SFR
MAY 1 7 1999
B
Visas   Departure/Sortie
PHILIPPINES
IMMIGRATION
3 FEB 1999
60
DAYS
FEB-04 1999
VISA
VALID UNTIL
1999
DATE OF ISSUE
1998-12
4605
USA 32
Southern Magnolia
MAGNOLIA GRANDIFLORA
PASSED
PASSED
PASSED

34

Zelda

After the Vegas incident, life was a stream of confusion. Mom was rushed to the hospital. We were told that she was exhausted and we needed to slow down. We were trying so hard to make Mom comfortable. Bobby and I had to make space where she would feel at home. But she insisted hospice was out of the question. Her exact words were, "Hell no, you are not letting me die in one of those places. I want to die near the ocean."

Mom still had her sense of humor, which was good because, let's face it, we didn't.

We didn't have anything.

"Where are we going to find a place? We can't rent and say, 'Hey, my mom wants to die here,'" I joked. Mom had slept all day. We had to go and check on her.

"I mean, we say she accidentally died there." Clara shrugged.

"So when I get sued, how will I hide my mom's illness?" I snapped, feeling frustration overwhelm me.

"Touché." Bobby glanced up from the computer screen.

I cupped my face in my hands. I was juggling a future death, a divorce, and a new relationship. Everything felt like too much.

It didn't help that James was trying to reach out to check on me with everything, from my mom to what I was doing. I had nothing to my name and not much in savings. At the same time, trying to chat with Edmund had been challenging. Either I was busy with Mom, or he was onstage. I hated seeing photos of him with women, but I had to trust him. He told me about the women who kissed him or tried to, and I couldn't hide how much I hated that. I didn't want to be the jealous girlfriend, but I felt so unbalanced.

"Oh, my goodness! I found something!" Clara yelled, her eyes wide.

"What?" Bobby responded.

"Look, I know this is a hospice facility, but it's on the ocean." She turned the screen. It was stunning. The website was filled with pictures of beautiful rooms, perfect ocean views, and paths to walk out.

"I think that fits the saying to go out with style," Bobby said.

"Dad!" I snapped at him. It'd been a couple of days since I started calling him the "d" word. "That isn't funny!"

"It is a little funny." Clara shrugged.

"We are talking about Mom's death. Please. I am unstable," I announced.

"We know," they said in sync.

"Listen. I want the best for Mom too. I want nothing more than for her to have the perfect last day of her life, but I don't have this kind of money," Bobby added.

"We can do a crowd-sourcing page. Like one where we make a sappy video, and people donate," Clara suggested.

"We don't know if they have availability. Or if Mom will go for that —" I felt a stinging in my heart, knowing we were cutting it close.

"Listen." Bobby cut me off as he reached for my hand. "If I have to sell everything I have to make your mom happy, I will. Clara, can you reach out to them and get details? I will see what I can do to get some stuff sold. Zelda, take care of yourself, okay? Focus on you for a minute. Go to sleep. You've been at it all day."

I felt defeated. I had no more tears. "Okay." I took a deep breath, stood, and stretched.

"I'm going to head out. I will get the details tomorrow." Clara stood from the table as she put her laptop in her bag.

"Yeah, I can come by—" I stopped. I remembered suddenly I was supposed to meet James at the apartment. "Shit—the arrangements!"

"Is it your day to go pick up your stuff?" Clara asked. With our lawyers' help, James and I agreed to sell the apartment and give the money back to his parents. I didn't want anything from him. He kept making issues about how much he would have to split, but I insisted I wanted nothing. Clara thought I was crazy, but that meant I was connected to him longer than I wanted to be. I wanted this divorce quick and quiet.

Today, I was supposed to start packing up my stuff from the apartment.

"Yeah! I will meet you after." I gave her a hug.

"No problem. See you, Bobby." Clara waved, then grabbed her stuff and headed toward the front. I kissed Bobby's cheek and squeezed his shoulder before heading to my room.

All I wanted to do was call Edmund and hear him for a moment, but I glanced at the time and knew it was too early for his concert to have started. He was in Los Angeles.

His phone rang once. Twice. Three times. Nothing. I took a moment before texting him.

ZELDA

> Miss you terribly. I can't wait to see you. Call me in the morning. Xx. Have a good concert!

THERE WAS no text back from Edmund at all. I saw he had read the text and found it strange that he didn't reply. I tried to brush it off, but something in my heart stirred up my emotions. It didn't help that I needed to see James. I tried not to think of it as I got myself ready to see James after weeks of no contact.

This was the last thing I wanted to do. I didn't want to face him because I was a coward. But also, I didn't want him to pull me back into what we were before. He kept delaying the divorce papers until he finally signed them this past week. I wanted nothing more than to be free.

I still had my key to the apartment, so I walked into the front entrance. It was still my favorite building I'd lived in. As I headed toward our apartment, I heard music playing inside the apartment. "Fade Into You" was playing, and I caught myself smiling. It was the first song we ever danced to. I knocked on the door two times before it swung open. James looked at me with hopeless eyes.

"Hi," I said.

"Hi." He leaned against the door. He looked as good as ever, but he shaved off all his hair to a buzz cut. He'd let his scruff grow along his chiseled chin, and his dark chocolate eyes were swollen from tiredness.

"Were you up all night?" I stood awkwardly on the threshold.

"Uh…" James exhaled as he rested his head against the door. "I have a lot going on with a big project at the studio."

"I can come another day," I said.

"No, come on in. I was going to leave anyway. To give you space." He moved, and I walked in, noticing the smell of the cologne I bought him a while back. It smelled amazing, and I couldn't help but remember the nights we had hugged each other.

The apartment was in disarray. I was always organized, and he was a tornado without any control. He grew up with someone cleaning up after him.

"Sorry, I didn't get a chance to clean up," he said as I glanced over my shoulder. He rested his hands on his narrow hips, watching me.

"It's okay. I can help out," I replied. It was the least I could do.

"You don't have to pick up the pieces, Zel," he snapped. I turned to him because that bite in his voice was unnecessary.

"I'm trying to help."

"Now? Why don't you go galivant like some groupie?" James narrowed his eyes as anger held them hostage.

"James, listen, I was—"

"I know about your rock star boyfriend, Zelda. You don't think I wasn't going to find out? How long were you with him?"

I knew eventually the truth had to come out. I needed to finally tell him about everything, whether I liked it or not. "I found a letter in the mailbox the first night we moved in. We were just friends until I started to feel things for him."

James swung his hands on his waist as he bit his bottom lip hard.

"Are you kidding me? I did so much for you while you were with that guy?"

"I'm sorry for what I've done, but you are also part of this." I snapped at him, "You pushed me away."

He took a deep breath as he rubbed his hands on his mouth. "I slept with Melody. We've been seeing each other for the past year."

I felt dumbfounded. My lips parted because I couldn't believe what I was hearing. I couldn't be mad at what he was saying, but a part of me was. That was when I caught myself laughing. "We were never meant for each other, James."

"I did love you, Zelda."

"Can we just talk about this another day? I need to focus on Mom. James, I'm trying to do everything for my mom before she dies," I snapped. That was when I felt something I hadn't expected.

James embraced me, swallowing me in his hold. He pulled my hands away from my face, and I cried against his chest. He pulled my arms around his neck while he rested his head against the nape of my neck. I tightened around his hold, feeling like he had a grip on me.

I felt the world crumble around me. The worst part of it all was that I was picturing Edmund holding me tight, telling me it would be okay.

"I'm sorry I caused you pain," I whispered in his ear.

"I had pushed you away and put myself first selfishly. I owe you an apology too. I will always be here, Zelda. Even if it was just a friend in need." James leaned away. I looked up at his brown eyes, but this time, his eyes were swollen with red. He cupped my face. "What do you need for your mom?"

"It's fine. I'll figure it out." I put on a fake smile. "I got this."

"Zelda, you don't have to 'get it' all the time. You're allowed to let the world crumble. We all do."

I released myself from his hold and took a deep breath. "I'm going to get some of my stuff."

"Don't," James begged. "You always run away."

"Because that's me. I am good at running!" I snapped.

"You can't keep running because, eventually, there isn't any place left to hide."

I stood there, not accepting what he'd said but knowing in my heart it was the truth. "I-I need to head home. Bobby needs a break, and I need to go in for the second shift." I swallowed hard. All my strength had left me. Before he could continue, I walked into the hallway.

My pocket vibrated as Edmund finally called me. I wanted to talk to him, but not in front of James. I glanced back over my shoulder as James moved to the couch. I reached our bedroom and answered the phone.

"Babe, I'm so sorry! My phone went missing last night, and I couldn't call you!"

"I can't talk." I was annoyed because he could have used any of the other guys' phones, but I brushed it off.

"Everything fine?"

"No." I hung up on Edmund without saying bye. I couldn't deal with him, not when I was with James. Quickly grabbing my bags and everything I needed, I walked toward the living room to see James's sketching.

"I'm heading out now," I announced. He stood and watched me. He didn't come toward me again, though, nor did he try to give me another hug. He looked frozen, watching me.

"Okay," he said. "If you need anything, please give me a shout."

I gave a small smile.

"For better or for worse, right?" he guffawed.

"I'm sorry for breaking your heart. I wish I was the woman you had wanted, but I can't be that. I can't be the woman who does everything for everyone."

James shut his mouth. "Just don't let this new guy walk all over you."

"I won't."

USA 32
Southern Magnolia
PASSED

35

Zelda

The following morning, I woke up to my phone buzzing on my side table. I glanced at the screen to see Edmund was calling. He tried to contact me last night, but I didn't want to talk to anyone. I wanted to hide under my covers. After James, I was emotionally drained. Regardless, I had put on a smile and helped Mom while Bobby had to go deal with selling some property to get the money for the hospice place.

Mom was not herself last night. She was out of it and in pain. I had to call her nurse to come back so we could give her more medication. Bobby rushed home. We both thought it was the end because the nurse mentioned her oxygen levels were dropping. I couldn't handle the thought of it all ending. But miraculously, her lungs pulled through, and she was back to her old self.

"Hello." My morning voice was muffled by the blanket over my face.

"Babe, can I see you?" Edmund asked. Before I could respond, I heard FaceTime beeping, and I brought the phone away from my ear. "There is my beautiful girl," he said, lying in bed. His curly hair was a mess, and his beard seemed thicker.

"How much did you drink last night?" I asked.

"A lot." He rubbed his face. "I'm so fucking tired."

"You're tired? My mom almost died last night," I snapped. I shouldn't have gotten mad, but I was annoyed. This past week, he was either drunk when he called or too busy to contact me.

"Sorry, Zelda. You don't have to snap at me. I get you're going through it with your mom."

"Going through it?" I sat up. "I didn't know my mom's death was a stage."

"You know what I mean, Zelda. Stop putting words in my mouth."

"Really? Ever since Las Vegas, all you do is drink and do drugs! I haven't heard you sober in a long time!"

"You know I would drop this all to be there for you, Zel! I told you! I love you."

I watched him as he sat up on his bed, bare chest exposed in the video. "I can't do this right now. I have to come up with money for Mom's hospice place that I don't have. So go back to fucking groupies and doing drugs!" I was bitter and regretted it the minute I said it. His eyes narrowed at me.

"You think that little of me? That I would do that to you? You're it for me, Zelda. You are the only one I love in this world. I will be your punching bag but don't shut me out. I'm sorry I've been distant this week. I promise to be here, no matter what!"

"You're not," I cried. "You're not! You read my text!"

"My phone was stolen, Zelda. I'm sorry."

"I can't do this right now. I need to go."

"Do you love me?" Edmund snapped. "Did you mean what you said that night? I promised you I would never walk away from this. You can go and do everything on your own, but I'm right here."

I ran out of tears, so I took a deep breath. "Edmund, have a good show tonight. We'll talk later." I hung up on him and threw the phone on the bed. I didn't need to deal with all this. I needed to walk away.

～

"I can't believe it!" Bobby was cupping his mouth with his hands while Clara beamed from ear to ear. They both were in the kitchen when I walked in. I still had bed hair, pajamas, and lacked coffee.

"This is too cheerful," I said.

"We got a room!" Dad yelled. "We got the money! We got a room! We are leaving next week. Zelda, Mom will get her last wish!"

"What—wait. How?" I threw my hands up. "How did this happen?" I glanced at Clara, confused.

Clara's smile disintegrated the minute she said, "James."

"What? No! I don't want anything from James!" I felt guilty about what I'd done and how we messed up. The last thing I wanted from him was his money. "Unacceptable!"

"James knew you would say no. He arranged it all."

Without waiting, I reached for my keys, grabbed my shoes, and headed out the door. I needed him to take it back. I didn't want it.

Anger poured out of my body. I felt guilty. James still cared, but I didn't know what his endgame was. Rushing up through the entrance to our apartment, still wearing my pajama shorts and an oversized sweater, I banged on his door as loud as I could.

James swung open the door. "Why!" I snapped. "Why are you helping? Why? Is this a romantic thing? To win me over? To hurt me?" Anger took over as I yelled at him.

"No! It's not like that," James confessed. "I owe you," he responded.

"Owe me? Are you kidding? For what?"

"When I sold your artwork," he said. "That piece and the collection. We made a lot of money. I decided to give it back to you. That was your property. I didn't ask for your permission. I figured this would be my way to make amends for my wrongdoing."

I watched him, completely defeated.

"I told you, for better or for worse, even if we are divorcing. I will help you through the dark."

I didn't know what to say to him. Instead, I wrapped my arms around his waist and held him as tight as I could. It wasn't longing; it was a lifeline I'd been handed. My life was being derailed. I needed to survive.

"I know we aren't together, but I took those vows seriously. For better or for worse. Always." I lifted my face and watched his eyes darken in the low light of the room. My lips parted, wishing to speak, to say something, but all I could do was watch him. Here he was trying to save whatever we were, but I was jumping.

"I need to go," I said, slipping out of his grip. I still felt his heat against my hand as I glanced back.

"I know I can't compete with the guy you're in love with," he confessed, "but even though you have another in your heart, you're still in mine." James exhaled, rubbing his chin. "Let me know about your mom."

Biting my bottom lip, I ran my hand through my hair, swallowed my pride, and headed out of the apartment. I tried to be the bigger person, but I was drowning. This was a mess, and nothing made sense, but everything happened for a reason.

Entrées/Entrees
6 JUL 19
8 FEB 19
B
Visas
PHILIPPINE S.O.
IMMIGRATION
3 FEB 1999
FEB
60 DAYS
U.S. IMMIGRATION
SFR
MAY 1 7 1999
RATION
FEB 1994
36
DATE OF ISSUE
1998
4605
USA 32
Southern Magnolia
MAGNOLIA GRANDIFLORA
PASSED
PASSED
PASSED

Edmund

"Take some cocaine for the emotions you're dealing with."

I couldn't remember what day it was, sitting backstage after another show. The nonstop performances, faces, and crowds were ripping my self-control on my emotions. Every day was on repeat, so I needed something to take the edge off. I fought the urge as long as I could, but I finally gave in.

Awakened by the demons and temptations, I thought I had the self-control not to allow those monsters to take over, but fighting for so long, my inner thoughts begged me to give up.

One of the groupies was setting lines on the table while Tommy waited to partake. I held my beer as my foot twitched, thinking about taking a bump. I'd been good with minor temptations here and there, but there it was again. In front of me. Calling for me.

"Fuck yeah," I said.

Andrew walked in with some guy next to him while one of the twins tapped away on the furniture, getting the women eager. It didn't take much to get Andrew pissed with what I'd been doing. But when he watched me as I went back on the couch, I knew I'd fucked up the feeling of freedom, the silence in my head, and the peace I was beginning to have.

"The fuck, Eddie? What are you doing?" Andrew sat on the couch. I stared at the ceiling.

"I'm exhausted; I needed an upper," I revealed. I needed to keep focus. All I'd been doing was keeping afloat, feeling alone in a hotel every night.

"That's not a fucking upper. That's a drug. One that is addictive with your fucking personality," he said matter-of-factly. I felt like half a man, barely capable of fighting for what was right in my life. This spiral I was in was a bomb, destroying everything around me.

"Listen, I won't do more," I pleaded.

"Better not! You have such a good fucking life right now. Why ruin everything?" Andrew reached for my face, squeezing my cheeks. My eyes finally met his.

"Why can't you worry about the other guys?" I said, pushing his hand off my face. His eyes squinted with pain. I was pushing my limits, but that was what I did. I always ruined good things.

"You are my family." His thick accent was defined. "You are my brother. I don't want to bury another friend."

I thought about what he said as I rubbed my face. "It's been too much lately."

"Have you chatted with your girl?"

Zelda.

I felt like an asshole. She tried to talk to me, but I kept pushing her away. I didn't know why I was doing it. I wanted to speak to her and hear her voice, but lately, I felt a darkness over me. I had a perfect girl, and I was fucking it up.

"No." She called me daily and sent texts and voice notes, but I gave her short answers.

"You need to go to your room. Go fucking talk to her before one of these groupies decides to suck your dick," Andrew snapped.

I shook my head as I stood. "I'm going to call her."

Walking out into the hallway, I reach for my phone as I tried to find a spot to call her. It was one in the morning, she was asleep, but I figured she would talk. It rang twice before she answered.

"Hey." Her soft voice was captivating. I could picture her sleeping with her hair tossed and her lips parted because she was a mouth breather. We would joke about the puddle of saliva on the pillow. I loved the shit out of her.

"Baby, I'm sorry to wake you."

"No! I wanted to hear from you. I missed you so much. I'm sorry that I've been so mad lately. Figured you were annoyed or —"

"Never. It's never your fault, my love. I'm sorry I've been terrible toward you. I'm exhausted from touring."

"Saw the ladies all over you, again…yesterday." Her tone was disappointed and cold.

"Yeah, about that…" Some women at a club had jumped me for a photo, which was annoying, but I did it. "Babe, it wasn't anything."

"Edmund, I know that. I know you wouldn't do anything. It's just weird."

I bit my lip and leaned my head against the wall. I watched people pass by in the hallway. "Can I see you?" I asked.

It was two seconds before I saw her face, saw her beauty that I miss so much. I wanted to hold her in my arms. I slid down against the wall. I cradled her in my hands, watching her lie in her bed.

"What I would do to you if I was there…" I licked my bottom lip. I could feel my pulse pump faster at the thought of her naked body.

"I see someone has hooded eyes again." Zelda widened her smile, and I adored her at that moment. Her smile was something out of this world. She improved my days with her fire. I wanted to soak it up. Lately, we'd been so distant that I barely got a chance with her.

"Is it that type of conversation? Because I should head back to my room then."

"No. I can't right now."

I pouted. "I guess I have to think of that sweet puss —"

"Edmund!" My eyes widened. "My walls are thin, and my parents are nearby."

"Why aren't you wearing your headphones?" I shook my head. "Silly woman."

"I forgot to charge them."

"Typical."

"I need to talk to you about something." Her face became serious. I took a deep breath. "What's going on?"

"Uh…" She paused and sat up. She ran her hand through her hair. "You remember the hospice place that we found?" she asked.

"Yeah, I was going to pay for it, but you said no. Do you want me to do it?" I asked. It was pricey. The advance payment I received for the tour was enough to cover it and then some.

"About that…" She released a breath. "James paid for it."

I was bewildered by her comment, pinching the bridge of my nose. "James did what?" I hoped I hadn't heard her correctly.

"I didn't ask him to. He talked to Clara and did it behind my back. I went to him and —"

"You went to him? What to thank him?"

"No. It wasn't like that, Edmund." She was frustrated. I was mad because I knew what he was doing. He wanted her back. If something like that would help, he would do it. James was playing dirty. He didn't care about her mother. Out of the time he'd known about the cancer, he didn't once attempt to help. I felt the bitterness overtake my thoughts.

"Am I supposed to be okay with it?"

"Yeah, because it's not what you think. I am yours. Why would I be running to him?"

"I offered to pay for your mom! You said no!"

"Because this isn't a transactional relationship, Edmund. I don't need you to give me money."

"We are together. I love you. I would do anything for you, Zelda. I am here for the long run, yet in comes Prince Charming to save the fucking day."

"Don't you dare do that!" she whisper-yelled. "I can't keep fighting with you. We barely speak. You're too busy partying, drinking, and having women all over you."

"Is that the real reason you took the money? Because I'm on the road, sleeping around? You think that's what I'm doing?" I bit back.

"No, I don't know what to do right now." I felt like I was losing the one thing I wanted more than life.

"What do you mean?"

Her eyes filled with tears, and she tried not to look at me. "Zel, look at me! What are you trying to say?"

"How can we keep going? I'm slowly sinking into this uncontrollable storm, needing you to save me, and you're chasing your dreams. I can't ask you to give that up."

"Do you want me to leave? I would do anything for you, Zelda. I would drop all this for you."

"I wouldn't want you to," she cried, covering her mouth.

My heart felt tighter. She had squeezed the life I had left out of me. "Don't end us, Zelda. Look how long it took to get us here. We are meant to be with each other. You are the only thing that matters to me. I would run away from all of this to have you."

"I know you would." She let the tears fall. "That is why I think we aren't supposed to be together. Why is it that every chance we get, something pulls us apart?"

"Don't say that."

"It's true, Edmund. Whenever we get a chance, the world flips over, and we can't be together. I love you, but I think I can't love you, like I'm not allowed to."

I hit my head against the wall so hard, pain ravaged my body. "I finally have you, Zel. We can make this work."

"Edmund." She shook her head. "How can we? I think about the letter I got and wish so hard that life wasn't so complicated, that we could be together. But I don't know how to be a part of your life."

"Stop! Just stop! I can't deal with this right now, Zelda." My anger took control. "Fine, go back to playing house with James and pop out some babies while you're a doormat. Go back to what you wanted so badly. You craved me when you were with him. You wished you had that freedom."

"I am not with him, Edmund. I would never go back to him! This is not fair! I can't keep feeling like I'm an inconvenience for you!"

"That's not fair? You're running away. You're scared of falling."

"No, I'm scared that if you decide to give it up, your demons will take over, and you will hate me."

If that wasn't a blow to the heart, I don't know what was. She knew my demons. I fought them every day, but to use that as a reason for why I would hate her? "Fine. Goodbye."

I didn't let her finish before I whipped my phone against wall across from me.

"Fuck!" I screamed as loud as I could, my rage echoing through the hallway. The only thing that would help me at this moment was the bottle of whiskey.

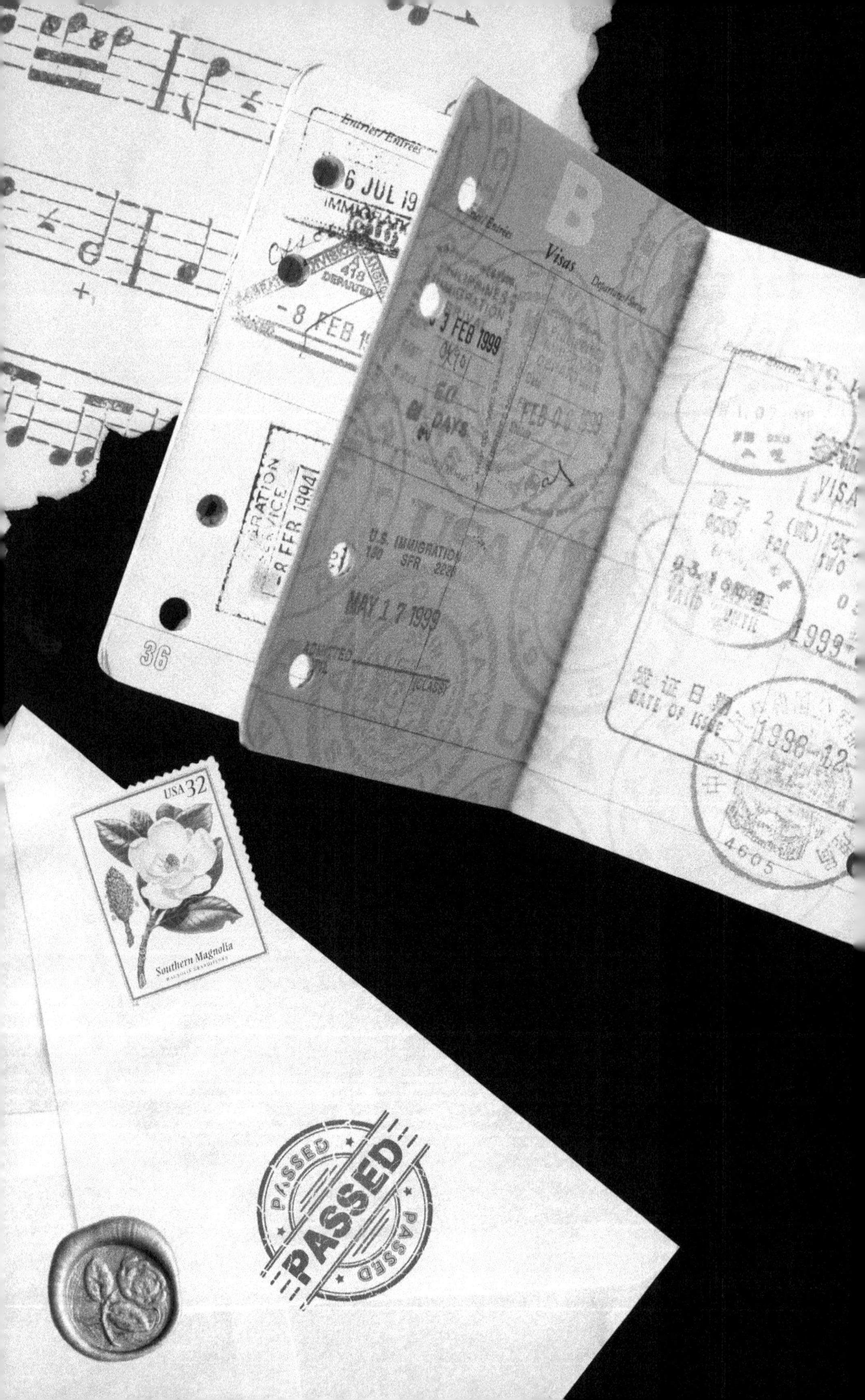
Entrée/Entree
6 JUL 19
IMMIGRAT
418
DEPARTED
-8 FEB 19
RATION
R FEB 1994
SERVICE
36
B
Visas
Departure/Sortie
PHILIPPINES
IMMIGRATION
3 FEB 1999
60
DAYS
FEB 06 1999
U.S. IMMIGRATION
SFR
MAY 17 1999
ADMITTED
CLASS
VISA
1999
入国
DATE OF ISSUE
1998-12-
4605
USA 32
Southern Magnolia
MAGNOLIA GRANDIFLORA
PASSED
PASSED
PASSED
PASSED

37

Zelda

When it rains, it pours.

"Listen, I'm okay with you listening to Celine Dion, but please don't butcher her songs," Mom snarled as she sat up on the sofa. Dad came out of the kitchen with two cups of coffee, and I dragged myself out of my bedroom.

Since my breakup with Edmund, my world had been in shambles. I'd listened to sad playlists repeatedly to make me feel better, but it didn't help. Even the romance novels I'd managed to crack open only made me want to cry harder.

Note to self: don't read sappy love books with happy endings.

"Do you want whiskey in your coffee?" Bobby asked as he sat in the uncomfortable egg chair. That chair came with us everywhere we went. It was the first piece of furniture we had managed to buy. He looked like he was trying every position to get himself settled, yet every time he moved, a squeak released.

"Listen." Mom squeezed the bridge of her nose. "You're dumb. I don't understand why you decided to end things."

"It's a lot right now, Mom. I have to deal with you and with James and—"

"I'm dying," she said. "I'm literally on my deathbed, and you're here leaving a man who loves you! He's gone through the trenches to make it work."

"I know James isn't your cup of tea, and I know we have end—"

"I'm not talking about James." She slapped her hands against her lap. "You know exactly who I'm talking about."

My mom was filled with rage. "Mom, our lives are complicated. I've tried to make it work, but things don't work every time we try. The universe is saying no!"

"You're just scared. That's all it is. You're scared of truly losing yourself to real love and not the organized one that is cookie-cutter."

"I'm terrified of allowing the unknown. I can't be like that! Like you!" I cracked. The words slipped out, and I regretted them instantly. Bobby sat shaking his head as Mom took a deep breath. "I'm sorry!"

"No..." She waved her hand. "You made your bed. I get it. I lived paycheck to paycheck. It was embarrassing to be a stripper or when we had to sleep in a car! That night under the stars, I told you that you better love someone who truly loves you and not allow yourself to be a shadow. You don't know how hard it was to be used all the time for men's pleasure. Men never wanted a washed-up woman with baggage.

"I wanted to give you a better life. I made terrible mistakes along the way, but I tried my best to make you the person you are today."

I fought the tears but couldn't stop at seeing her anger. I was in the wrong. "Mom, it isn't like that. I loved my childhood; it was imperfectly perfect. Sometimes I wished it had been stable. I hated that you had to work so hard."

"If we live our life in a box, we are living six feet under. You're terrified of the unknown. Any time you go a little bit off course, you shut down. I can't let you go on like that because you will be no different from me." Her frail body suddenly had some color.

"Mom, stop talking like that." I couldn't hold it in any longer. I rushed to her side, and she pulled me into her chest.

"I'm going to run out of oxygen one day, and Bobby will be here. The sun will still shine, but I need you to take a chance, baby girl." Mom pushed my hair away from my face. "There is a reason you got that letter." She kissed my temple.

"Mom, I think everything is too tough right now, and I need to figure it all out." I flashed her a fake smile, but I knew it was not what she wanted. She knew all my secrets, all my desires, and the look that she had in her eyes was devastating.

Bobby forced me out of the house that night because he wanted a night free of sappy music. I called Clara to crash at her place, but she was busy, so I was heading to my favorite place in the world—the bookstore.

Walking the streets, I listened to Letters to Augustus and scrolled their socials. I wished I had him in my arms. I wished I had never broken his heart. He had not messaged me back since our conversation, but I saw that there were posts of women on his lap and another woman kissing him.

I messaged my future *ex*-husband.

I saw him sitting at the bar, drinking an old-fashioned. I headed up to him, hoping to talk. "Real Love Baby" played through the bar speakers while people conversed in their own world. I held tight to the strap of my purse, feeling nervous as I tapped James's shoulder. He turned to look over his shoulder. He flashed his typical smile, the one that was comforting in times of need.

"Zel," he said as he spread his arms out, letting me embrace him. Wrapping my arms around his neck, I felt a stableness I'd always wanted. James kissed my cheek as I tried to move away from him.

"Uh... James, hey," I said. I scratched my head, trying to understand what to do next.

"You can sit." He patted a stool, and I flashed him a small smile. Taking off my jacket, I hung it onto one of the hooks under the bar while I straddled the seat next to him.

"I'm glad you called me. I've been wanting to check in but didn't know what to do, to be honest," he confessed.

"It's been hard lately. I mean, with Mom and Edm—" I regretted his name leaving my lips. He haunted me, even his name made me think about him. My judgment was clouded by him, which led me to believe that I may have made a mistake in letting him go.

James sucked in a deep breath before he sipped his drink. "You two still okay?"

I was undecided if I wanted to tell him that I ended it with Edmund. I saw it in his eyes, hungry to take advantage of the situation.

Being with someone, you get to understand who they are over time. James always had to be right. As much as he was kindhearted, he had to always come out on top. That was one characteristic I had concluded that I never loved about him.

"We are taking a break. I need to deal with Mom and our..." I paused, looking at him as he cradled his drink in his hand. He glanced down at the amber liquor and rubbed his chin.

"Are we calling it quits? Are we truly ending it? What you did... anyone else would be extremely pissed off."

"I'm not asking for you to take me back. I wanted to talk because everything happening has been stressful. What you did for my mom... I don't understand why."

"I told you. I did it because I care. I still have feelings for you, Zelda. Even if I'm starting to feel for Melody." He shot back his drink and slammed it against the walnut lacquered bar top.

"I'm sorry for all that I've done. I didn't mean to do it."

"Why did you?"

I paused, thinking about it all, wondering how to answer him. "I can't really answer that. I don't know."

"That's the coward in you," he said.

"Pardon?" I asked. "Why would you say that to me? I'm not a coward, James. Everything was too in control with you. I never could breathe," I snapped, causing others to notice.

"Zelda, relax—" He reached for my hand, but I pulled away.

"This." I stood from the chair. "This is why I didn't want to stay. This is the reason you made me feel completely and utterly useless. I could never be on your level. You wanted me to be a trophy wife to you," I continued.

"Please stop making a scene," James responded.

"Right there!" I pointed at him. "This is why I went for Edmund."

I turned away from him, reassured that I'd never return.

38

Zelda

After over twenty hours in the car with Clara, we arrived at the hospice center with Mom's favorite items, including the ugly egg chair. This place was like a dream in the Coral Cove, near the Florida Keys.

It was filled with color and small-town charm. Mom and Bobby flew in with her nurse because driving was out of the question. However, Clara and I had a much-needed road trip filled with memories, singing, and too many shakes.

"This place has some yummy views," Clara said as she put her sunglasses on. I watched her while I saw several workers pull stuff out of a truck.

"Well, he's definitely yummy," I teased, tapping away on the steering wheel.

"The biggest hit in the US is a band from the UK; here are Letters to Augustus," the deejay on the radio announced.

Clara reached for the volume, but I tapped her fingers. "It's okay."

"Have you heard from him lately?" Clara asked.

I shook my head. "No, we haven't spoken since that night," I replied.

Ever since the talk with James, both have been silent. In the past week, Mom slowly disappeared. We had a meeting with the nurse about the status of Mom. Her nurse, Lisa, indicated she didn't have many days left. I tried not to think of the end, but it was hard. I wanted nothing more than to spend this time with my mom. I didn't want to lose the one person I love deeply. I tried to convince myself that my world was not crumbling because one of us had to keep strong in the darkness.

"I'm trying my best to live life without thinking of men right now," I admitted as anxiety crept over my heart.

"Zel, whatever you do, I will be there." She gripped my hand tightly and flashed a weak smile.

Coral Cove Hospice was on the coast. Tree arched above the road heading to a colonial mansion. There was a fountain right in the middle of the driveway, with an entrance filled with greenery, feeling a sense of calmness. Around the main building, little homes on the property were dedicated for the patients to live in until their passing. Expensive was an understatement. Luxury cars parked were perfectly lined up. This place was for rich people to die.

It didn't take long to figure out where my mom was located because she was blasting Fleetwood Mac from her little house. We brought our suitcases and left the chair for Bobby to bring in. Lisa came out the door.

"Hey." She closed the door and walked toward me.

"How was the flight with my mom?" I asked, placing my bag down.

"About that..." She looked uneasy. "Zelda, she's not doing well. She's weak, and we had a scare today."

"What do you mean?" I asked.

"Her oxygen levels dropped dramatically upon arrival. We got them stable once we placed an oxygen mask to help increase her levels. She's excited to see you." She reached for my hand. "I'm going to check in with the doctor's office in the main house. I will be right back."

I nodded before heading into the house. I couldn't comprehend how the place looked, so I rushed to my mom. She sat in the living room with the sliding doors open. Music played while Bobby put some stuff away.

"Why didn't you call me? Why didn't I know," I snapped. Mom looked like a ghost with her skin becoming blue. Her hair was discolored, and her body was disappearing at a rate I couldn't comprehend. I felt scared.

"She didn't want that," Bobby responded.

Mom pulled the mask off her face. "It was a little thing. Don't make it a big deal." She sounded out of breath as she spoke.

"Little thing? Lisa said you almost died! I wasn't around," I snapped. Clara came into the space and dropped the bags.

"Clara, I told you"—Mom paused to take a breath in the mask—"to do something with her. You should have brought her back to her boyfriend."

"I'm not getting into this," Clara replied as she walked toward Bobby.

"No, Mom, you are my focus right now. No one matters in this world except you!"

Mom rolled her eyes. "Zelda." She pulled my hand as I sat on the stool next to her, struggling to speak. "You are my world." She smiled as she pressed her hand against my cheek. Her skin was translucent, and her eyes were set deep. The spirit she'd had for years had slipped away. She was skin and bones, lying there. I'd tried hard these past months not to look at her too closely and not to see her bones or how hollow she looked. I tried my best to keep her image of what I remembered. How she looked singing all those late nights as I was a child when we'd jump on beds and have movie nights. It was us against the world, and nothing else mattered. But she begged me to leave, pushing me away during her final days.

"Don't worry." She breathed through the oxygen mask. She could barely speak.

"Mom"—I pressed my lips on her forehead—"I'm going to be here until your last minute on this earth. I'm not leaving you. You hear me?"

Her eyes were heavy. "Okay." She squeezed my hand tight. "Did you bring the egg chair?" she muffled in the mask. I let out a little laugh.

That chair will be in her will.

~

NIGHT HAD FALLEN, and I pulled a bottle of wine out and walked to the beach. Clara had passed out, so I didn't want to wake her. I was a tad tipsy because I needed an escape. Crashing onto the sand, I felt the waves tickle my toes before they sucked back into the abyss. I wished I could take all the pain away. A cool breeze hit my face, and I tugged my sweater closer.

I cradled the phone in my hand, hovering over the one phone number I was begging to call. It felt like such a heavy pull that I couldn't handle it. That was when I did something I would regret.

I called Edmund.

It rang twice before I heard a voice, not his, but a girl's voice answering.

"Hello?" She was annoyed.

I couldn't speak. "Uh…"

"Hello?" she asked again.

A tear slipped down my cheek this time. "Uh…is Edmund there?"

"Eddie? No? Is this that woman who dumped him? Listen, I'm taking care of him now. Fuck off!" She hung up.

I took a deep breath and released it as I let the tears pour. This could be the universe saying I shouldn't have attempted it.

"So fucking dumb!" I cried, screaming as loud as I could. The roar of the waves muffled my voice.

I finished the bottle and looked at my phone. Some social media caught my attention when I landed on James. It could've been the intoxication, but I did the second worst thing a person could do and called my ex.

James picked up after one ring.

"Hey," James answered.

"Why didn't you focus on me instead of your art? Why did you always concentrate on pleasing everyone else besides me?

"It's late. Can we talk about this later?" James sounded tired.

"No! I want to know! Why did you make it so complicated? I needed you when I quit my job, when I didn't know what life was to bring for me. I needed that!"

"You had your boyfriend to help with that," he replied bitterly.

"Don't play that card. This was before him. You cared about yourself and not me. Never me. I was always the second best to your dreams."

"Zelda, you're drunk. You need sleep."

"No, I needed you!" I regretted those words. I couldn't take them back. But maybe life was about compromising. Nothing was like romance stories where everything was so perfect. No book boyfriend would pick your ass up in a moment of weakness and save you.

"What are you saying, Zel? You want to try again?"

"Yeah. Let's start again."

Entrée/Entrée
6 JUL 19
IMMIGRATION
418
- 8 FEB 19
RATION
SERVICE
8 FEB 1991
36
B
Visas
Departure/Sortie
PHILIPPINES
IMMIGRATION
3 FEB 1999
OK 191
DAYS
PHILIPP
CLARK
FEB 04 1999
U.S. IMMIGRATION
130   SFR   222
MAY 1 7 1999
ADMITTED
CLASS
VISA
1999
DATE OF ISSUE
1998-12
4605
USA 32
Southern Magnolia
MAGNOLIA GRANDIFLORA
PASSED
PASSED
PASSED
PASSED

39

Zelda

Mom wanted nothing more than to see the universe. That was what I would give her before it was too late. I arranged a night out in the sand, and Bobby helped me set it up as dusk settled in the sky. Lisa said it could be any day, and I didn't want to think of it. I wanted to spend more time with her. But I knew that everything was coming to an end. I would try my best to make it a night where she got to see the universe.

"Had a rough night?" Bobby sat next to me. I pressed my hands to my face. I tried to make this picnic amazing. We had a bunch of pillows, food, and her favorite movie set up on a projector. I tried to make this night perfect, but all I thought about was what was in my head.

"What gave it away?" I placed the bowl of chips on the table.

He shook his head and reached for his pack of smokes.

"That can kill you." I said matter-of-factly.

"Yeah, everything kills in this world." He scratched his salt-and-pepper bearded chin. "Life is like that. Everyone is going to die." He seemed pale and weak. Everything was too much to handle.

"Are you okay?" I asked.

He licked his bottom lip. "Did your mom tell you about how she met me?" he asked.

"Yeah. High school and it was about—"

"No, how I really met her?" he interrupted.

I shook my head in response.

He smiled as he scratched his head. "She was at a drive-in. I saw her in another car with another guy." He let out a snicker. "I saw her, and I knew I wanted her so bad. I wanted her in my life. I didn't care how or when, but I knew she made me feel like no other person in this world would ever make me feel. I met other women. I've been with others…" He paused. "It's funny how that works. You can be with others, but something about that one person changes the world for you."

I smiled, but I couldn't hold back the tears. "I'm sorry you didn't get more time with her."

"I'm sorry too. I wish you could have her forever, my sweet girl. And I'm sorry I wasn't there for you all these years, but I'm not leaving you. I'm not going to break any promises. I'm here until my last breath. You understand?"

I nodded, crossing my arms against my chest.

"I know you talked to James last night," he said.

"What?" I shot him a confused looked. "How?"

"Honey, the front desk contacted me this afternoon asking for authorization for him to come by today. I said fine, seeing as how I guessed you asked him to be here." He lit his cigarette.

"I'm going to give it another chance." I gave him the answer I knew was right for me.

"Why?" he snapped. "Why him? When I saw you with Edmund—"

"Edmund and I can never be, Dad. I can't be with him because we're too complicated. We're an atomic bomb together."

"Your mom and I were a supernova. I wouldn't want anything else in this world. Why wouldn't you want that?"

"Because I'm scared! Life can't always be a supernova life."

Bobby took a deep breath as he looked out at the ocean. "It's your choice, Zelda, but you're making a big mistake."

~

WITH THE HELP of Lisa and Bobby, we blindfolded Mom and carried her to our night picnic. Clara filmed the entire experience as I blasted "I Will Always Love You" from my mom's favorite movie, *Bodyguard*.

"Is Whitney singing?" Mom cheered as loud as she could from the arms of my dad. He gave her a kiss on her cheek, and I took her blindfold off.

"What is this?" She leaned her head against my dad's chest. "All for me?"

"Yeah, Mommy." I reached for her, holding the tears back as I kissed her cheek. Dad placed her on the giant pillows turned chair we made for her. I stood next to the projector while Clara poured drinks. Lisa tried to get Mom comfortable as she checked her vital signs. The wind settled, and the stars were brighter than ever. It was perfect.

"Hello, everyone," I said as everyone took their seats. As I was about to continue, I looked out toward the house and saw James standing on the porch. He looked boyish and shy. I stood frozen.

"What is she looking at?" Mom whispered.

Dad whispered back, "James is here."

"Not Edmund?" She tried to hide what she said, but Clara and I made eye contact.

"Who invited him?" Clara asked.

"I did," I responded as I flashed a smile and waved at James.

"Oh, for the love of God. Even on my death night, I must go out with drama?" Mom shook her head. I flashed her a dirty look, but she frowned. I didn't want to displease her, but she saw what I was doing. She knew all too well that I had to do this. To make my life proper.

James walked over to us, pulling his hoodie down. His hands were in his pockets as he walked toward me and kissed my cheek. "Thank you for coming."

"You needed me. I'm here."

"Take a seat next to me." Clara patted the pillow next to her.

"Welcome to our night-time showing of one of mom's favorite movies, *Bodyguard*. Bobby, Mom still loves Kevin Costner. I wanted to do this because we would watch this together religiously." I took a deep breath before continuing. "So let us enjoy every minute we have left with you. I love you." I wiped my tears as I watched my mom blow me a kiss.

Everyone giggled as I started the movie. I sat next to Mom while Bobby held her in his arms. She rested her head against his chest. She reached for my hand, and I held her.

"Remember"—Mom took a deep breath—"I used to force you to sing this while we cleaned?"

"Yes, and unfortunately, this song was played at every event I ever went to," I teased.

"It's the best song ever. I'm telling you."

I kissed her head and sat closer to her. James chatted with Clara, and I didn't want to leave Mom. I didn't want to focus on him.

As the movie continued, I glanced at Lisa to make sure to see Mom's vitals were doing decent on the portable machine. Lisa shook her head, which let me know they were dropping. I tried to hold it together. I needed it to. But I couldn't.

"Zel?" Mom called for me, and I leaned into her.

"You comfy? Do you need anything?" I asked.

"No, I have everything I need. You checked off my last bucket list item." Her eyes were glossy, and her lips were blue. She took slower breaths, and I tried not to think about what was happening. I fought every bone in my body not to let her see my tears because I wanted her to be happy.

"I did. I made sure we did it all." I squeezed her hand.

"But I want you to do one thing for me. If you can," she said as I glanced up at Bobby who was in tears, knowing that she was coming to her end.

"One day, you will stumble upon a message from a guy who wanted to have something with you. Who truly wanted to be with *you*. Please answer that letter?" She smiled.

"Okay, I will. I love you, Mom."

"I will always love you last."

I held her hand as long as I could, and we watched the film. The tightest of her grip slowly loosened, and Lisa reached for me. I knew what she was going to say. I knew what she was going to tell me.

My mom was gone. She had left me and headed to the stars. Looking at her with her eyes closed, I screamed.

"Mommy! Mommy, no!" I cried, reaching for her. "I'm not ready!

Please come back! Please come back to me!" Bobby reached for me as I hugged her as long as I could. I couldn't let her go just yet. I couldn't let go of my star, not even if she was meant to align with the rest of the universe.

Entrées/Entries
6 JUL 19
IMMIGRATION
418
DEPARTED
-8 FEB 19
RATION
SERVICE
FEB 1994
36
B
Visas
Departure/Sortie
PHILIPPINE
IMMIGRATION
5 FEB 1999
60
DAYS
DEPARTURE
FEB 0 6 1999
U.S. IMMIGRATION
130   SFR   2228
MAY 1 7 1999
ADMITTED
CLASS
VISA
VALID
1999
DATE OF ISSUE
1998-12
4605
USA 32
Southern Magnolia
MAGNOLIA GRANDIFLORA
PASSED
PASSED
PASSED
PASSED

40

Edmund

Awoken by the sounds of vibration from my phone resting on my side table, I rubbed my face trying to remind myself that I was in my apartment . Since I was back home from my tour, home felt foreign to me. I reached for my phone. It was too early in the morning as I didn't recognize the number.

"Who is this?" I snapped.

I was about to hang up when I heard a voice. "Please don't hang up. Please." The voice was familiar. "It's Clara."

I paused and sat on the edge of the bed. "Is Zelda okay?" My heart rushed with panic.

"Eloise passed a couple of days ago. Zelda wouldn't let the mortician take her. They had to pull her off Eloise. She wanted to hold on to her for a little longer. I know you two left things a mess, but maybe you can come save her."

I felt a pain in my chest, knowing that Eloise was gone. "I'm booking a flight. I'm coming for her."

"Okay, I know this is last minute, but the funeral is in two days. I needed to tell you because I promised Eloise you'd come to the funeral."

"I guess she liked me," I teased as sadness clouded my mind.

"Yeah, she was rooting for you."

"I will try my best. Please send me all the details."

"I will."

"Thank you, Clara. I'm sorry for your loss. I know she was also a big part of your life."

Clara was crying. "Thank you."

As the phone call ended, I pressed my hands to my face, feeling pain in my heart, knowing how empty Zelda was right now.

WE WERE in Edinburgh for a couple of shows at local spots, but I called Andrew the minute I found out about what had happened. We paused the tour for this. I had requested a sub for the time being, but everyone insisted they couldn't do it without me. I didn't know what was in the cards for me, but if she told me to stay, I would. I'd stay there for her. I wanted a life with her. Nothing else mattered.

Clara messaged me as I made my connection at Heathrow. I didn't want to be bothered, so I wore a hat and sunglasses in the airport. I hated fame; all I cared about was playing piano. I wished I had worn a mask from the beginning so I didn't have to deal with people. I was grumpy, not like Tommy or the twins.

I knew in my heart that Zelda was my favorite person in the world, and I'd let her go. I never fought for what I wanted.

I took my seat in first class and looked out the window. It was a rainy day, perfect for my feelings. Holding my leather notebook, I flipped it open and knew what to do, the one thing Zelda would respond to.

I wrote her a letter. A love letter from an idiot man who finally decided to get a grip and try.

I saw the text from Clara pop on my screen, so I swiped to respond.

CLARA

I need to tell you something before you come.

EDMUND

What's up?

CLARA

James has been here since the death. He's with her... again. I didn't know if you'd come. I know my friend, and she's making a mistake.

For fuck's sake, I thought.

I wanted to punch the wall, but being kicked off the flight was the last thing I needed.

"Flight attendants, please be seated," the pilot announced as I leaned my head into the headrest. The man next to me typed away on his laptop. I ran my hands through my hair, feeling the color drain from my face. It was going to be a battle to get her back, but it was a battle I was willing to fight.

~

ONCE BACK IN JFK AIRPORT, I rushed to the restroom to change into the suit I had in my carry-on. My hands shook at the thought of seeing her. I slept maybe an hour because my mind reeled at the thought of her with him. I washed my face, trying to help my bloodshot eyes. My beard wasn't trimmed, and my hair was a mess, so I let it down. I fixed my tie and looked at myself in the mirror. I hadn't worn a suit since boarding school. It was a death sentence in my eyes.

Andrew planned for a rental, so I picked up the keys and headed to the funeral. I glanced at my watch and realized I was already late. I threw my suitcase in the back and started the engine. The roar of the Audi R8 took over, and I knew I needed to get there.

Clara sent me the location of the burial, so I threw it in the GPS as I became a Formula One driver, cutting through the traffic. This was my love, my hope, my heart. I needed to be there. I needed to make sure that when she fell, I caught her. I would treasure her every minute I had left in this life.

I parked and saw a crowd of mourners surrounding a casket. I leaned against the headrest, unsure of what to do. She was standing near the casket as she wept in his arms.

His arms, I thought.

I squeezed the steering wheel as I felt my chest tighten. I was tired of fearing loving someone. I wanted to be the man she held. I swung the door open and watched as the mourners dispersed slowly before they lowered the coffin.

Walking up the hill, I noticed Clara walking over toward me. "I think this was a mistake. I'm sorry." She threw her hands up, trying to hold me back. "I don't think we should do this."

I shot her a confused look. "What are you talking about? I came from Edinburgh to see her. I want to see her, Clara."

"No. She's not good. She's literally..." She turned over her shoulder as we heard the scream, heard the pain, heard her cry.

Pushing Clara's hands away from my chest, I rushed toward Zelda who was on her knees, watching her mother be lowered into the ground. James was there, but I did not care. I kneeled next to her, and I pulled her into my chest as tight as I could. Her cries exploded against my chest.

"I'm here," I said into her ear, wrapping her tighter. She held me like I was her lifeline.

"I'm alone. I have no one," she replied.

"No." I pushed her hair away from her face. "I'm here. I'm always here."

"No, you're not." She pushed from me. "You're all the same. You left! You gave up on us!"

"That's not true. I love you, Zelda. I'm here! I will always be here."

"Get away from me, Edmund. Go kiss one of those women from your photos," she snapped.

"Zelda, I'm not going anywhere! Please, baby," I pleaded with her as I rested on one knee. She got up from the ground. I reached for her hand, but she pulled away.

"I don't need a fling. I need stability. James and I are back together."

I glanced over to James, who was talking to an older couple, when he finally noticed us. "Don't you dare, Zelda. Not him! You don't love him. You should be with me."

"Edmund, how will that work? You are a rock star, and I'm here. You will be living a life that isn't for me."

"I'll give it up," I confessed.

She shook her head. "No because you will regret it, just like my mom. She died never being able to do what she wanted. You will hate me. You will regret it!" Zelda turned away from me, but I gripped her hand.

"Please, Zel, you know I will leave everything for you. I regret losing you. Give us another chance," I pleaded. I begged. I did everything I could to get her back to me.

Zelda slipped from my hold. "I need you to go."

"You don't mean that—" Anger rose from my gut because I knew she wasn't saying it. It was *him*. James.

"She said to leave, Edmund. Go back to wherever you came from. No one wants you here." I stood. James swarmed me with such force that I knew what he wanted.

"Who do you think you are? Coming out of nowhere and deciding to be in her life?" I said.

"I'm her husband. I know what is best for her." James shoved me, and rage ignited. I punched him in the face, and he fell to the ground.

"Edmund! What is wrong with you?" Zelda screamed, rushing over to James. Bobby came over with Clara not far behind.

"You need to leave. This isn't the place! I buried my wife and the mother of my daughter. Do you think this was the right thing to do? Get the hell out of here!" Bobby snapped as he pointed toward the road. I threw my hands up in the air.

"I'm sorry!" I yelled. "I'm sorry, Zelda." I bit my bottom lip. It was too late to have her again.

We had come to the end of our story.

41

Zelda

I'd been a zombie. I didn't know how life was supposed to go on when a part of you died. A piece of my heart was taken away, and I was supposed to live on.

Every minute of the day, I was reminded that I was completely and utterly alone in this world. Mom had managed to leave behind a newfound relationship with Bobby, but I still had to learn how to love a new person. For thirty years, my mom was the person I adored the most. She was the only person I called every day. I told her how I felt and what I ate.

After the incident with Edmund, I promised I would never speak to him again. I deleted everything that had to do with him. I wanted to erase all that he was to me in those years. I didn't want to hear or speak of him. Edmund, in my eyes, was also dead. I wanted to go back to the life I had before.

Bobby decided he was not leaving New York because he wanted to be there for me. Every day, he helped me get out of bed, made me breakfast, and tried to give me candy. Some nights, I could hear him resting against the bathroom door while I wept for my mom. Those days were the hardest.

Clara had been there trying to pick me up from the darkness, but I kept pushing her away. As much as I loved my friend being there for me, I hated dragging her down. I was damaged goods.

James hovered so much that I told Bobby to let him know that he needed to step away. How could a person think I should move on or keep strong when I couldn't get out of bed?

I walked out to my mom's living room, and it was quiet. Bobby went out to get some groceries. I passed my mom's room, and I took a second to smell her perfume. That was when I heard a knock on the door.

I took a deep breath, feeling nervous at the thought of James coming by. I heard another knock. Rolling my eyes, I headed to the front of the apartment. I looked into the peephole and recognized it was the building manager. I swung the door open, trying to make myself presentable.

"Hey, uh, Sofia, right?"

"Zelda," I responded. This man wasn't like the building manager I shared with James. He was lanky and rigged with a chiseled jawline and translucent skin. He looked like he lived his life in a cave, and his eyes were ice cold.

"Look, clear out your mailbox. We've had several complaints."

"My mom died—"

He threw his hands up. "Three months ago. But you can still do stuff."

"I'll go today."

"Thank you."

Without waiting, I closed the door. "What an asshole," I muttered.

AFTER TWO ATTEMPTS TO go to the mailbox, I finally had the courage to make my way down to the front of the building. With cleaner clothes and my hair pulled away from my face, I unlocked the box. The door swung open fast, pouring its contents. There were many letters on the floor. Seeing my mother's name printed on each one made my chest tighten with sorrow.

Wiping the tears from my cheek, I headed up the stairs with the letters in my arms. I felt her next to me, pushing me up each step toward her apartment. I went inside, closing the door and wanting nothing more than to throw it all away, but I couldn't, so I sat on the island.

One by one, I opened each letter, separating them into junk and important. Then I saw it. One letter I hadn't expected to see.

I saw my name tattooed on a red envelope. My fingers traced his handwriting. I missed him so much. I wished I could hold him, but I knew that I couldn't. My life was not meant to be with his. Even though I wanted it, we were two different worlds. I took a deep breath. I wanted to open it and see what he said, but I couldn't. I just couldn't do it. So I placed all the letters aside.

I remembered that he was a chapter in this life, but it was the end of our story.

I slipped open the drawer of my mom's desk and saw a little cut-out purple star I made as a kid. Mom insisted that I was a star in this big giant galaxy. I was worth one day to be someone's star. I rubbed the rough little material of the star, and I could hear my mom's words encouraging me not to hide the letter.

Taking a deep breath, I pulled out the letter from Edmund and opened it slowly.

Zelda,

I hate how we left things, and that life seems to break us every chance it gets. We keep pushing each other away. It's as if every chance we get, somehow, we are too afraid to fall for one another. I wish one day someone will love you the way I do, the way you deserve. One day, maybe you will finally be at peace with being who you are.

I can't force you to love me when we aren't right. Maybe I need to let you go to experience what kind of love I could have too. Maybe one day in the future, we can see each other for what we have. A cosmic love.

Love you always,

E.

I didn't want to keep fighting over and over to be something I was not. But I needed to find myself.

Entrée/Entrée
6 JUL 19
IMMIGRAT
- 8 FEB 19
Visas
B
IMMIGRATION
3 FEB 1999
60
DAYS
U.S. IMMIGRATION
SFR
MAY 1 7 1999
ADMITTED
CLASS
36
VISA
GOOD FOR TWO
VALID UNTIL
1999
DATE OF ISSUE
1996-12
4605
USA 32
Southern Magnolia
PASSED
PASSED

42

Six months later

Zelda

The cool breeze of fall was settling, and I finally got a part-time job at a local café while taking baby steps to live again. Reflecting on the past couple of years, it was a clusterfuck. I'd experienced things I couldn't comprehend. All I could think about was what goes down must come up.

I was attempting to regain the fire I once had in my heart. The one my mom insisted I always had. My mom had wanted nothing more than for my life to be happy. I had to take chances even if they terrified me. What she did with my dad was utterly absurd, but I knew she didn't want me to be alone. So I created a new Zelda.

Every Friday, Bobby pushed me to do father-daughter date nights to get to know each other. At first, I was hesitant. I tried everything to close him out, but he wouldn't have it. He insisted on being there every moment.

On lonely nights, he held me like a father should. He patted the tears away and strengthened me when I didn't think I could be. Bobby reminded me that I was capable.

On this Friday night, we tried rock climbing, and I laughed for the first time in a long time as I hung off the wall. I had no idea how to climb correctly, and I felt a rush of enjoyment. It was like seeing sunshine after a hurricane.

Bobby and I dragged our fatigued bodies to a pizza joint near Mom's apartment. We sat at the window, devouring the slices like it was the first time we ate. "I'm proud of you." He chewed what he was eating. Watching him more, I could see our similarities.

I picked off a pepperoni and ate it. "It feels good to get out," I admitted. "I sometimes feel guilty." The darkness was slowly slipping away, but I always felt the depression reminding me I couldn't let go.

"I'm hurting so damn much. I wished I'd had more time with Eloise, but she would probably tell us we are being ridiculous." He let a small laugh out.

"It's true," I answered as I looked out the window, seeing the people pass us by. I sometimes heard her voice in my head. I could feel her picking me up like she was standing there.

"How does it feel to be officially divorced?" Bobby patted his lips with a napkin, then sipped his drink.

After the funeral, James tried to help me, but after three months, he was done. He went right back to his art. He mentally checked out; he didn't want to help me anymore. James was too self-absorbed. I was intruding on his life. Besides, he confessed that he was in love with Melody. We knew that we couldn't make it work. James wasn't my forever. He was never the person I thought I could have the rest of my life with. I tried so hard to make it real. I was so foolish to think it was worth it when I knew my heart told me otherwise.

"I'm actually feeling good—" I released a deep breath before continuing. "It was never meant to be. I kept telling myself that we should be together when we shouldn't. I had to come to terms with the fact that James wasn't the right person."

"So you know who the right one is for you?" he asked. I could feel him watching me rip a piece of the crust. I took a sip of my drink and looked down at my hands, trying my best not to make eye contact with him.

"Edmund is famous and has a massive career. There are plenty of women begging for him. He doesn't need me." I lied to myself because it was the only way to forget him. I was his past, never his future.

"Really? Because that boy was a firecracker, and you're his lighter."

"Aren't you a poet? Where did you get that?" I laughed.

His face lost his smile. "Your mom." He paused for a second as his eyes welled with tears. He looked like the pain in his heart was all over his body. "Your mom would say that in high school. That I was the lighter for her firecracker. We managed to have an explosive romance people begged to have. We were fireworks." He looked out the window, and his eyes glossed over as he rubbed his mouth. "God, your mom…" He wrapped his arms around his chest. "Her laughter was like music; it brought me peace every time. Our souls were parallels. Not everyone gets that, but if granted, never let it go."

I gave him a minute before reaching for my father's hand. "Dad." I came for him, hugging him. "Thank you for telling me that. I know Mom will always be here."

"But she gave me the best thing in the world," he cried as he leaned away and held my face. "She gave me you. Our souls came together to create you. I know I didn't get a chance to see you grow. I wish I had known about the pregnancy. But I'm so proud of who you became. I want you to take a chance before you become like me. When time runs out, you can't have more. So you're going to do one thing for me."

"What, Dad?" It felt like we were the only ones in that pizza joint for a second. He pulled away, moving a strand of hair as he beamed.

"I have a letter for you." He pulled it out from his pocket.

Narrowing my eyes, he handed the letter over to me, and I held it. "What is this?" I examined the purple envelope with my name on it. I recognized the handwriting as my mom's. My eyes widened. "Is this…?"

"Yes." He nodded. "She insisted I give that to you when you found peace. It's time."

Flipping the envelope, I pulled out the contents. The smell of my mom triggered goose bumps down my neck. I felt like she was right there with me, and it was hard to breathe.

Zelda,

My love, my everything. My heart, my soul. My sunshine. My heaven. This was a hard letter to write, not because I'm a blubbering idiot. No—because you won't leave me alone! I had to lie and tell you I needed something for my back so you would leave. You can be annoying sometimes (I'm joking, my love). Here it goes—I love you.

When I held you for the first time, you wrapped your fingers so tightly. I could see your light, your fire. You made me a mom, and that was the best thing that ever happened to me. I know I did some shitty stuff and tried my best to make things right, but I feel guilty for those moments we had to be in the dark. I did everything to make sure that light in you never died.

I know sometimes you were embarrassed by what I was doing or how I tried to keep us going, and I regret that. I do. I wish I had told your father; I wish I had given you a better life. It killed me that I made so many wrong mistakes, but I was terrified. I was fearful of losing you. So I want to apologize for all of it. You are the strongest person I know.

Every part of me knows you can do anything in this world. I hate that I won't be able to see it. But I will be in the forget-me-nots that you love, the little butterflies that fly at your window, or the rainbows after the storms.

Life will be scary; it's going to be messy. But that's the best part. It will be challenging. It will bring you up and drop you down, but keep going. Take hold of it and run with it.

You need to go after that man. You know who I'm talking about. The man who loves you. He came to visit me when you weren't around. That was a fucking shit show! Clara arranged for you to go take a break. He came, and we talked. Zelda, that man is so good. I see him loving you till the very end. You tried to make James work, but he needed to be right. It's okay. He was good for now, but not forever.

Edmund told me how much he loves you and wishes to make things work. I told him he needs to make himself better to love you. I warned him that one day you'd go back to him. You're going to walk up to him and tell him that you two belong with each other. It's going to be scary, but it's worth it, my love. You will fight with each other and tell each other how much you are frustrated. You'll get married and have babies. One day, when your daughter struggles, you will tell her the same thing.

Now, here is the hard part. I hate this part. I don't want to say goodbye. It feels final. Please rely on your dad and Clara for guidance. I left you with the perfect people who will take care of you. But I will come and visit you. I promise, my love-bug. I love you forever and always wherever I am. So this isn't a goodbye. No, this is forever. This is, see you later.

Go live, my love.

I love you last,

Your mom.

P.S.

Look up at Bobby. He has something for you.

I took a deep breath. The pain in my heart drenched my soul at knowing my mom wasn't there. "I love you, Mom," I whispered as Bobby cradled my face in the palm of his hand.

Bobby sniffed back the tears. "Here you go." He passed me a ticket to Scotland. "She really wanted you to go."

Wiping my tears, I glanced down and scrunched my nose. "One way?"

"The only way to be with the one you love."

"What if he doesn't want me?" I said.

"Never know until you see."

Entrée/Entrées
6 JUL 19
IMMIGRATION
418
DEPARTED
-8 FEB 19
IMMIGRATION SERVICE
RFER 19041
36
B
Visas   Départ/Arrivée
RÉPUBLIQUE FRANÇAISE
FEB 0 0 1999
3 FEB 1999
60
DAYS
U.S. IMMIGRATION
130   SFR   22
MAY 1 7 1999
ADMITTED
CLASS
VISA
VALID FOR TWO
1999
DATE OF ISSUE
1998-12
4605
USA 32
Southern Magnolia
MAGNOLIA GRANDIFLORA
PASSED
PASSED
PASSED

43

Zelda

"So that is how my situation got this far." I leaned into the plane seat after I finished telling the older lady next to me my life story. Donna sniffed into the tissues loudly.

"Oh, honey! That is devastating." She blew her nose. "Does he know you're coming?" She widened her eyes with curiosity. After getting the letter from my dad, I knew I had to try one last time. Even if I ended up brokenhearted, at least I tried.

"No, he doesn't. Everyone has managed to get everything ready for me to see him," I replied to Donna, who looked like she just finished a book that ended on a cliffhanger.

I had called Clara, crying my eyes out. She knew what to expect. She invited me to come by to plan for this journey. She had already spoken to Andrew about it. I also found out she'd been secretly messaging him for a while. Imagine my shock when I saw them Face-Timing each other to arrange everything for me.

Andrew mentioned they were performing at a venue in a couple of days and that he would arrange tickets for me to attend. Andrew filled me in that Edmund had been alone. Every night, he returned to his room and didn't partake in anything. He was still in love with me, Andrew had mentioned.

Maybe it was a lie, but I didn't know the truth. Clara planned my outfit. She had everything ready for me to get there.

"When is the concert?" Donna asked, then sipped her wine.

"Tonight."

~

I WALKED to the venue in my leather jacket and long floral dress. It was colder at night, so I bundled up. I was trying my best to remember why I was here. I had to push the pain of my past and feel the fire take over my bones. Edmund was the only thing I wanted in this life. Whether he liked me or not, I needed to make peace before it was too late.

There was a line at the entrance, but because of Andrew, I had a VIP pass that allowed me to head to the other side. "Mom, give me the strength," I said as the bouncer checked my purse before letting me in.

Inside was packed. I followed one of the workers who took me to the back. I saw Edmund heading down the stairs backstage and push through the setup team. He stood there with his bandmates as they pumped themselves up. My lips curved into a smile, and my cheeks blushed from staring at him.

Swallowing my fear, I walked to him. I had to do it. I had to finally do what my heart was begging for all this time. Ultimately, I'd always been his, even when I didn't know I was. I knew Daisy did this in some cosmic way; she gave me to him.

Edmund wore his fitted tee, dark wash jeans, and his hair down. His beard was trimmed, but he had this sweet smile I wanted to kiss again. I wanted to ravage him. I reached for his shoulder, and he slowly turned around.

He towered over me, watching me for a second before his lips parted. I couldn't hold back any longer. I wanted him. I wanted to be with him. Wrapping my arms around his neck, I felt happy for the first time in a long time. His hands cupped my cheeks as shivers rushed down my back. Kissing him was everything I'd ever dreamed of, as I missed his taste. Our breaths mingled, twisting as we came up for air like we were back at that lake. Our lips were tender as everything finally came to a standstill. I felt a mix of emotions, and my cheeks burned with fire as my eyes widened.

Edmund made me vulnerable to falling in love. His eyes were filled with admiration as we stood there in silence.

"I told you I would be right where you left me." He leaned against my forehead, pulling me closer as his hands released my face and tugged at my waist. "I knew you would come back to me."

"I know, but—" He dove into another kiss. I tasted him again, feeling ecstasy as our world faded.

"Everything was a mess. All I wanted was to run to you. I wanted to be by your side. I know I lost you, but I would be here whenever you decided to return to me. I don't care about everything else. We've got time to make it work together." He pushed my hair away from my face. "I have my whole life to make you happy, and I can't wait for it."

Tears slid down my cheeks as I stretched my lips to a grin of pure excitement. I'd been pushing so hard to have something perfect, but here is what my perfect was. A man who looked at me like I was his lifeline, his everything. "I love you," I said.

"I love you." He winked, then kissed my forehead.

"Hey! Let's go! We need to go on!" Tommy yelled as we both glared at him. "Oh." Tommy finally looked at me, confused. "Are we making this official... again?"

"We are making this official," Edmund said firmly.

Turning to look up at him, I said, "Go! They're calling for you."

"I guess it's time to sing that song."

"What song?" He squeezed my waist and headed toward the stage, but before he did, he winked at me.

"Thank you, Daisy," I said as I watched him climb the steps and heard the audience roar.

From the side balcony, I watched Edmund play the keyboard passionately as he peeked my way. I was entranced by him as the music rumbled through the crowd.

Suddenly, it felt like the world was still. The voice singing was not Tom. It was Edmund.

"I know you're surprised to hear my voice," he said into the microphone as he played some notes, "but the next song is special. A woman wrote me a letter one day, and she hadn't left my mind since. In fact, she is right up there." He pointed, and the spotlight went to me. "I've been waiting for so long for her, and she is finally mine."

Cheers. All that was heard was cheers.

He played the melody. "That's my girlfriend up there. She doesn't know it yet, but I wrote her this song. I hope she likes it." I was utterly lost for words. He cracked a cocky smile, following it up with his famous wink.

"The song is called Zelda.

"Through the darkness, you brought the light,

"Your force guided me to ignite,

"The thunder of you serenaded my soul,

"Begging me to finally feel in control,

"With every heartbeat,

"The symphony keeps playing,

"But you're an unknown,

"But you're an unknown."

It felt like we were alone. His voice was haunting as I watched him sing to me. It was his love letter. His breath was heavy and raspy as he sang the highs and lows. I watched him allow himself to become vulnerable in front of me.

The man I had fallen for in the most unconventional way sang to me.

"For you, I let the darkness go."

Edmund played the final note, and the audience sat in enraptured silence. I stood, clapping as hard as I could, feeling the sting in my hands as I watched him make his way to center stage. He turned to me, blowing kisses at me as I did the same with tears falling. I rushed down the balcony steps and headed to the stage. Andrew pulled me up the stairs. I ran toward him, and he turned to me with open arms. It was my perfect love story.

Wrapping my arms around his neck, he pleaded, "Don't ever let go, Zelda." He kissed my lips so gently and sweetly. Kissing someone in front of thousands of people, especially while being madly in love with Edmund, was a high I'd never felt before.

I leaned back, and the rest of the band surrounded us. We all took a bow at the end of the show. Edmund kissed my cheek as we made our way off stage.

I understood how Mom had declared, "You need someone to drive you to feel the fire."

The End

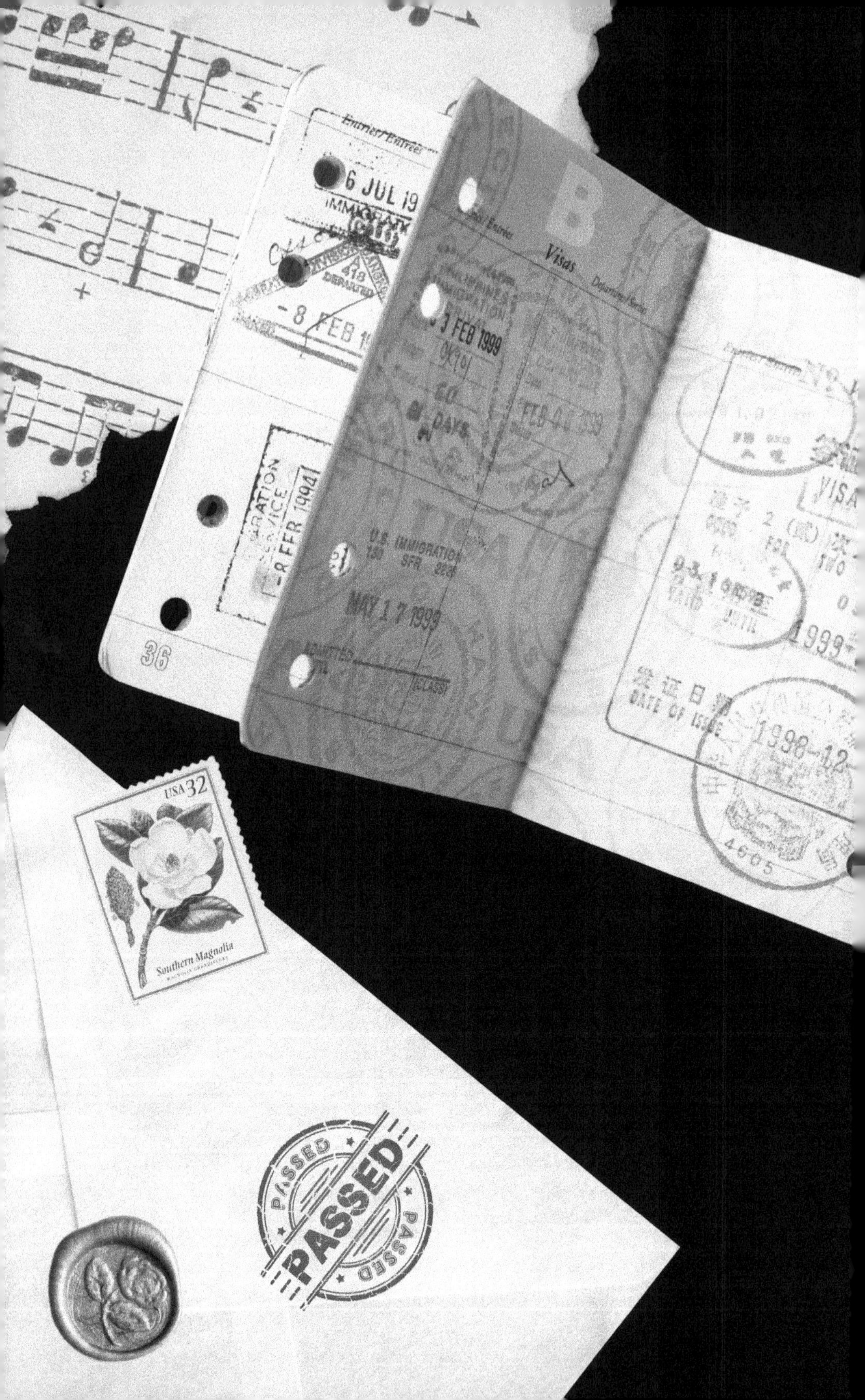
USA 32
Southern Magnolia
MAGNOLIA GRANDIFLORA
PASSED
PASSED

EPILOGUE

One year later

Edmund

The past year had been challenging. Traveling to see each other was intense, but it was worth it when I saw those eyes. With the time change, the band, and Zelda applying for citizenship, we made it work.

Two months after the show, Zelda sold her mother's apartment. The band, Clara, and Bobby helped pack her life in New York. Zelda stayed with Bobby for a while in his hometown in Florida, wanting to spend more time with him while I was on tour. And I called her every night—whether for a minute or hours, I made the time. She told me she'd met cousins, aunts, and uncles, which helped her realize she had this massive family waiting to love her.

After ten years of purposely avoiding Christmas with my family, I returned home with Zelda on my arm, carrying gifts for everyone. My mom cried. She held me tight, telling me she loved me no matter what. My dad told me he was proud of me. When we sat next to the fire and Zelda held my new niece, I knew she was my home. She was my world.

In the new year, Zelda discovered where Daisy was buried. She was placed in her hometown outside of New Orleans. We made a trip there to pay our respects to the woman who made this happen. We even met with her parents. After that, we traveled, just building more memories together.

The sun poured into the hotel room as I watched Zelda sleep peacefully. I kissed her bare back, then wrapped my arms around her waist. She released a soft moan as my face settled into her hair, breathing her in. She put air in my lungs. She created a fire that drove me to be a better person.

I knew I was the luckiest man in the world when I slid my hand over her swollen belly, feeling our baby growing inside her. Zelda turned her head to face me and cupped my cheeks. "Good morning," she said, slowly opening her eyes. I watched her as the golden light hues created a halo around her head. She was mesmerizing.

"I've got something for you." I licked my bottom lip.

She fully turned over. "What is it?"

I winked at her, knowing it made her weak. "Hold on." I reached for my wallet and pulled out the letter I'd held for so long. The letter she gave me the night she told me she was leaving Scotland.

Zelda's eyes widened. "Which letter is that?"

"It's the one where you say goodbye." I sat up, looking down at her.

"Oh God!" She hid under the sheets, but I pulled them down. "Please don't!"

"This one is my favorite." I unfolded the paper and glanced down at it. "Can you read it to me?"

When she left the first time, I went home in complete disarray because I'd let the love of my life go, knowing all too well she was the one for me. When I got into bed, Andrew placed the letter on my pillow, yet I couldn't read it. It took a long time to read it, but when I did, I cried. I kept it in my wallet, knowing it was a part of her heart.

Zelda sat against the headboard and wrapped the sheets around her exposed body. "Fine." She gave me a soft smile as she reached for it.

"Edmund,

"You're a dream to me. I've always dreamed about someone I

would love but couldn't see his face. Now I know it's you. You're the boy I will forever be madly in love with.

"I know life is pulling us apart, and we can't be together, and I have to let you go. But I can't, Edmund. Nothing in this world will ever come close to my love for you.

"You're so incredibly talented. I've never met someone so good who hides in the darkness. Come out of it, my love. Please.

"If I never get a chance with you, know that I will remember our love till my last breath.

"I love you, Edmund. Always."

Zelda wiped her tears as she looked up from the paper. "You kept this in your wallet?"

"Yeah, darling, I knew one day that nothing would pull me away from you." Before I could speak, Zelda crawled onto my lap and kissed me as hard as she could. Her sweet taste, her melodic voice, and her love were all I needed to keep living.

After spending the day with her father, I told her I wanted to see the sunset at the beach. We packed up our rental and headed out. We were on our second to last day before it would be official; Zelda was going to live with me in Scotland.

The roof was down on the Bronco, and Zelda traced her fingers in the breeze. I watched her from the corner of my eyes. Her grin was brighter than the sun. She was happy. Zelda was content, and I would try my best to keep it that way. I pulled into the parking lot, then she grabbed the blankets. "Did you pack treats?" she asked.

"Of course." I rolled my eyes. I got my small speaker and bag for the beach.

Zelda ran to the water, dancing in her loose summer dress while the waves crashed the shores. The sun was kissing the horizon, making the sky an array of pinks and oranges, dusted with purple. Zelda came careening onto the blanket, and I pulled her between my legs and rested my lips on her bare shoulders.

"So I got the news," she confessed as she interlaced her fingers with mine.

Pulling them to my lips, I kissed them. "What's that?"

"Our daughter will definitely —"

"A girl?" I lifted my head with excitement because I didn't know about our baby's sex. My eyes widened. "Baby?"

She turned around and pushed me down, coming to lie on me. "We're having a girl."

Zelda kissed me as I cupped her face, feeling a burst of happiness spread through me like wildfire.

"Darling, marry me," I whispered against her lips.

"I guess I could marry you," she joked. I wrapped my arms around her tight, embracing her like I was meant to be all this time.

ACKNOWLEDGMENTS

All I can say is, whoa. I have written my first book and am at a loss for words. I never thought it was possible because I never believed I could do such a thing. These last years have pushed me to take a chance. This past year was a rollercoaster of emotions, but I wouldn't have done it without the village behind me.

I want to start with my editor, Brittany, from E&A Editing—thank you for helping me along the road with this book. Your thoughtful messages and cheerful encouragement have made me a better writer. I can't wait for the next book; I promise I won't send you too many messages (Who am I kidding?).

To Jenny Sims from Editing4Indies, I am grateful for your help with the details and for ensuring this book was ready for the world to see.

To the incredible designers at Opulent Designs, you took what I had in my head and made it come to life. It's stunning! I was incredibly honored to see it for the first time. I've always loved your design and can't wait to work with you on future projects.

To my friends—Michelle, Melissa, Shelly, Katie, Kate, Lily, Kelsey, and Amber, I can't thank you enough for your support and love during this year. Thank you for always having my back. You have truly inspired me to be a better person. I couldn't have done it without you.

My familia, the list is long. Let's start with my parents. Mom, Dad, and Jennifer, thank you for constantly pushing me to pursue my dreams. I know it's been a whirlwind for a couple of years, but you were always my number one support. I can't thank you enough for always ensuring that I could do anything if I put my mind to it.

THANK YOU

Ai miei nonni, grazie per avermi sempre sostenuto! Spero che questo possa arrivare in italiano, così potrete leggerlo (if I butcher this, I'm sorry! I tried).

Zia Nadia--I have permanently written that in this book. I love you and thank you for all the help and support. I can't express how much it means to me. You're like my older sister, and I always look up to you for help and encouragement.

To my husband and daughter, you have been my number one fans. You have supported me through the long nights writing this story. My heart is whole, knowing you were always there to help me meet my deadlines. I know it hasn't been easy, but you are my world. I love you so much.

Lastly, to my readers, the people who have followed my journey or those who just decided to pick this book up, thank you for taking the time and effort to do so. You are helping this dream to become a reality. Thank you for the reviews; even if they are mixed feelings, you made the effort to take the time to read the book. I'm so grateful to you.

Thank you all for all the love and support. I look forward to my journey in the world of writing.

Vee.

ABOUT THE AUTHOR

Vanessa Stock is an independent Canadian author with a passion for weaving romantic tales. With every stroke of her keyboard, she strives to create worlds where love knows no bounds and the power of connection transcends all obstacles. Whether it's the allure of a chance encounter or the depth of a lifelong bond, her stories are a journey through the heart's most profound emotions. Join Vanessa on this adventure, and let's explore the limitless possibilities of love together. She resides north of Toronto with my husband, daughter, and their puppy Maverick. When she's not writing, she likes to design spaces and binge the latest crime shows.

As I closed the final chapter of this story,
a new adventure is waiting on the horizon.

Do you like Motorcycle romance?
Because I do…